MIDSUM
MURDER

MIDSUMMER MURDER

CLIFFORD WITTING

G

GALILEO PUBLISHERS,
CAMBRIDGE

Galileo Publishers
16 Woodlands Road, Great Shelford
Cambridge
CB22 5LW UK

www.galileopublishing.co.uk

Distributed in the USA by SCB Distributors
15608 S. New Century Drive
Gardena, CA 90248-2129, USA

Australia: Peribo Pty Limited
58 Beaumont Road
Mount Kuring-Gai, NSW 2080
Australia

ISBN 978-1-912916-733

First published 1937
This edition © 2022

Printed in the EU

To Marjorie Witting

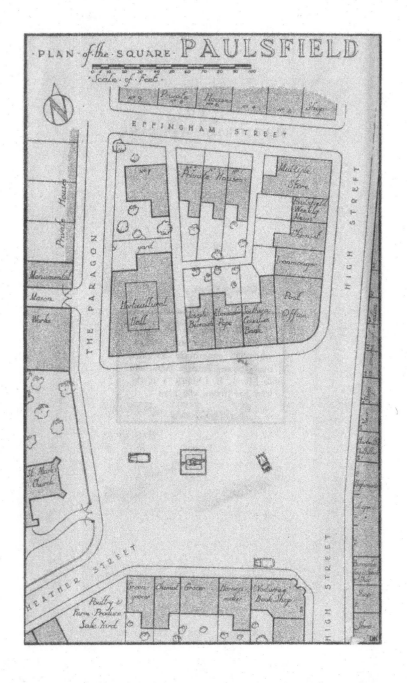

CONTENTS

I.

At High Noon

PAULSFIELD (3,853), Downshire. *(Map* 33 *C.*7). London 5$\frac{1}{2}$ miles.
L.H. 10.30-2.30, 6-10 w.d.; 12.30-2.30, 7-10 S. M.Day—Alt.
Tues. E. Closing—Wed. Post—7.45 a.m., 7.15 p.m.; S. 6.30 p.m.
Littleworth 4$\frac{1}{2}$ □ Padging 6□Burgeston 2$\frac{1}{4}$, Lulverton 4, South-
mouth-by-the-Sea 7□Meanhurst 1$\frac{1}{2}$, Whitchester 8□.

(Automobile Association Handbook).

DURING the summer previous to the events recorded
by John Rutherford in *Murder in Blue,* there took place
in Paulsfield a series of happenings to which Police-sergeant
Martin was afterwards to refer as "that 'orrible to-do in the
Square." It has hitherto been the author's fixed determination
to write nothing on that subject: the whole thing seemed too
extravagantly silly to be believed. But since that painstaking
historian, John Rutherford, saw fit to pass on a casual remark
by the Sergeant, the demands to hear more about the to-do
in the Square have become increasingly pressing; and, after all,
for those who died in that July and for those who lived on,
in fear for their lives, through those flaming days and sulky
nights, and in particular for Detective-inspector Charlton, it
was anything but silly.

So the story shall be set down.

It began on the first Tuesday in July, which was market-
day in Paulsfield. The church clock in the Square was verging
on midday and, beneath a sky as blue and cloudless as a sky
can be, the tumult of the fortnightly gathering, that was so
anathematized by a large proportion of the town's inhabitants,

1

was at its zenith. Sheep and pigs in pens and cows tethered to railings, bleated, grunted and lowed, according to their persuasion. A perspiring red-faced man stood on a box, with his bowler hat pulled down to shield his eyes from the sun, extolling in a mighty voice the wearing qualities of his lace-curtains, sheets and table-napery; and in the Poultry and Farm Produce Sale Yard, just off the Square in Heather Street, an auctioneer monotonously offered eggs for "lemarf" a dozen. Cheap-jacks were doing big business with their pretty rubbish and in front of the Horticultural Hall, in the north-west corner of the Square, a Punch-and-Judy show was in mid-act, in direct competition with an adjacent barrel-organ, from which a disconsolate man was churning out "Coal-Black Mammy." A blackavised Latin, whose forbear may have seen Naples, but doubtless deferred his demise until he had reared a large family just off Tottenham Court Road, deftly dispensed cornets and wafers from an ice-cream barrow which had once been a riot of gaily painted vulgarity, but which was now not even vulgar.

It will be as well if local colour is not laid on too thickly at this early stage in the story, which must be got moving as soon as possible; but it is really necessary to add a word or two about the road-repairing in the High Street. The old part of this principal thoroughfare of Paulsfield ran almost due southward from the "Queen's Head," the only inn in Paulsfield worthy of the name. At this particular time, the portion of the High Street that bounded the eastern margin of the Square was up. Two narrow passages had been left at the north-east and south-east corners of the Square to allow traffic to pass, but half the strip of road between had been dedicated to a handful of the Council's employees, two of whom were adding to the general hubbub with samples of that devil's trombone, the pneumatic-drill.

It has been pointed out by a writer of great discernment (his name is not remembered, nor the exact wording of his remarks) that in photographs taken by intrepid newspaper men during civil wars, revolutions, riots and earthquakes, when it would be expected that all those present would be participating in the excitement, there is always at least one man caught by the camera in the act of lighting a cigarette, blowing his nose, tying up his shoe-lace or doing some such commonplace thing. In the same way, on this Tuesday morning in Paulsfield Square, there was one man who took no part in the market-day confusion.

In the middle of the Square was the statue of a former Lord Shawford, who, if he did not storm Quebec or snap his fingers at Napoleon, had certainly won fame for something that had seemed quite important at the time. The present holder of the title was always a little vague on the point, perhaps with reason. The figure, which faced the High Street, was mounted on a horse standing, with one foreleg raised, on a plinth, which was now shared by the man previously mentioned, who was scrubbing down the now piebald animal's left thigh with brushes that he dipped from time to time into one or the other of the two buckets balanced by his side.

His lordship's torso and cocked hat, which was always held in great favour by the pigeons, had been cleaned the day before and now the workman was slowly working his way round the animal, isolated from those about him by the iron railing around the base of the plinth, and completely oblivious of the noisy crowd eight feet below him.

It was at exactly one minute to twelve that a bull got loose. They often did on market-days, sending all the timorous ladies scuttling for shelter into the shops around the Square. The tradespeople made a pretty thing, though they would never admit it, out of these sudden visitors, who hardly liked to leave their sanctuaries without buying a tube of toothpaste or half-a-pound of grapes. This bull was certainly intent on its one brief hour of glorious life, for in fifteen seconds it had the whole market in an uproar. Some of the more flimsy stalls were overturned, the organ-grinder and the showman simultaneously stopped their performances, gaitered men with sticks ran here and there, women and children screamed and shopkeepers came to their doors, smiling and rubbing their hands.

And amid the chaos of it all and the fiendish din of the remorseless drills, the man who was cleaning the statue suddenly sagged, then fell between the railings and the plinth, and lay crooked and still.

★ ★ ★

The police station at Paulsfield is on the left-hand side of the High Street, going northward from the Square. Inspector Charlton of the C.I.D., attached to the Downshire County Constabulary, had driven there that morning from his base at Lulverton and was chatting to Sergeant Martin, when the uproar from the Square took him to the open door.

"Something seems to be afoot," he said over his shoulder to Martin. "The party's getting rough. Even those confounded drills don't drown the shouting."

"Them drills are worse than the Wipers salient in '17," said Martin, who had passed his early years in Camberwell and had never lost the accent. "P'r'aps somebody's gone bughouse and corpsed one of the operators," he added hopefully.

"Who's on duty in the Square?"

"There's a temporary man—name of Hawkins—on detachment duty from Littleworth. 'E's controlling the one-way traffic in the High Street and Johnson's doing ordinary market-day duty."

"Downshire's most handsome flattie," smiled Charlton, "and the stealer of a thousand hearts."

"But a good man, for all that," said Martin stoutly; then went on carelessly, "Probably the rumpus is a bull got loose. It's the usual thing on market Tuesdays. You'd think you was in Barcelona."

"The Council ought to hire a few matadors," Charlton suggested, "to deal with such emergencies."

"The only thing you ever get out of the Council," snorted Martin, "is a double-blank."

Charlton looked at the Sergeant strangely.

"Do you notice," he asked, "how everything has gone suddenly quiet?"

Martin mopped his brow with a large handkerchief.

"Thank the Lord for mercies small," he said piously.

"Those so-and-so's with the drills knock off for dinner at twelve—and I hope it chokes 'em."

"And has the whole noisy market gone to dinner, too?"

Martin drew in his breath sharply.

"Something's happened," he said. "Don't say a bull..."

"I'll go and see," said Charlton, but as he stepped through the doorway to go down the steps, a uniformed man—the relief constable from Littleworth—who had come running from the Square, pulled up by the railings outside the police station.

"What is it, Hawkins?" asked Charlton, who knew him.

"There's a man been shot in the Square, sir," was the answer.

Charlton turned back to Martin.

"Get Dr. Weston on the 'phone," he said. "If he's out, get Hayling. D'you know who did it?" he then asked Hawkins.

The constable shook his head.

"Nobody seems to 've seen it happen. 'E was cleaning the statue one second and the next 'e was lying behind the railings. He's been shot through the head."

"Get back there. I'll follow you," the Inspector said. "Which of your men are on duty, Martin?"

"Johnson's, as I said, in the Square, Didcott's round by the Common, Chandler's at 'is dinner and Harwood's off till the evening. That's all four of them."

"When you've got the doctor, ring up Lulverton and Littleworth stations and tell them to send men along at once and post them at the four corners of the Square to stop anybody from leaving."

As Martin lifted the telephone receiver, murmuring something to himself about stable doors, Charlton hurried down the steps and along the High Street. When he neared the Square, a little bald-headed man, who was standing in the entrance to a chemist's shop, asked anxiously what the trouble was, but Charlton elected not to hear.

P.C. Johnson was standing by the statue, holding back the crowd as efficiently as one man could be expected to do, and saluted as the Inspector pushed his way through to him. Behind the railings was the twisted, overalled body of the workman, with a half-smoked, pinched-out cigarette still behind his ear and a neat, slightly bleeding hole in the right temple, a little below the level of the cloth cap that remained miraculously on his head.

"Get some trestles and poles," Charlton murmured to Johnson, nodding in the direction of the High Street excavations, "and have this railed off."

Johnson shouldered his way through the gaping crowd.

The iron railings round the statue were about five feet high and a step-ladder was still leaning against them, where the workman had placed it earlier that day. As Charlton was bending down beside the body, a sharp imperious voice was heard demanding to be allowed to pass, and a short, belligerently moustached little man pushed his way brusquely to his side. He looked up.

"Morning, Dr. Weston," was his greeting. "Here's some more work for you."

"As if I haven't enough already," snapped the doctor.

"What's the silly fellow been doing?"

"Just getting shot," Charlton informed him calmly.

"Will you climb over the railings, or can you give him the once-over from this side?"

"I am not a circus performer, Inspector," said the doctor, as he knelt down by the bars.

Charlton bent over him and whispered in his ear:

"Don't move him—I want to get some photos."

In a few moments, Dr. Weston rose to his feet and dusted the knees of his impeccably creased trousers.

"Is he dead, sir?" asked a man in the crowd.

"That's more his concern than yours," was the acid reply.

"I'm his brother," said the man.

"I beg your pardon," said the doctor quietly. "Yes, he is dead. Shot through the brain."

"What sort of weapon have I to look for?" Charlton asked in a low tone.

"I can't be sure. When you've got the coroner's authority for a P.M., I'll extract the bullet."

"Much of a job?"

"It'll take time. Not like probing a wound in the body. It looks to me like a pistol. A rifle bullet would have probably gone right through his head. It certainly wasn't a shot gun, but it might have been a low-powered rook-rifle."

After which inconclusive, but eminently sound reply—for it is only your fictional medical man who can announce with certainty, after a swift glance at the wound, that the deed was done with a Mannlicher 7.63 mm. or a Webley .455 self-loader—the doctor burrowed his way through the crowd like a self-important ferret.

Johnson returned with some civilian assistants—the road-menders, murder or no murder, had gone to their dinners—and swiftly erected a barricade with trestles and poles. Charlton knew too much of human nature to expect an excited crowd to "stand well back, please" at the polite instance of two members of the police force.

When there was a clear space around the statue, he produced from his pocket a tiny camera, which, when he acquired it, nearly put the General Rates up a halfpenny. Six exposures satisfied him and he was folding up the camera when the ambulance arrived. At a word from him, the body was lifted over the railings by the uniformed men: then the doors were slammed and the car driven away.

During the time that all this had been going on, the relief constables from Littleworth and Lulverton had arrived by motor-cycle and car and were now stationed at the four corners of the Square, where they were having a busy time. When the general interest had centred round the statue, there had been few who had wished to leave the Square, but when the ambulance had turned into Heather Street, the excitement died down and the crowds began to disperse, in the same way as the onlookers make instantly for the exits, when the referee's whistle announces "No side."

"It's a net that lets through more fish than it keeps back," Charlton thought to himself, "but what more can a poor 'busy' do?"

"Get a megaphone," he said aloud to Johnson, who had rejoined him. "Is there one at the station? No? Well, slip off and buy one and bring it back here."

Johnson soon returned from Burnside's, the sports shop in the High Street overlooking the Square. After a few words from Charlton, he climbed the ladder against the statue railings and stepped onto the plinth.

"Will everyone now in the Square," his much amplified and unexpectedly refined voice came through the megaphone, "please move well back from the High Street. We regret having to detain you, but it is unavoidable. Every effort will be made to cause as little delay as possible. Will all those who have urgent business elsewhere kindly form up outside the Horticultural Hall, so that they may be dealt with first. All stall-holders, please, to stay by their stalls and all those in charge of animals to remain in their positions." The Great British Public is a docile thing. In France such a request would probably have led to an immediate rearrangement of *La Chambre des Deputés* and in South America to two revolutions, three counter-revolutions and a *coup d'état*; but now, in Paulsfield, England, the crowds moved obediently away from the High Street side of the Square, which enabled the ordinary business of the town to go on without undue obstruction.

Charlton hurried back to the police station. Martin looked up from his writing.

"Murder?" he asked.

"Looks like it. Might have been an accident, of course."

"I've rung up the Super at Lulverton and reported the matter. I told 'im you're here and he said 'e leaves things to you. What steps 'ave you taken?"

"I've locked, bolted and firmly secured the stable door," said Charlton with the shadow of a smile.

Martin looked at him quickly and an involuntary question slipped from him:

"Surely you didn't hear what I said? I didn't mean you to, sir. I'm sorry, sir."

"I have not heard you mention stable doors this morning, Martin. I have merely ventured to guess at your reactions to my suggestion about picketing the Square."

"You scored an inner that time," said Martin ruefully.

He and the Inspector were on the best of terms, but Martin knew well enough that it did not do to run foul of a senior man in the force, especially when that man was Detective-inspector Charlton.

"Now, Martin," said Charlton briskly, "let's get on with the job in hand. The man was shot through the brain and the ambulance has taken the body away, leaving; the Square full of potential witnesses. I know it's a pretty big task, but the only obvious course is to question the whole lot of them. Most of them were there when it happened and we've got to get all the information we can, while it's still fresh in their minds. I realize that between the time that shot was fired and the time when the men arrived from Lulverton and Littleworth, there was plenty of opportunity for anybody to leave the Square. But I don't think many did leave: the tendency was for the

Square to fill up. The body behind the statue railings drew everybody like a magnet."

"Everybody but one," said Martin dryly.

"Precisely. That gentleman's well away by this time and probably buried deep in the next valley glades. But those people in the Square *must* be questioned."

"You've got your work cut out, Inspector. Looks like being a busy afternoon for you."

"Not for me, Sergeant," said Charlton sweetly. "It is *you* who are going to be busy."

"But . . ." Martin began, then wisely started again:

"You want me to take down partic'lars? Certainly, if you wish it, Inspector."

"I think you'd better get in touch now with the caretaker of the Horticultural Hall and use that for the questioning. Pass them through the front entrance in the Square, take down what they've got to say and then let them out again through the exit in the Paragon."

"The whole five thousand of them?" asked Martin hoarsely.

"The total population of Paulsfield is only three thousand eight hundred," Charlton answered with a smile.

"Who's going to look after the station?" demanded Martin, suddenly seeing a loophole.

"I leave that to you, Martin," was the reply. "Now you ring up the caretaker of the Hall, while I jot down a questionnaire for you. We mustn't waste time. Our witnesses are probably loping up and down the Square like so many caged tigers."

"Let 'em lope," said Martin and pulled the telephone towards him.

II.

Question Time

MEREWORTH was not, perhaps, as famous as Eton, Harrow or Winchester, but her sons were to be found in many exalted walks of life. Most of her flannelled fools and muddied oafs certainly developed into completely respectable nonentities. That was inevitable: the greatest Public School in the land could have done no more with them. But there was a generous sprinkling of those who were "on Fame's eternall beadroll worthie to be fyled": surgeons, explorers, missionaries, scientists, rowing blues and many others who made names for themselves in the world. That, in several cases, the name was Mud was not really the fault of the bounteous mother. There was Paul Mullion, who became a Secretary of State for certain Affairs; young Richard Garroud, who wrote one good book that lived and thirty bad ones that enabled him to do the same; Percy Harridge, who became chairman of the South Western Bank, Ltd., and sat on more boards than a confirmed gallery first-nighter; Eric Jameson, who won a great reputation at the Bar and eventually took silk; Arthur Scott, who won an equal, if not quite so savoury, reputation in a front-page divorce case and eventually took cyanide; Jack Langdon, who dabbled in Long Firms until the Home Office found room for him in the rather gloomy building to the north of Hollowstone: and that quiet and gentle thunderbolt, Detective-inspector Harry Charlton, who helped to secure him the accommodation.

In Downshire, they called Charlton the "Doctor." A malefactor once complained that the big man had lured him into saying more than discretion should have allowed by the soothing magic of his bedside manner. The little dip did not

11

put it in quite those words, although his vocabulary was far from limited, but after that, the "Doctor's" bedside manner became a legend in the County Constabulary and among those with whom his calling brought him into touch. He had, as John Rutherford said, a comforting air. After a few minutes in his company, one felt that Pippa had hit the thing off to a nicety. Many a shifty-eyed gentleman with a guilty conscience warmed more and more towards him as their cosy little *téte-á-téte* proceeded. Here, thought each, is a man after my own heart, who doesn't bluster or bully or snarl disbelief at every little fib—a man broadminded enough to look at a thing by-and-large, with not too close an attention to niggling detail, helping a chap along with a friendly smile and now and then an encouraging word or two. Then, when the warm glow of good fellowship suffused the victim's soul and he was about to feel in his pocket for a tiny offering to the Police Orphanage, the Inspector's deep, caressing voice softly asked a question; and all the joy went out of life, leaving behind it only the coldness of naked terror.

He might have become a great K.C. As it was, he became a competent police officer and sang at his work. Not exactly sang, of course, but he enjoyed it, although he never tired of telling what an unromantic job it was. Much of it was certainly just dull routine, at which even the cheeriest enthusiast would not have sung; but when murder spoke with most miraculous organ, as, even in sleepy Downshire, it sometimes did, Charlton hummed a blithesome stave and happily laid aside the Case of the Rifled Cigarette Machine or the Strange Disappearance of Her Ladyship's Nauseating Pekingese.

He usually wore a dark grey suit, the otherwise faultless cut of which was marred by a bulge on his right hip, occasioned by nothing more alarming than the expensive little camera which has already been mentioned. His niece and chatelaine, Molly Arnold, had once complained about this protuberance, saying that it looked too horribly sinister, to which his only reply had been that that was the idea. The girl did not know—there were few who did—of the tiny Browning pistol that, ever since the unpleasantness with a bunch of Lascars in Southmouth docks, had reposed in the lower right-hand pocket of her uncle's waistcoat.

He was in the early fifties, clean-shaven, with thick greying hair brushed back from his forehead, large well-kept hands—but it will be as well if we return to our interrupted narrative.

While Martin was putting in hand his mass-examination, the Inspector was not idle. The Sergeant might elicit some useful information by means of the questionnaire; some bystander might even have seen the shot fired: but Charlton thought it was unlikely. There had been no excitement in the Square when it happened; no shouts of "There he goes!" or "I saw him run down Heather Street!" Instead, there had been an awesome hush, a silence of stupefaction. It was completely inconceivable to Charlton that any person standing in the Square could level a weapon, take aim and fire, without attracting general attention. Average Englishmen, he knew from experience, had as keenly developed powers of observation as a mumchance congregation of turnips, but even they could have hardly failed to notice such ostentatious behaviour.

The obvious alternative was that the shot had been fired from a window—probably an upper window, as, with the exception of the Church and the Horticultural Hall, all the buildings round the Square were shops or business premises. Murderers, thought Charlton, as he walked along the High Street towards the Square, share with a celebrated film-actress the desire to be alone: they like to carry out their spot of homicide as privately as possible. Apart from that, it seemed to him that a person sitting by an upper window would be more likely to notice anything that happened below than one who formed part of the market-day crowd. Some watcher might have seen suspicious goings-on in a room across the Square or a flash of flame as the murderer pulled the trigger.

At this stage in his meditations, Charlton arrested the course of his thoughts. He was already taking it for granted that the dead man had been murdered—an extremely reasonable premise, perhaps, but not the open-minded way, he chided himself, to begin an investigation.

When he reached the Square, he saw a queue of people stretching from the door of the Horticultural Hall, passing very slowly into the building under the courteous direction of P.C. Johnson. With the exception of the stall-holders and a few cow-men watching over their charges, the rest of the Square was deserted, the patrols still being on duty at its corners. A few shopkeepers stood in their doorways, possibly trying to arrive, by feverish mental arithmetic, at the amount they stood to lose through this unprecedented dislocation of their business. All the customers who had been inside the shops at the time of the picketing had been politely required to join the queue.

The man from Littleworth saluted as the Inspector walked past him into the Square and made his way towards the statue. The barrier of poles and trestles was still in position and Charlton rested his hands upon it, as he studied the horse and its rider, who faced, as has already been explained, towards the High Street. Elsewhere in this book is a plan of the *mise-en-scène,* a study of which may help the reader to follow the course of the Inspector's investigation and, perhaps, to foresee its conclusion.

As Charlton stood leisurely puffing at his cigarette, his eyes took in several facts, from which he drew certain-conclusions. The conclusions will be discussed later on: the facts were these:—

(1). The stone horse, like the figure astride it, was a good deal bigger than life-size. It was a full twenty-one hands, or, for those whose knowledge of horses begins and ends with the office sweep on Derby Day, seven feet from the animal's shoulder to the ground.

(2). The difference in colour between the stonework before and after cleaning was extremely marked.

From the condition of a section of the horse's near thigh, it was clear that the hard scrubbing necessary to shift the grime had been completed by the workman and that the rinsing with clean water was in progress when the shot brought him down. It was possible to fix almost the exact spot reached by the brush on its curving downward journey before being arrested by the murderer's bullet. The hot sun had dried off the moisture, but from a height of about five feet above the plinth, there were clean streaks where the rivulets of water had trickled down.

(3). Two buckets were still standing on the plinth. Charlton reached up and carefully brought down the left-hand one. It was three-quarters filled with cloudy water. The second bucket, which was standing on the corner of the plinth, contained about the same quantity of a liquid approaching the consistency of thin mud. This bucket had a brush in it, but the brush for applying the rinsing water was lying on the ground behind the railings.

When these facts had been duly recorded in the Inspector's mind, he turned from the statue and walked towards the red-faced linen-salesman, who was now sitting on his box with a cigarette, as crushed and dejected as he, hanging by a miracle of adhesion from his lower lip. Charlton's questioning of this man and the other stall-holders, cheap-jacks, hawkers and farmhands was later added to the data obtained by Sergeant Martin.

The red Shorthorn bull that had caused the disturbance was, by that time, securely tied outside the Post Office. Charlton asked the drover if the animal had snapped the rope that had been looped round its neck.

"No," said the man. "When a bull be fixed to they railings, un do be fixed. Good strong manilla it be and an inch thick.

Two turns round the top rail and then round the bottom rail with a double-'itch, and un never do free 'isself."

"How did this old fellow escape, then?"

The man's explanation was that he had led the animal towards the railings by means of a bullstaff, which was a stout ash pole with a spring link at one end of it for fastening to the copper ring in the bull's nose. But just as he reached the railings, the man stumbled and lost his hold on the staff. The bull, which had been made uneasy by the pneumatic-drills, reared back, swung round and lumbered across the Square with the staff swinging from his nose-ring and driving him to frenzy by bumping on the ground, battering his forelegs and getting under his feet. A few of the crowd made grabs at the wildly whirling staff, but only succeeded in annoying the bull still further. Then his foot came down on the staff and the nose-ring, thinned and weakened by wear, broke.

"The pain of it mazed un," said the drover, "and before un got back 'is wits, us looped a couple of ropes round 'is horns."

The road-excavators, as has been said, had gone to their dinners, except one man, who was cooking a sausage over a brazier when the Inspector approached his shelter. It is, in parenthesis, a remarkable thing that Council employees cannot stir a finger, even to the extent of anointing a square foot of highway with a lick of tar and a sprinkling of sand, until they have erected a shelter and lighted a coke fire. The man was sitting facing the High Street in the entrance to the shelter—a large tarpaulin contraption whose interior, when viewed from the outside, was murky—watching with a fish-like eye the sausage sizzling in the pan.

Charlton spent only a short while with this taciturn man, whose attention it was difficult to attract for long from the contemplation of his sausage. Like a High Priest importuned in the midst of a solemn sacrifice, he abstractedly answered Charlton's questions. No, he had not seen anything. Had he heard a shot? What, with them drills going? Had he heard a shot? Hadn't he just said he hadn't? Where were his mates— at their dinners? He pondered on this for some time and then announced that that was so, adding, with unexpected garrulity that they were all Paulsfield men, while he came from Burgeston. Would they be back by one o'clock? This question also needed consideration. They would be back *at* one. Charlton pictured them with their watches in their hands, avoiding any possibility of resuming work a split second before the time laid down by their Union. Would he give a message to the foreman? This was answered by what may be loosely described as a noise, which Charlton interpreted to mean that, entirely without prejudice or any obligation to himself, he would, provided that it put him to no personal inconvenience, give a message, on the understanding that he didn't forget all about it, to the foreman, if and when he saw him.

The Inspector smiled blandly down at him and murmured a few words. Their effect on the man would have given pleasure to his enemies. Even the sausage seem to give a terrified splutter.

"It wasn't me, sir!" he said. "I swear it wasn't me! I was only in there'aving a glass o' beer, on my Bible oath!"

"Then it must have been some naughty little goblin who passed the slip," the Inspector smiled. "Not that it really matters. Ten pounds is a mere fleabite and three months soon go by. Will you give a message to the foreman for me?"

It now seemed that nothing would please the workman to a greater degree. He expressed himself more than anxious to do anything possible for the Inspector. Ask the foreman to see the Inspector? Why, of course, he would be delighted. A dull pop interrupted his protestations. The sausage, fretting at this inattention, had o'erbrimm'd its clammy cell.

It will be seen from the plan that there were not many buildings around the Square, each side of which measured approximately fifty yards. The churchyard with its square-towered building occupied the whole of the western side. On the northern side was the Horticultural Hall, where, besides flower and vegetable shows, held under the auspices of the Paulsfield Horticultural Society, were housed such other entertainments as concerts, dancing displays and sales of work. To the east of the Hall was a passage leading into Effingham Street. Then there were two shops, a branch of the Southern Counties Bank, Ltd., and, on the corner, the Post Office. On the south side of the Square were five more shops, the one on the High Street corner being "Voslivres," which was kept by John Rutherford. It might be said that there were no buildings on the eastern margin of the Square, in so far as they were on the other side of the High Street. It was possible to see the statue from several buildings that did not face the Square, but those to the north were part of a new block of shops, none of which had been let. The fronts were boarded up, with spaces between the planks that allowed a view of the empty interiors, and the flats above were, as yet, unoccupied.

To the south of this block were three shops. The big one in the middle, which was Highman's, *the* drapers of Paulsfield, had originally been three shops, but had been transformed into one magnificent establishment, with a fascia that was a riot of chromium plate and a vast acreage of window space, a large proportion of which was devoted to the restrained display of one hat. To the south of this—yes, it shall be said—this *monstrosity* was Burnside's, the toy and sports shop, and to the north, Mr. Harbottle's small premises, which were dedicated to the outfitting of gents and boys. A more ill-matched pair of neighbours than Highman's and Harbottle's was hard to imagine, reminding one of the picture, "Dignity and Impudence," except that, in the case of the shops, Dignity was the smaller.

Southward from Burnside's were two more shops from which the statue was visible, but from these and all the other buildings in the High Street, Charlton had little hope of collecting helpful information. Their very position had protected them from the isolation that had been imposed on the other shops in the Square. One could segregate the Square, but the High Street was another matter. It was still only half-past twelve when Charlton tore himself away from the effusive navvy, but many customers must have come and gone since the workman met his death.

Highman's and Burnside's devoted their whole buildings to their businesses, but the shops to the south had living accommodation over them. Charlton visited them all, but discovered no useful witnesses. From his examination of the statue, he had decided that Mr. Harbottle was likely to prove more productive than the other traders and dwellers in the High Street and his conversation with the outfitter is repeated here in full.

The dapper, bald little man, with a tape-measure worn with a certain nonchalance around his neck and a coat-lapel bristling with pins, expressed himself eager to tell Charlton all he knew about the affair, but as he appeared to know nothing, was not of any great assistance as a witness. Mrs. Harbottle, he regretted, had been out since eleven o'clock and the children were at school—or rather, he hastened to add, were, by this time, probably on their way home to dinner. Would the Inspector care to wait until Mrs. Harbottle returned? No, the Inspector hardly thought he would. He took it that at midday there had been nobody upstairs? Mr. Harbottle was pleased to confirm this. And had he had any customers in his shop at midday? Yes, Mrs. Middleton had brought her son in to be fitted for a blazer. It gave him pleasure to inform the Inspector that he was the officially appointed retailer for the blazers, ties and caps that distinguished the pupils of Paulsfield College for the Sons of Gentlemen. The name? Middleton. Mrs. Middleton of Chesapeake Road. Number twenty-four. Mrs. Middleton. That, the Inspector thought, was all, thank Mr. Harbottle very much. Mr. Harbottle said that it had been an honour and how was the Inspector off for shirts?

It said something for Charlton's Sales-Resistance that when he left the shop, he carried no parcel neatly tied by the chubby hands of Mr. Harbottle.

Charlton passed along to the empty block of shops and made sure that it was deserted. He peered through the boarding into each shop and walked right round the block, checking all the doors and window fastenings. It took him five minutes to satisfy himself that nobody without a key had entered or left the block.

He crossed the High Street to the Post Office.

It is the custom for Londoners to jeer at the provinces for their cinemas, shops, omnibuses and primitive sewage, but there is one subject on which they ought to show a decent reticence—Post Offices. When it comes to Post Offices, Suburbia must yield place to Arcadia. Choose any country town you like, ask to be directed to the Post Office and there will be pointed out to you a fine, commodious building with a pleasing interior, in which it is a pleasure to wait for a stamp until the busy fingers of the young woman at the counter have completed the requisite number of K's and P's to finish the row. But tour the suburbs of the metropolis and rarely will you find a Post Office that is not run as a side-line by a newsagent, an ironmonger or a grocer. It is a dismal experience to chafe while Mrs. Hither Green is supplied with half-a-pound of short-back, and then to issue hastily into the street, with the mingled odour of paraffin and Stilton in your nostrils, murder in your heart and sawdust on your shoes.

Paulsfield Post Office was a clean white building with a black and white checked rubber floor and a quadrant-shaped mahogany counter. Most Post Offices are not nowadays on corners, because the P.M.G. discovered that he could get fine prices from the Banks for such sites; but in Paulsfield the Post Office still held that proud position.

None of the three girls or the other officials then on the premises had anything to tell Charlton. They could see very little through the windows, the lower halves of which were frosted, and they had first heard about the tragedy from a customer. The upper part of the building was let off as a private flat with its entrance in the High Street, but the occupier was away with his family on their summer holiday.

The Southern Counties Bank next door was a little more helpful than the Post Office. The cashier was a smiling young man, who asked if the Inspector would care to speak to the manager. Charlton said that he would certainly like to do that, but in the meantime could he, the cashier, tell him anything about the shooting? He had noticed, he said, that the window-screens obscured most of the view of the Square, but perhaps the cashier had heard the sound of a shot?

Several heads had, by this time, bobbed up over the screen behind what is technically known as the cashiers' run, and the busy tap-tap of a typewriter had ceased.

"Those drills rather prevented us from hearing anything else," the cashier admitted, "but *you* said you heard something, didn't you, Bloar?"

Bloar was more definite than that.

"I *know* I heard something. The drills were going full-blast, but there was one explosion that was certainly not made by a drill—it hadn't that flat, thudding noise with a sort of loose rattle about it. Wood heard it too. Didn't you, Wood?" Wood nodded. He was a long mournful boy, obviously new to the Bank, who hardly looked as if he would survive his three months' probation before melancholia got a firm hold on him. Charlton marvelled that there should be room for so many pimples on one face.

"I said to Wood," Bloar went on, "that somebody's car tyre had gone off. They do sometimes, you know, when the sun has been on them too long. I had a friend—"

"This gentleman doesn't want to hear about your friend, Bloar," the cashier pulled him up.

"To the contrary," smiled Charlton. "I have found that the only interesting things that ever happen, happen to people's friends or to their cousins in Manchester. When a man says, 'I once had an unusual experience,' you can depend upon it that he is lying. Did the explosion seem to come from close at hand?"

On this point Bloar was not so forthright.

"I shouldn't like to say," he said dubiously. "It sounded pretty loud, but it might have come from anywhere. I expect the Square echoes a lot."

"What do you say, Mr. Wood?"

This sudden mention by name deprived the young gentleman of speech for some moments, but at last he managed to gulp out that he had heard a bang and that was all he could really say.

"What time did this explosion occur?"

"A very few moments before midday," said Bloar.

"In the ordinary way, I go to lunch at twelve and I was actually glancing at the clock when it happened."

A word or two with the manager and the accountant, who came out of the inner office at this point in the conversation, did not help much. The two of them had been discussing the question of an advance and had noticed nothing.

The upper floors of the building, Charlton learnt, were empty. The previous tenant had moved out on the June quarter day and the new man had not yet taken over.

He thanked the manager and his staff for their assistance and as he pushed open the door and went out again into the Square, caught Bloar's excited question:

"D'you know who that was? That was the 'Doctor'!"

He smiled and murmured to himself:

"'Nor Fame I slight, nor for her favours call;
    She comes unlook'd for, if she comes at all.'"

He glanced up at the name over the next shop. It was "Alexander Pope."

III.

Gold-Rimmed

A S ONE walked into his shop, Mr. Alexander Pope was a confectioner on the left and a tobacconist on the right. At the back was a door panelled with blue and red stained glass, with a lace curtain fixed across the parlour side of it. Whenever the bell summoned Mr. Pope into the shop, a swift glance at his customer told him which way to wheel, if such a military phrase can be used of Mr. Pope's splay-footed shuffle. If the customer stood against the tobacco counter, Mr. Pope went left; if the customer stood against the sweet counter, Mr. Pope went right: and if the customer elected to stand in the middle of the shop, Mr. Pope was reduced to a condition of delicious uncertainty and stood like a setter whose best days are done.

It could be said of Mr. Pope that he did not spare himself. One bought, let us say, a quarter of a pound of toffees and then required ten Gold Flake. This compelled Mr. Pope to walk right round to the tobacco counter. When the cigarettes had been duly handed over, one suddenly remembered those glycerine gums for the wife's throat; and Mr. Pope shuffled back to the confectionery department. Then it occurred to one that Jones, who was coming round for bridge, always smoked cork-tipped, and once again Mr. Pope set out upon his dismal pilgrimage. It should be added that he did it with the best grace in the world. He had been doing it for twenty-five years, so presumably had got used to it.

The bell rang as Charlton pushed open the door and walked into the shop. He had time, before the proprietor arrived, to note the interior and the circular marble-topped table bearing a vase of artificial carnations, at which one could sit and drink a still-lemon or a stone-ginger. Nobody ever did, but that was the idea. When Mr. Pope came through from the parlour, Charlton asked for ten Player's and while leisurely tearing off the cellophane and taking a cigarette from the packet, said to Mr. Pope:

"A nasty thing to have happen almost outside your door—this shooting, I mean."

"It was indeed," replied Mr. Pope. "A most unusual thing to happen on market-day. I have been here a quarter of a century, yet I cannot recall another such occasion."

This was not intended to be funny: there was not much humour in Mr. Pope's make-up. He was tall and drooping, with scanty hair and a moustache that seemed to have tarried, like a forest of dead trees, long after the roots of it had died. Charlton guessed him to be sixty-five or six.

"I have no doubt," the tobacconist went on, "that the police have the situation well in hand."

"I am Inspector Charlton."

"Oh, indeed? I am very pleased to make your acquaintance. I suppose you are looking into this tragic affair?"

"Yes," the Inspector agreed, "and I am hoping that you can help me."

"*I* help you? Why, by all means, Inspector, but I quite fail to see how."

"I am wondering whether you saw anything of what happened. I notice that it is possible to see the statue over those curtains behind the stock in your window. Did you see this man working on the statue?"

"I saw him earlier to-day," said Mr. Pope. "He had been up there all the morning. I am under the impression that he was cleaning down the stonework."

"That is quite correct," said Charlton without a trace of a smile, "but did you see him at the time the shot was fired?"

"That question I can answer with a definite negative, Inspector. A minute or two before the church clock struck

24

twelve, I had occasion to—leave the shop unattended. It is sometimes very awkward when one is in business by oneself. When I came downstairs again, I immediately noticed something untoward had happened in the Square. That, I am afraid, is all I can tell you."

"Did you hear the sound of a shot?"

"That is a very interesting point, Inspector. I think I can safely say that I did. I was upstairs in the—back of the house and I have the most definite recollection of noticing an explosion. Even where I was, I could still hear very clearly the commotion of those pneumatic-drills. Why they cannot continue to use the old-fashioned sledge-hammers, which were not only rhythmic, but also dignified, I am at a loss to understand. I could still hear the drills, but this isolated explosion seemed not to be a part of the road-making activities. It was closer and more—individual. I hope I make myself clear?"

"Eminently, Mr. Pope. Can you give me any idea of how close this explosion seemed to be?"

"If I had to give an opinion on that point, Inspector, I should say that it was comparatively adjacent—but I hasten to add that that is only my opinion. If a man's life depended on my evidence, I should hesitate to appear too definite."

"What was the time when you heard this shot?"

"About noon. Perhaps a minute either way."

"You have a family, Mr. Pope?"

"Alas, no. My wife died five years ago and since then I have lived here by myself. A very lonely existence, I am sorry to say."

Charlton expressed his sympathies, which were sincere. He had taken rather a liking to Mr. Pope, with his old-fashioned phrasing and his air of one whom the world had left behind. He seemed not so much a decayed gentleman as a superannuated solicitors' chief clerk. There seemed nothing more to be gained from him, so Charlton bade him good morning.

Between Mr. Pope's establishment and the Horticultural Hall was a second-hand shop, although Joseph Beamish, its

proprietor, preferred to announce on his sun-blind that he was
a curio and art dealer. Putting it with alliterative frankness, the
contents of the window was just jumbled junk—the jetsam
of a thousand households: china, glass, silver, brass, chess-men,
ping-pong balls, geometry-sets, cameras, barometers, pictures,
all higgledy-piggledy. Along the pavement outside were
ranged a couple of boxes filled with books. Tin-tacked to the
fronts of them were cards bearing the respective legends "All
in this box 2d." and "Prices marked inside covers." Sensitive
purchasers, who sought afterwards to remove evidence of a
book's small cost, cursed the seller heartily for not using an
ordinary H.B., for the prices inside the covers were pencilled
in with the ineradicability of Omar's moving finger; but Mr.
Beamish, that disillusioned man, had discovered many years
before that an indelible pencil firmly used dissuaded customers
of questionable probity from putting in some swift work with
an eraser, thereby relegating a novel valued at tenpence to the
humble level of "All in this box."

The musty smell of old things leapt out at Charlton as he
walked into the shop. Most of the interior was cluttered up
with odds and ends, and one had to move with circumspection
to avoid disaster. Pinned to a soiled white card hanging on
the wall was a set of corporal's stripes. Charlton asked himself
who, in the name of all that was wonderful, could possibly
want those and had decided that they might, perhaps, have
some appeal for a lance-corporal, when Mr. Beamish came
down the staircase that led straight into the shop. He was a
small, spare man, of about the same age as Mr. Pope, with stiff,
upstanding hair that was nearer white than grey, and Charlton
summed him up as a snufftaking, unsystematic old dodderer—a
fairly accurate valuation. He suffered from deafness—not the
spasmodic infirmity that can so discomfit incautious relations,
but a real blanket of deafness. We will not try to enhance
the humorous merits of this book by the insertion of comic
dialogue based on the faulty hearing of Mr. Beamish. He was

deaf; one had to shout to make him hear: mercifully, we will leave it at that.

Charlton explained his mission.

"I am afraid," was the reply, "that I know very little. During the course of my morning's work, I happened to glance out into the Square and saw a crowd round the statue. I immediately said to myself that the workman had fainted— affected by the hot sun; and then, I'm sorry to have to admit, I lost all interest in the matter. My business, Inspector, makes great calls on my attention. I had, of course, noticed the man earlier this morning and he was up there most of yesterday."

Charlton asked if he had heard the sound of a shot.

"I fear that I hear nothing very clearly, Inspector," said Mr. Beamish with an apologetic smile. "I suffer from deafness— closure of the Eustachian tube."

"I should have thought," said Charlton, "that the sound of a loud explosion of that kind would have been caught, even by a person hard of hearing."

"In that, you are perfectly right. If a shot was fired, there is every likelihood that I heard it, but I assure you that it did not impress itself on my mind. You, I take it, Inspector, are not deaf and everyday sounds are quite audible to you. They form a background of which you are hardly conscious. A loud noise attracts your attention, but a loud noise does not attract my attention, for loud noises are the background of which *I* am hardly conscious. If I were given to swearing," Mr. Beamish finished on an unexpectedly humorous note, "I could tell you precisely how loud a noise would have to be before I really noticed it!"

The Inspector smiled.

"I think I see what you mean," he said. "Where were you, Mr. Beamish, at the time the shot was fired?"

"That I can't tell you until I know when it was fired. I have only my sister's assurance that the shooting actually took place. She came in from shopping about five minutes past twelve and told me that the poor man had been shot through the head."

"I'll put it another way, Mr. Beamish," said Charlton patiently. "Were you in this shop at midday?"

"Yes," Mr. Beamish replied, "I was. I had been taking advantage of a lull in business by getting things tidied up. In a shop of this kind, it is so easy for everything to fall into confusion. I had just got everything ship-shape when, as I said, I chanced to look out into the Square."

The Inspector mastered a strong desire to smile at Mr. Beamish's conception of ship-shape, and asked whether he had been alone at midday.

"Quite alone. I have not had a customer since eleven o'clock. Several people examined books in the boxes outside, but none of them made a purchase. Of course, my sister was upstairs at midday."

"But I understood you to say that she did not return from her shopping until five-past twelve."

Mr. Beamish smiled.

"I fear I am misleading you, Inspector," he said "Your question was justified. I have *two* sisters, one who is a widow and the other who is still a spinster. It was Miss Beamish who went out shopping—she looks after the domestic side of our modest establishment. My other sister, Mrs. Archer, who seldom leaves the house, was, to the best of my belief, in her bed-sitting-room."

"She is an invalid?"

"I would hardly say that, Inspector. Her husband died in 1923 from wounds received during the Great War and my poor sister has never really recovered from the shock. When this great tragedy overtook her—she was wrapped up in my brother-in-law, who was a splendid fellow, mentioned twice in dispatches and won the D.S.O.—Erica came here to live with Ruth—my other sister—and me, and has lived here ever since. The front room on the first floor has been given over entirely to her and nothing pleases her more than to pass her days quietly in it. Besides being a great crossword enthusiast, she loves to spend these beautiful summer mornings sitting by the open window, watching the world go by."

"Would it be possible to have a word with her?" asked Charlton.

Mrs. Archer looked like being helpful.

"I am sure she will be delighted to see you," said Mr. Beamish, "but I beg of you not to alarm her with this tragic happening."

"But," protested Charlton mildly, "I can't avoid touching on it. I *must* ask her one or two questions."

"Then do it as gently as possible. Say that the man was injured in an accident. I have cautioned Ruth not to speak too much of it. I'll introduce you as Mr. . . . . Forgive me, but what is your name again?"

"Charlton."

"I'll introduce you as Mr. Charlton. That is less likely to disturb her. Will you be kind enough to step upstairs? Bless my soul, where did I lay my glasses?"

Charlton drew his attention to the spectacles lying on top of a gramophone cabinet and Mr. Beamish then led the way up the staircase, the side wall of which was decorated with knob-kerries, assegais, war-shields and tennis rackets.

When he followed Mr. Beamish into Mrs. Archer's sitting-room, Charlton saw two women sitting opposite each other at a table. Both of them were somewhere between fifty-five and sixty, but they were of distinctly differing types. One was tall, with dark hair hardly touched with grey and startlingly light blue eyes that stared keenly through a pair of gold-rimmed spectacles. She seemed to possess a more masterful personality than the other woman, who was shorter, fairer haired and stouter, and preferred pince-nez glasses. Neither of them had ever been beautiful. It would be ungallant to say that neither of them had ever been attractive. If it was, or ever had been, necessary to say which of the two had more physical charm, the vote would have undoubtedly gone to her of the pince-nez spectacles.

They were playing a game, which the Inspector immediately identified as the friend of his earlier years, "Word Making and Word Taking." Between them on the tablecloth were scattered squares of cardboard with red backs. Separated from these was another smaller cluster, but these were turned face upwards, showing the letters printed on them. Immediately in front of both players were words that had been already formed. Gold-rimmed had four words and Pince-nez five. Charlton noticed that Pince-nez's letters were not in so precise an alignment as Gold-rimmed's.

They were both so intent on their game that they seemed not to notice the arrival of their brother and the Inspector. One of the words in front of Gold-rimmed was ICE. Pince-nez took a square from the table and turned it over. It was an N. She reached across the table and laid it in front of ICE.

"There you are, dear," she said in mild triumph. "N-I-C-E. That gives me six words and makes me one game up."

"Oh, no it doesn't," said the other tartly. "Nice is a town in the South of France and it definitely says in the rules that geographical and proper names are not allowed."

"But it isn't Nice, it's nice," Pince-nez protested.

"Nice is a town and towns are not allowed," said Gold-rimmed; then went on without looking round, "What do you say, Joseph?"

"I don't like to express an opinion on such a technical point," smiled Mr. Beamish. "But please spare a moment from your game, my dears, and allow me to introduce Mr. Carlton, an old friend of mine."

"You have met him this morning for the first time, Joseph," said Gold-rimmed, "his name is not Carlton, but Charlton, and he is not Mr., but Detective-inspector of the County Police."

"He prefers to be styled Mr. when he makes a friendly, out-of-business-hours call," said Mr. Beamish.

"Don't *soothe* me, Joseph," said Gold-rimmed. "Inspector, I am Mrs. Archer and this is my sister, Miss Beamish. Won't you sit down?"

"Thank you," Charlton replied, and took a chair. "I happened to be passing this house this morning and I took it into my head to drop in——"

"To see if we knew who murdered Thomas Earnshaw," Mrs. Archer finished his sentence in rather more brutal terms than he himself would have used.

"That, frankly, was my intention," he agreed. "You have certainly supplied me with some information already: his name."

"There is one more widow in Paulsfield to-day," said Mrs. Archer.

"Erica, my *dear,* don't be so heartless," said Miss Beamish.

"I am not being heartless," her sister retorted. "I am stating a fact. The Inspector has come to us for information and I am the one to give it to him. If there is any inhabitant of Paulsfield whose name and history I do not know, he must have moved in this morning."

She turned to Charlton.

"You did not know the murdered man's name, Inspector. Perhaps there are other interesting things I can tell you about him. Ruth, I think I catch a suspicious smell of burning coming from the kitchen. Wasn't that the shop bell, Joseph?"

Lady Macbeth did not drop a plainer hint than that, and when her brother and sister had taken it, Mrs. Archer pulled her chair a little nearer to the Inspector.

IV.

Mrs. Archer is Helpful

"INSPECTOR CHARLTON," said Mrs. Archer, "I am a plain-spoken woman and you, I feel sure, are a plain-spoken man. We both of us call a spade a spade."

In which she gravely misjudged Charlton. He called a spade a spade only when his main interest lay in the trowel or the watering-can. There were few people to whom he ever revealed what was passing through his mind. Sergeant Martin was one: Dr. Weston another. This, of course, applied only to the professional side of his existence. In private life, on the few occasions when he could enjoy that luxury, he was very different.

He inclined his head at this intended compliment.

"My brother and sister think that I am not right in my mind," Mrs. Archer went on. "Many years ago, my husband died and I'll admit that for some time afterwards my reason was in danger; but now I am as sane as you are. I'll admit, too, that I have my odd little ways, but Joseph and Ruth take them for signs of insanity. You can call me eccentric if you like, but if all eccentrics were measured for a strait-waistcoat, we should have no art, literature or police force."

Her pale blue eyes glinted humorously behind her glasses and Charlton smiled in reply.

"I spend most of my life in this room and from the window I see everything that goes on. I know everybody and I see them coming and going, day in and day out. Nothing happens in Paulsfield that I don't hear about. If Mrs. Jones has a baby, I know before she does whether it is a boy or a girl."

"It's wonderful how you keep in touch with things without leaving the house," said Charlton, for want of a better remark.

He was waiting for an opportunity to turn the conversation in a less autobiographical direction.

"You think so?" asked Mrs. Archer eagerly. "I have, of course, the telephone"—she nodded towards a corner of the room— "and Ruth is clever at picking up tit-bits for me. Then I have the *Downshire County Herald* and the *Paulsfield Weekly News.*"

"The 'Screamer,'" smiled Charlton.

"I know that's what everybody calls it," Mrs. Archer agreed, "but it gives very accurate reports of births, deaths and marriages. I have little social gatherings here every Wednesday afternoon. I get a lot of information from them. Do you see those?"

She pointed to a corner by the window overlooking the Horticultural Hall, where there stood a nest of four drawers, on which the telephone was placed. They were marked "A—C," "D—L," "M—R" and "S—Z."

"A card-index," she said with the relish of a small girl discussing strawberries and cream. "An index of the population of Paulsfield, with a card for every man, woman and child. All the drawers are fitted with 8-lever Chubb locks and there's only one key for them, which I never let out of my possession."

"A very interesting hobby," said Charlton approvingly, "and more useful than collecting match-boxes or bottlecorks."

Mrs. Archer looked like being even more helpful than he had hoped.

"You want to know something about Thomas Earnshaw?" she said. "Let me see what I can do for you."

As she rose to her feet and walked across to the card-index, the Inspector took a glance round the room. It afforded a pleasant change from the disorder of the shop below. The furniture was well-made and in good taste. Standing against one wall was a glass-panelled bookcase filled with a collection of books that showed a catholic taste in literature. A big black Bible stood next to *Jesting Pilate* and *The Three Just Men* rubbed shoulders with *Candide.* In a large bowl on the table were roses that filled the room with their scent. On the sills outside the open windows that looked on to the Square were green-painted boxes of geraniums, and from the walls hung a few original etchings. Along one side was a divan bed, by the side of which was a chromium-plated clock with a square face, and a volume of essays by Hilaire Belloc on top of a copy of *Punch*. In the corner by one of the front windows was a radio-gramophone with the *Listener* lying on its lid.

"Here we are," said Mrs. Archer after a short search, and returned to her chair with a card.

"'Thomas Earnshaw,'" she read. "'Elder son of Minnie, wife of Frank Earnshaw, builders' foreman. Born 1893. War service in Mesopotamia (conversation, 1932)'—I had a chat with him then. 'Employed 1924 onwards by P. Urban District Council as labourer. Married 1923 Ellen, eldest daughter of John and Mary Baggs (q.v.).' That means 'which see.'"

"Thank you," said Charlton gratefully.

"'Daughter, Kate,'" Mrs. Archer continued, "'born 1924. Son, Henry, born 1926. Daughter, Grace, born 1929, died same year. Kate won prize for under-ten-years sewing competition at St. Mark's sale of work, Nov., 1933. Hobby, fretwork (conversation, 1932).' Not, I'm afraid, a very exciting record, Inspector!"

"'The short and simple annals of the poor,'" he smiled.

"Which, I think somebody once said," remarked Mrs. Archer, "were anything but short and far from simple. Would you like to see the card?"

She handed it to him and he glanced through the particulars, until he came to a red-ink note at the bottom. After that's day's date, there had been written the following:—

"Shot in Paulsfield Square by   (q.v.)."

"Your records are certainly up to date, Mrs. Archer," he said.

"As soon as you find out who did it, I shall fill in the name."

"I suppose you don't have particulars of anyone living outside the boundaries of Paulsfield?" Charlton asked, and Mrs. Archer shook her head.

"I am a specialist," she said proudly.

"I ask you that," he said, "because I notice that you have written 'q.v.' after the space for the name of the person who shot Earnshaw. That suggests that you are assuming it to be an inhabitant of this town."

"A reasonable assumption, for all that," said Mrs. Archer slightly acidly. "Tom Earnshaw has lived and worked in Paulsfield all his life, except during the war years. His interests are in Paulsfield, his relations and friends are in Paulsfield and if he has made any enemies, he has made them in Paulsfield."

"Have you any record of his relations, Mrs. Archer? I believe there is a brother."

Mrs. Archer looked as if she begrudged him this information. She did not, however, ask him how he knew.

"That would be Albert," she said. "There were only two sons. Martha, the sister, is on the kitchen staff over at Meanhurst Grange, Lord Shawford's place. The mother and father, old Frank and Minnie Earnhsaw, are dead, I think. I'll look at their cards and make sure."

She went over and extracted various cards from the drawers.

"These will give us the whole story," she said, as she came back to her chair. "If you have a notebook, Inspector, you may care to make a few jottings. Frank Earnshaw married Minnie Phillpotts and she bore him three children: Thomas, Martha and Albert. John Baggs married Mary Jenkins and she bore him four children: Ellen, Frank, Mary and Jane. Thomas Earnshaw married Ellen Baggs and she bore him three children: Kate, Henry and Grace. Albert Earnshaw married Jane Baggs—yes, I had forgotten that: the two Earnshaw boys married two of the Baggs sisters. Frank Baggs is a bachelor and gets a living doing rough gardening and odd jobs—making rabbit-hutches, creosoting fences, cutting keys and so on; and Mary, the third

35

Baggs sister, has stayed a spinster. This also applies to Martha Earnshaw, who, as I thought, is in the employment of Lord Shawford."

"You say," said Charlton, "that Albert Earnshaw married Jane Baggs. Are there any children?"

"Yes, one—a boy of six, named Albert after his father."

Charlton made a rough genealogical tree, the details of which, for the sake of clarity, are reproduced here:—

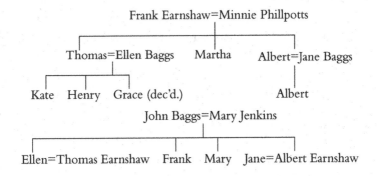

Frank Earnshaw=Minnie Phillpotts

Thomas=Ellen Baggs   Martha   Albert=Jane Baggs

Kate   Henry   Grace (dec'd.)   Albert

John Baggs=Mary Jenkins

Ellen=Thomas Earnshaw   Frank   Mary   Jane=Albert Earnshaw

"John Baggs and Frank and Minnie Earnshaw," explained Mrs. Archer, "are dead. Mary Baggs is still living in Paulsfield with Frank, the son, and Mary, the daughter."

"Can you give me any other particulars about Albert Earnshaw, the dead man's brother?"

"He is a plasterer working for Oakden's, the building contractors."

"There's nothing—interesting about his career?"

Mrs. Archer's eyes twinkled.

"By which I suppose you mean scandalous?" she asked. "I'm afraid not. The whole history of the Earnshaw and Baggs families is entirely commonplace and dull."

"I'm greatly obliged to you, Mrs. Archer, for this extremely useful information. Now may I trouble you to turn your mind to this morning. Did you see or hear anything of the shooting of Earnshaw?"

"I'll tell you all I know about it," said Mrs. Archer, "which I'm afraid isn't much. I was sitting in that easy chair there, doing the crossword puzzle in the newspaper. From time to time, I glanced through the window to see what was going on. I was just filling in a word that had been teasing me for some little while. The clue was, 'There's metal in this wood,' and the word turned out to be 'forest.' Rather clever, don't you think? Well, I was just pencilling it in, when I heard extra shouting break out in the Square. I leant forward to see what all the excitement was about and saw a bull careering across the Square, with all the people falling over each other to get away from it. I guessed that it had broken away from its tethering outside the Post Office. When I saw it, it was charging along more or less parallel with the High Street. Then it swerved to the right and I was beginning to fear that somebody was going to get hurt, when I heard a loud explosion and saw, out of the corner of my eye, the man who was cleaning the statue throw up his arms, then sort of crumple up and fall in a heap down behind the railings."

"Did the explosion strike you as coming from any particular point?"

"It was very loud, but I shouldn't like to say where it came from. An explosion like that is very elusive and seems to come from everywhere at once, especially in a limited space like the Square. I should say, at a fairly rough guess, that it was fired quite close to me."

"You say, 'especially in a limited space like the Square.' Am I to assume that you received the impression that the shot was fired *in* the Square?"

"Yes, I did get that impression, but really I was so flustered by the bull and Earnshaw falling like that off the statue, that I didn't think very much at the time about the explosion."

"Did you happen to notice anything else, Mrs. Archer, that may be of assistance to me?"

"I noticed one small thing, but I don't think it's very likely to lead to anything. Almost immediately after Earnshaw fell, the men got the bull under control and it wasn't until then, I think, that anybody besides myself noticed his body behind the railings. It was little Jack Harris, the newsagent's youngest boy, who saw him and drew the attention of Mr. Chase of Handen Street to him. Mr. Chase peered down at Earnshaw and then sent Jack off to find a policeman. That good-looking young constable, Tom Johnson, was in the Square and Jack soon found him. By this time, people were beginning to crowd round the statue. Johnson bent down and had a look at Earnshaw's head and then sent Jack running off to the other policeman, who was directing the traffic along the High Street. He's not a local man, so I don't know his name," she added regretfully.

"And this small thing that you noticed, Mrs. Archer?"

"Oh, yes. Everybody was crowding round the statue, except the people who couldn't leave what they were doing. It's a natural instinct, when anything has happened, to go and see what it is and when there's a crowd obviously attracted by something, it's against all the laws of human nature not to go and join that crowd. Don't you think so, Inspector?"

"It's a very strong temptation, certainly," he agreed.

"Well, there was one man in the Square who wasn't human."

Charlton leant forward.

"I didn't see where he came from and I didn't recognize who he was. I only saw his back. He was walking briskly along the pavement just outside here in the direction of the High Street. He was dressed in a grey flannel suit and wore a brown soft felt hat. He was carrying something in his hand, but I couldn't make out what it was. It struck me, at the time, as strange that he should show so little interest in the excitement round the statue. He was obviously in a hurry and, by leaning out of the window, I could see him turn to the left into the High Street. As he walked past the Bank, he looked at his wrist-watch. I got the general impression that he was young."

"Very interesting, Mrs. Archer," said Charlton. "A matter

that needs looking into."

There was a knock at the door and Mrs. Archer called, "Come in."

It was Miss Beamish.

"Erica, dear," she said, "I don't want to hurry you at all, but if we don't have lunch soon, it will be completely ruined."

Charlton jumped to his feet.

"I'm afraid I'm interfering with your domestic arrangements, Miss Beamish," he said with an apologetic smile, "but I won't keep Mrs. Archer any longer."

"Won't you stay and have something with us, Inspector?" asked Miss Beamish. "I'm sure we should all be delighted."

"It is very kind of you to suggest it," he replied, "but I'm afraid that my duties won't allow it. Before the police ban is lifted from this Square, I have a good many places to visit. If I stay here too long in such pleasant company, somebody will write to the papers about the slowness and general inefficiency of the police force! I should like, though, before I go, to take a few moments of your time, Miss Beamish."

"Certainly," she smiled.

"Can you give me any information about this shooting?"

"None at all, I'm afraid, Inspector. I was shopping in the High Street and as I walked home across the Square, I saw a crowd round the statue and asked a man at the back what had happened. He said that a man had been shot. That rather alarmed me and I hurried back here."

"Thank you, Miss Beamish. I think that is all I have to ask you ladies. I hope I shan't have to worry you again."

"We hope you will," said Miss Beamish coquettishly. "Don't we, Erica?"

"Not on quite such an unpleasant errand, anyway!" smiled Charlton, and wished them good morning.

"A charming man," said Miss Beamish, when he had gone, "and not a bit like an ordinary policeman."

"*And* a bachelor," said Mrs. Archer musingly.

"I caught him looking at you once or twice, Erica," said Miss Beamish with a rougish smile.

"Ruth," retorted her sister, "don't be a fool."

The queue outside the Horticultural Hall had considerably decreased when Charlton came out into the Square. On the corner of the Paragon opposite the Hall was a building occupied by a firm of monumental masons. There were no windows on its frontage, all the necessary illumination being obtained from the type of sloping windows on the roof that are known as "top-lights." On the other side of a carriage-way, which itself was out of sight of the statue, was a showroom, in the window of which were displayed such examples of the stonemason's art as are identified with the Latin phrase, *Reqniescat In Pace.*

Charlton stood in thought for a moment or two and eventually decided not to visit the stonemasons. He skirted the tail of the queue and made for the church.

The sexton, however he may have discharged his duties, was entirely useless to Charlton. He had been in the part of the churchyard farthest removed from the Square and had heard nothing and seen nothing. The church, he said, had been locked and empty. Charlton left him and walked past the patrol at the Heather Street entrance to the Square. He considered the empty space between the greengrocer's on the corner of the Square and the first house in Heather Street. This was the Poultry and Farm Produce Sale Yard and it was cut off from the street by an iron railing with a gate in it. Together with the adjoining houses it afforded a view of the statue, but at such an angle that Charlton thought it unnecessary to carry his investigation so far. He turned, therefore, and went into the greengrocer's.

It will overstock this story with characters if a conscientious account is given of Charlton's visits to the buildings on the south side of the Square. Suffice it to say that he gained no fresh information from the greengrocer, from his neighbours, the chemist, grocer and harness-maker, or from John Rutherford's assistant, George, who, during his employer's absence on business, was looking after that delightful little bookshop, "Voslivres." None of them could really vouch for having heard the sound of a shot or seen anything unusual. George did his best to lighten the Inspector's task with a few ingenious theories, but that was all. Charlton left him almost in mid-sentence and George drifts out of our story. A pity, perhaps, for we all feel a certain fondness for the lad. We may see more of him another time.

Charlton walked briskly across to the Horticultural Hall. Sergeant Martin was sitting at a table with a police-constable by his side. His manner was harassed. His hair was ruffled and there were ink-stains on his hands and round red face. But he rose smartly to his feet when he saw his superior.

"How are you getting on?" Charlton murmured to him.

"Not so bad," said Martin. "Only another fifty thousand to do. Ought to be through by the week-end."

"Carry on with the good work," Charlton encouraged him. "I'm just off to attend to an urgent matter that brooks no further delay. If I don't see to it, serious consequences may result."

"A clue?" asked Martin eagerly.

"No, Sergeant. Lunch."

V.

The Photograph

A GOOD deal later that afternoon, Charlton was with Sergeant Martin in the private office at the police station. A bundle of foolscap sheets secured by rubber bands lay, as evidence of the Sergeant's industry, on the desk.

"Did you get Trench's authority for Weston to carry out the P.M.?" Charlton asked.

"Fixed it up before I went to the 'All," Martin replied. "We ought to hear from the doctor pretty soon what kind of a gun it was done with. I think meself it must've been a revolver or an automatic. A rifle would've nearly blown 'is head off."

"It might conceivably have been a bit of long-range sniping," Charlton suggested, "but it would have had to be very long-range for the bullet to stay inside the head. Did you get any help from your conversazione this afternoon?"

"Not what you'd write a long chatty letter to the old people about."

"I was going to suggest that you got the answers classified under different headings for me, but now I think it's hardly necessary. I've formed a pretty shrewd idea of the general direction from which the bullet came; and my own personal opinion of statistics is that they enable you to see at a glance what the position would be if the figures were correct."

He pulled some papers from his pocket.

"Here," he said, "are the notes I took about the people who weren't covered by you. You'd better put them with the others and file them all away. I expect most of your examinees picked out the sound of the shot from the din of those drills, but did anybody have anything useful to tell you—see a flash or catch sight of a Sinister Figure crouching at a window?"

"Not a perishing one of them," said Martin disgustedly. "The only real fact that I could get from all that questioning was that the shot wasn't fired by anyone who was in the Square—*standing* in the Square, I mean. You can't whip out a gun in a public place like that and bring a man down like a ping-pong ball off a squirt of water, without being noticed— and not one single one of the folks I questioned saw anybody else up to any no-good."

"Which considerably reduces our list of suspects. Even assuming that the murderer did fire the shot while standing in the Square and escape our rather inadequate net by a swift and unobtrusive scram, we do know that all the persons who supplied the names in your copper-plate records are as innocent as a new-born babe or any other revolting simile that may occur to us. If the name of Ezekiel Hammertoes is on your list, the man who gave you that name did not shoot Earnshaw. Ezekiel Hammertoes may be a false name, but that would form the subject of an entirely different investigation." Martin roughed up his scanty sandy hair in his attempt to follow Charlton's airy verbosity. At last he said:

"Supposing this Mr. Hammertoes wasn't in the Square when the shot was fired, but came and mixed with the crowds afterwards? There was a longish period when we couldn't stop them coming in, any more than we could stop them going out. Supposing 'e shot Earnshaw from the church tower and then slipped out and mucked in with the mob? I know one of the questions I asked 'em all was, 'Were you in the Square when the bull got loose?'; but there wasn't anything to stop 'em from saying they were when they weren't, was there?"

"Occasionally, Martin," said Charlton solemnly. "I see in you the makings of a Detective-inspector."

"Not much hope of that," said Martin equally gravely. "I always get the fidgets out of uniform—never know where to put me thumbs."

"It's certainly a possibility," said Charlton with a thoughtful frown. "I was hoping that we had accounted for a fair proportion of the town's population, but now I'm afraid we haven't. He would have to get rid of the weapon, of course, before he mingled—you kept your eyes open, I hope, for any suggestive bulges?"

Martin nodded.

"I know your selection of the church tower was only a random one, Martin, but let's consider the points that a shot could have been fired from. This shot—pull me up if you don't agree with me—must have been fired from somewhere."

"That is a reasonable hypothesis, Inspector," said Martin, with the merest subtle hint of Charlton's gentle voice.

Charlton looked sharply at him, but Martin's rubicund face showed no more than respectful attention. "And it must have been fired," he went on, "from some point in a direct line with Earnshaw's head. Bullets don't travel round corners."

"Unless they ricochet," corrected the Sergeant.

"A good point, Martin—a very good point. The bullet might have been intended for somebody else. But we'll leave it to tell its own tale. If it did ricochet, it'll be knocked out of shape. Let's assume that it didn't ricochet: that it was fired directly at Earnshaw. Let's assume, further, that it was fired by a man who, having hidden the weapon, went and mixed with the crowd in the Square. We'll take it that he wasn't standing in the Square when he fired the shot. Where was he, then? Any part of Burnside's and Highman's was almost as public as the Square, and Harbottle, the outfitter, was serving customers, with nobody upstairs. I have accounted for the Post Office, the Bank, Pope's, Beamish's, the church and all the shops along the south side of the Square."

"What about the shops past Burnside's?"

"Nothing doing, and that new block this side of Harbottle's was locked up and deserted. Where, then, was this man lurking?"

"That reminds me," said Martin. "There was one thing I was told that'd p'r'aps be worth following up. It's nothing definite, but it might get us somewhere. You remember you told me to ring up the caretaker and borrow the Horticultural Hall? Well, there isn't a caretaker. There's only a cleaner, who comes to do the place out every so often. The secretary of the Horticultural Society, old Mr. Farquarson, lives in Effingham Street and keeps an eye on the place from there. I rang ' im up at his home and 'is help— 'e's a bachelor and she comes in every day to do for him—told me that she thought 'e was in the Square. So I went round to see if I could find 'im—and I *did!*"

The Sergeant paused dramatically.

"Where d'you think 'e was?" he asked. "Lined up in the queue, waiting to go into 'is own Hall! Johnson 'ad got 'em all safely gathered in and old Farquarson was one of them. I know him pretty well—met 'im several times—so I stepped up to 'im and took 'im on one side.

"'Mr. Farquarson,' I said, 'I'm sorry to put you out like this, but I'm wondering if you'll let me have the loan of the 'All for a couple of hours.'"

"'E's a nice old chap, though a bit odd in his ways. Always wears an overcoat and carries an umbrella, even when it's ninety in the shade. 'E said 'e'd be pleased to, but 'e'd like to have a word with me first. We walked up together to the main entrance, he got out the key and the two of us went inside.

"'Sergeant,' he said, 'I've got something I want to tell you,' he said. 'It may mean something and it may mean nothing,''e said. 'It's about this murder.'"

"Was the last remark made by Mr. Farquarson?"

"Yes. 'It's about this murder,' he said."

"Ah, that makes it clearer," said Charlton.

That was another little score settled.

"'E was indoors this morning," explained Martin, "up in—"

"Where exactly is his house?" interposed Charlton.

"Number seven, backing on to the Hall. He was up in one of the back rooms this morning, when he heard what 'e called 'a sharp explosion.' He looked quickly out of the window and caught sight of a motor-van in the Paragon that was just beginning to move away from the High Street."

"Did he get the number of it?" asked Charlton sharply.

Martin shook his head.

"'E said 'e thought the explosion was made by the van and didn't give it a second thought until he knew about Earnshaw being shot. I thought, as I said, that this was worth following up, so I included a question about the van in with the others I asked."

"Good man. Any luck?"

"Not much. Several people said they'd seen it, without kind of taking it in. One chap said 'e thought it was painted red. 'E'd walked past it a few minutes before, when it was standing in the entrance to the Paragon. Nobody noticed the number or any name on it."

"I'd better see the people in those houses in the Paragon. They might have seen it go by. It may have been outside the monumental masons' for some time, so I'll go round and see them, as well. Mr. Farquarson must also be interviewed. It's wonderful what people can remember, if you only jolly them along."

"There was another Earnshaw in the Square this morning," announced Martin.

"Albert, the younger brother," added Charlton.

"Where did you pick that up?" Martin asked in some surprise.

"A little bird told me," the Inspector replied, and then thought with a smile that he ought not, perhaps, to have put it quite like that. "Do you know anything about him?"

"I just asked 'im the same general questions that I asked the others. I thought that if we wanted to get a few more partic'lars out of him, we could always go round and see 'im."

"I mean do you know anything of his history? I know he's a plasterer for Oakden's and is married, with one child, but that's about all."

"Blimey!" said Martin coarsely. "You don't know 'is wife's maiden name, I suppose?"

"Jane Baggs," said Charlton obligingly, "a younger sister of the shot man's widow."

"And you want *me* to tell *you* something about Albert Earnshaw?"

"As far as I can tell, Albert Earnshaw bears a blameless reputation. I was wondering whether you had his name in your visitors' book: 'Thoroughly enjoyed my stay. The cuisine was excellent and everything was done for my comfort. Coming again next year. . . .'"

"'Inspector Charlton was the soul of courtesy,'" said Martin with a broad grin. "No, nothing doing."

"I thought not. I have never yet met a dishonest plasterer—their day's work is too hard for the prosecution of any illegal sidelines. Have you ever tried any plastering, Martin?"

"Only my corns," said the Sergeant.

"It looks the simplest job in the world, but it's really jolly difficult. To get the plaster slapped on the wall—or, worse still, the ceiling—before it sets and then to smooth off the surface as flat as a billiard table, is really skilled labour. If you or I did it, Martin, the finished work would look more like a relief map of the Himalayas. And have you ever thought of the terrific strain on the arm muscles?"

"No," said Martin woodenly.

"That's the trouble with you," said Charlton severely.

"You haven't mastered the art of digression. By all means let us investigate a brutal murder with all regard for decorum, but let us sometimes tarry by the way to pick a sweet wild flower or two."

The Sergeant accepted this reproof with the utmost composure. As a matter of fact, he was thoroughly enjoying himself. The Inspector's verbal fireworks always filled him with a deep content.

"Do we know anything about Thomas Earnshaw?" Charlton went on. "We know that he was a labourer for the U.D.C.; that he leaves a widow and two children; that his daughter Kate won a sewing prize in the St. Mark's competition of 1933—"

"That little bird of yours was a mine of information," said Martin admiringly.

"But do we know of any reason," Charlton persisted, "why he was shot down? What kind of man was he? Who were his friends? Had he any enemies? That is what we must find out."

"As far as I can tell, he was just an ordinary working man. Lived with 'is wife and kids, did 'is football coupons every week and went to matches of a Saturday afternoon. Had 'is glass of beer, quiet and respectable, and enjoyed 'is two ounces a week of eightpenny Empire. Anyway, that's what young Chandler told me when 'e came back from 'is dinner. Lives in the same street."

"There was no Breath of Scandal about him, I suppose? No question of a revengeful husband—a trusting traveller in vacuum-cleaners?"

"I asked Chandler that," said Martin, "and he said not as far as he knew. Earnshaw always struck 'im as a steady-going sort of chap, fond of 'is wife, kids and home. Slippers on, pipe going and what's on the Regional?"

A constable knocked on the door and poked in his head.

"Dr. Weston's here, Sergeant," he said.

"Show him in."

"Ah, you're here, Charlton!" said Dr. Weston, as he came into the room. "That's good. I hoped to catch you. I've got that bullet out."

"Splendid!" said the Inspector. "Sit down, won't you?"

The doctor felt in his waistcoat pocket and pulled out a pill-box.

"It looks like a pistol bullet," he said as he unwrapped the cotton-wool that protected it. "A nickel-jacketed pistol bullet."

He handed it to Charlton.

"I'm afraid," he said with a regretful shrug, "that I know very little about firearms."

"If it comes to that," said Charlton with equal frankness, "neither do I. It's a popular belief that we 'busy-fellows' know all there is to know about them, but I don't mind admitting, within the privacy of these four walls, that this little messenger of death tells me precisely nothing. I don't even know whether it is a pistol bullet. I notice one very helpful point about it, though—it isn't very much deformed. That puts the kibosh on your ricochet theory, Martin."

"The best thing for you to do," suggested Dr. Weston, "is to consult a firearms expert. It's wonderful the things some of those chaps can find out."

"Or you could send it up to the Yard," said Martin, ill-advisedly.

"I could also send it up in a balloon, Martin," retorted Charlton, "but I don't propose to do so."

"I'm sorry," said Martin abashed, and giving himself a metaphorical kick in the pants.

"I'll take it over to Captain Harmon at Whitchester," Charlton decided. "He's helped me quite a lot in the past. Do you remember that beautifully planned accident with a .22 rifle at Lulverton in 1934?"

The doctor passed him over the pill-box and cotton-wool and after carefully wrapping up the bullet, he put the box away in his pocket.

"From the track of the bullet, Doctor," he asked, "can you give me an idea of the direction from which it came? I don't mean from which point of the compass, because that would depend on how Earnshaw was standing when it hit him. I mean—how can I put it clearly? Well, assume that we had a photograph of Earnshaw in profile, with the bullet wound facing the camera. Did the track of the bullet suggest to you that it had been fired straight at him, from a lower level, from a higher level, from a point in advance of him, from a point to the rear of him—you see what I'm trying to get at?"

Dr. Weston smiled.

"The trouble with you police," he said, "is that you expect too much."

"I don't see why. You've extracted the bullet. Didn't it leave a sort of track behind it?"

"My dear Charlton, the human head is not a lump of P'lasticene! There's no knowing what a bullet will do, once it has pierced the skull. If that bullet now in your pocket had gone right through Earnshaw's head and come out from the other side, it would have been some sort of guide; but as it stopped in his head, it's impossible to tell what jolly little pranks it may have got up to before it came to rest. The contents of the skull are not of the uniform consistency of modelling-clay, Charlton, although, after many years' contact—"

The Inspector held up his hand.

"All right, Doctor!" he smiled. "I've been in the police force too long not to have heard that one before!"

"I'll let it pass, then," said the doctor with an answering smile. "But joking apart, you might just as well ask me to establish the course taken by a bullet through the water after it has pierced the side of a storage-tank. The only thing I can say with certainty is that the bullet didn't enter the head at any great slant. If you can imagine a line drawn straight through Earnshaw's head from front to back, the path of the bullet did not form a particularly acute angle with that line."

"And the same thing applies, I suppose," said Charlton with a nod, "to a perpendicular line drawn through his head. That doesn't help much, I'm afraid. The field is still a very wide one."

"I should think," suggested Martin, "that it'd be better to drop the g'ometry and try to find out how Earnshaw was standing when the shot was fired."

"I've been thinking about that, Martin," said Charlton. "I had a good look at the statue earlier to-day and I noticed one or two things about it."

He mentioned the points enumerated in Chapter Two.

"Does anything strike you about those facts?" he asked.

"The first thing that occurs to me," said Dr. Weston, "is that, whatever position Earnshaw was standing in when he was shot—unless he was standing on his head—he was protected from a great many points of attack by the horse. That is obvious."

"That cuts out all the south half of the Square," said Martin.

"Not exactly, Sergeant," the doctor corrected him. "It certainly cuts out the south *side* of it, but Earnshaw was vulnerable from certain parts of that half of the Square. He could have been shot at an angle."

Martin murmured something about angles that would have pained Euclid.

"That doesn't really matter," said Charlton. "From the inferences I have drawn, I should say that the shot was not fired from anywhere to the south of the statue. Here we have this right-handed man standing on the plinth—"

"We are doubtless intended to ask," said the doctor, "how you know that Earnshaw was right-handed. So I will put that question."

"Because the two buckets were on the corner of the plinth. If Earnshaw had been left-handed, he would have had them on the other side of him. Here, then, we have this right-handed man standing on the plinth. He is not up there to admire the view or to examine the sky for aeroplanes, portents or what-you-will; but to clean the statue. How would he stand to do that? Definitely not with his back to the statue. He would surely have been facing it or, more probably, slightly turned away from it, to give his scrubbing arm freer play. As he was right-handed, he would turn to his right, bringing his left shoulder nearer to the horse's body. He was shot through the right temple. Ergo, the shot was not fired from any point to the south of him. If he had been left-handed, of course, he would have turned slightly the other way, which would have placed his head in such a position that he could have been shot, as you suggest, Doctor, from a certain area to the south-west of the statue.

"I think we can limit our zone still further. I don't imagine that he could have been shot from the High Street—the east side of the Square. I have suggested that he might have turned slightly away from the statue to facilitate the cleaning. He might even have stood at right-angles to it. But he wouldn't have twisted himself round any further, unless something attracted his attention and made him look over his shoulder."

"The bull, for instance," said Martin.

"That thrice-cursed bull!" said Charlton impatiently. "With him claiming everybody's eyes and those pneumatic-drills beating a rataplan on everybody's eardrums, we're left with no coherent witnesses at all! The murderer probably took the drills into account when he planned the thing, but he could hardly have anticipated an escaping bull."

He paused suddenly and looked at Martin.

"How did the bull get loose?" asked Dr. Weston.

"Probably slipped the cable," was Martin's prompt reply.

The thoughtful frown left Charlton's face.

"For one who has never been further to sea than the end of Southmouth pier," he grinned, "your phrasing is unexpectedly nautical."

"Slipping the cable," said the doctor, who was a keen yachtsman, "means not waiting to weigh anchor, but releasing the other end of the cable and letting the whole lot go overboard. In this case, it is a piece of false metaphor. What

Martin really intended to imply was that the animal managed, in some way, to liberate itself."

"The way you two pick a man up!" said Martin despairingly, to the great delight of the leg-pullers.

"I have it on good authority," said Charlton, "that when a bull be fixed to they railings, un do be fixed. What happened in this case was that the drover was just going to tether the animal, when he stumbled and dropped the bullstaff."

"Let's get back to what you noticed about the statue," said Dr. Weston. "You mentioned something about the brushmarks."

"Oh, yes. I was coming to that when Martin suggested that Earnshaw might have looked over his shoulder at the bull. I could see on the horse's thigh the exact spot reached by the brush before Earnshaw lost interest in his work. It was the rinsing brush and I could follow how he had brought it down the side of the animal with a sweeping movement to wash off the grime. When the motion of the brush was arrested, it was almost horizontal—I could still see where the trickles of water had run down from it. Their parallel courses covered an area about nine inches wide, which was the length of the brush."

"Where does that get us?" asked Martin.

"It amounts to this: You can't give a wide, swinging motion to a brush held in front of your chest. You have to keep it almost at arm's length. So Earnshaw was not standing immediately in front of the part he was cleaning. He was to the left of it; and if he was looking at what he was doing, he was facing almost due west. The trouble is that it may not have been the shot that stopped his work; it may have been the bull. One can picture him pausing when he heard the excitement outside the Post Office and glancing back over his shoulder."

There was a knock at the door and, at the Sergeant's summons, young P.C. Chandler came into the room.

"The evening papers 'ave just come down, sir," he said to Charlton. "I thought you'd like to see this." He laid the paper on the desk in front of Charlton. On the front page were two large photographs: one of the statue in the Square, with a huddled bundle lying behind the railings; and the other of the same statue, with a man standing on the plinth, his right arm stretched out across the horse's thigh.

VI.

Somebody's Biscuits

THERE was silence in the room for quite a while, the three of them being too astonished to speak. Then Charlton said:

"I can understand some smart freelance getting a snap of the body behind the railings and putting it on the first train up to London, but the other one is beyond me."

"'E's standing just like you said," remarked Martin in admiring tones.

Charlton glanced at the top of the page, then pulled the telephone towards him.

"We must clear up this little myst—Hullo! I want a call to London, please. Central ten thousand . . . Yes, I'll hold on."

The number was obtained and he was put through to the proper extension.

"This is Detective-inspector Charlton of the Downshire Police, speaking from Paulsfield. I want to ask you about these photographs in your Late Extra Final edition . . . Yes, the statue . . . Oh, no. That's all right. I only want to know where you got them from . . . Just a moment. I'll make a note of it . . . I'll read it back to you: Arthur Ransome, I, Effingham Street, Paulsfield . . . Thanks very much . . . Yes, you're right! Pretty snappy work! . . . That's what *I'm* wondering . . . Good-bye!"

He hung up the receiver and turned to Martin.

"This fellow Ransome didn't wait to develop the negatives, but put the camera on the 12.16 up to Waterloo and then 'phoned the story through. I think I'd like a little chat with Mr. Arthur Ransome!"

"Are you going now?" asked the doctor. "Perhaps I can give you a lift?"

"Thanks very much, Doctor, but it's only a step to Effingham Street."

When the two of them had left the room together, Chandler looked at Martin.

"Did you see what 'e did?" he demanded. "Walked off with my paper!"

"Ask him for a penny next time you see 'im," suggested the Sergeant.

A sweet-faced woman of fifty or so opened the door of number one, Effingham Street and Charlton asked if Mr. Arthur Ransome was in.

"Yes," was the reply. "Do you want to see him?"

"If you please. I am Detective-inspector Charlton of the County Police."

The woman's smile faded rapidly from her face and her hand went to her mouth.

"There's nothing wrong, I hope?" she asked fearfully. "I'm his mother."

"Please don't alarm yourself," said Charlton soothingly. "I only want to see your son on quite a small point."

This did not entirely comfort Mrs. Ransome, but she asked him to step into the front room. After she had closed the door on him, she called her son's name from the foot of the stairs. Charlton heard him come down and hold a whispered conversation with his mother. Then he entered the room with an air that was a little too off-hand to be genuine.

"Good evening, Inspector," he smiled. "Won't you sit down? What can I do for you?"

He wore horn-rimmed spectacles and his hair rose along his crown like a wave breaking angrily on a beach. His fountain-pen was clipped in the breast-pocket of his grey flannel jacket.

Charlton held out Chandler's newspaper.

"I think you took these photographs?" he said.

"Yes, that's right," Ransome agreed, and then repeated his mother's question: "There's nothing wrong, I hope?"

He spoke with an American accent that seemed entirely natural to him, yet he had lived all his twenty-two years in Paulsfield.

Charlton shook his head.

"Nothing at all," he said, and Ransome smiled with relief.

"I was afraid I'd broken some law," he admitted.

"Not a bit of it," said Charlton reassuringly. "The only reason why I'm here is to ask you how you came to secure such a terrific journalistic scoop. Any fool can hurry along with a V.P.K. and take pictures after a crime, but only a genius can be ready on the spot before it happens."

"Not much genius about it," said Ransome. "It was just blind luck. I'm always on the lookout for news and views in this neighbourhood. I do pretty well out of the *County Herald* and the local paper; and some of my stuff has appeared in the big dailies. They like a photo *and* a story. The trouble with the evening papers is to get the stuff to them early enough. They're fairly clamouring for it before midday—there isn't much coming in then. But we're a good fifty miles from London. . ."

Charlton gently stemmed this torrent of enthusiasm.

"Tell me," he said. "How did you get that first exposure?"

"I was ambling round this morning, looking out for copy, when I saw a man cleaning the statue. This immediately gave me an idea for an illustrated par for the *Weekly News*. Something brightly written with a snappy title: 'The Hero of Eckphen has a Bath' or 'A Dark Horse Goes Piebald' or something on those lines. I had my camera with me, of course, and I went round and took up a position outside the Horticultural Hall, which seemed about the best place. I got the statue into focus and took my picture—and had hardly done it before I saw Earnhsaw fall down behind the railings. I thought he'd probably fainted with the heat and decided it wouldn't do any harm to take another snap of him: 'An interrupted Bath' or 'Unusual Accident in the Square.' So I did. Luckily there wasn't anybody standing in the way. Everyone seemed to be more interested in the bull that had got loose. You can't see it in the first photo, because it was on the other side of the statue, but you'll find it in the second one. They captured it just afterwards."

"Did you hear a shot just before Earnshaw fell?" Charlton asked calmly, in spite of his inner jubilation.

"Yes, I'm almost sure I did. The drills in the High Street were kicking up a hell of a row and I was concentrating on what I was doing, but I can remember hearing some sort of unusual explosion."

"Did it come from behind you?"

"I'm afraid I can't tell you."

Charlton left it at that. The other thing was far more important.

"You are sure that you took that photo of Earnshaw immediately before he was shot?" he asked.

"He seemed to fall a split second after I snapped him."

"Thanks very much, Mr. Ransome. You've helped me a good deal. Will you let me have copies of those two photographs?"

"Sure thing," replied Arthur Ransome, already foreseeing for himself a great future.

"Just one more question before I go. You took those photographs standing outside the Horticultural Hall. What did you do after that?"

"Somebody shouted that Earnshaw had been shot and I saw the chance of a big news story. I decided to get a few more details—the dead man's name and all that—and then I realized that there wasn't much time to get the photos off. So I thought I'd first of all rush the camera round to the station and get it put on the 12.16 fast; then ring up the paper, tell them to pick up the camera at Waterloo and that I had a front page story on the way: 'Dramatic Shooting in Paulsfield Square. An Arrest is Imminent.'"

"Flatterer!" murmured Charlton.

"After that, I proposed to hurry back to the Square, get the full story and 'phone them again."

"When you left your position outside the Horticultural Hall, which way did you go to the station?" Ransome looked rather hard at the Inspector.

"Why on earth do you want to know that brusquely demanded.

"Does that really concern you?" said Charlton in the sweet tones that had made many an old lag Wince like a hurt child. "Which way did you go to the station?"

"I went along the High Street," said Ransome hurriedly, "round by the 'Queen's Head' and across New Road at the traffic-lights. The station is the Meanhurst road, a hundred yards or so past the crossing."

"So they tell me," said Charlton politely. "And how did you get from the Hall into the High Street?"

"I walked along the side of the Square, past the second-hand shop and the Bank."

"Your camera was under your arm?"

"No. I was carrying it in my hand."

"Were you wearing the same clothes as you are now?"

"Yes."

"And a cloth cap with a check pattern?"

"No—a brown soft hat with a pulled-down brim."

"Thank you. That is all I have to ask you. You may be wanted at the inquest."

When Charlton left the house a moment or two later, Mr. Arthur Ransome, that ambitious young man, was suffering from the lowering after-effects of a dose of the Doctor's medicine.

As he walked back to where his car still stood outside the police station, Charlton asked himself, "Where next?" Ransome was, without much doubt, the man seen by Mrs. Archer, so that point was settled. There were several other things to be done before he called it a day: see old Farquarson about that van; visit Mrs. Earnshaw and Albert, her brother-in-law; and have a word with the people in the Paragon. The identification of the van seemed to be the most important item. There were interesting possibilities about it.

He reached the car, climbed in and laid out the newspaper on the steering-wheel.

If Ransome's evidence was to be depended upon, the photograph showed exactly how Earnshaw was standing when the bullet struck him: with his head pointing almost, but not quite, due west. There was a slight tendency towards the south. Dr. Weston had said that the bullet had entered the head at no very acute angle. On the testimony of those two, then, and apart from all other considerations, the only buildings in the Square that could be identified with the murder were the Horticultural Hall, Beamish's, Pope's, the Bank, and perhaps the Post Office and the monumental masons'.

The van had been standing, according to witnesses, in the entrance to the Paragon. It would have been quite a simple matter to snipe Earnshaw from the back of it, although the angle would have been rather sharper than Dr. Weston had suggested. There could have been two men concerned, one in the driver's seat and the other crouched in the dark interior of the van. Canvas flaps pulled cautiously open a crack, aim taken at the unconscious victim, a word to the driver with his finger on the starter, simultaneous pressure on trigger and button, a rapid revving up of the engine—and Here's Ho! for the open road.

Quite an attractive little arrangement.

But he decided to leave that investigation until later and get the routine work done first. He went into the police station and got the address of Mrs. Earnshaw from Martin. The tearful widow was at home with her two children when he arrived; and he was gentle and sympathetic. He asked his questions delicately and, when he left her, she felt happier than before he came.

Looking back, however, not as a human being, but as a cold-blooded investigator, on his ten minutes' talk with her, he was forced to admit that he had gained nothing from his visit, except increased astonishment that anybody should have seen fit to shoot Thomas Earnshaw. As Martin had said, he seemed to have been just an ordinary working man. The widow had told him, without entirely realising that she was doing so, that, for not a single moment of her married life with him, had she ever had cause to suspect her husband. He had left home early each morning, come home to his midday meal, gone back to the afternoon's work, returned for a high tea and then settled down with a newspaper or listened to what the B.B.C. had to offer.

On Sundays, he dug his garden, chopped firewood or did fretwork. At General Elections, he voted for the Labour candidate without exactly knowing why. There were thousands like him in Downshire and millions like him in England. Had it not been for them, the war might have been *fought* on the playing fields of Eton.

Albert Earnshaw, the plasterer, whose address Charlton got from the widow, was another one of those millions. He had nothing more than his sister-in-law to tell: he merely confirmed all that had been said already.

"Poor old Tom," he said, "'adn't got an enemy in the world. Easy-going 'e was—what you might call placid. Did 'is bit in the War, same as I did. Then came back to Blighty and settled down. War was all right, we said, just for a few years, but that was enough. No more 'igh jinks for us. A wife, a job and a comfortable bed at nights—that was the idea. All the fun we wanted, we'd get out of the 2.30 at Bogside and Southmouth going up into the First Division."

"Did your brother bet much?"

"We did it together. A bob each way on what the book said, once a week while the flat was on. We never touched the sticks—too darn risky. And a tanner every Friday in Littlewood's. We went to a 'flapping' meeting once and tried the dogs; but when we'd both dropped three 'alf-crowns, we said never again. The whole thing was a bit fishy."

"You should stick to the N.G.R.C. tracks," Charlton advised.

"Tom and me," Albert Earnshaw went on, "used to pick out the best things of the week and when it came off for us, we each took our missus to the pictures. We were on Nifty Sarah at Shanklin Park to-day."

"It came in at 100 to 8."

Earnshaw's face lighted up.

"Did it?" he asked eagerly. "That'll bring in Tom and me a matter of—Oh, my *God!*"

Charlton left him. It was not the time for more questions.

Mr. Farquarson, the secretary of the Horticultural Society, received him in his study, which was a welter of books and papers. On the corner of his littered desk was a pile of account books, on whose dizzy pinnacle clung a portable typewriter that had apparently been moved from the blotting-pad while letters were signed. The secretary was a benign old gentleman in the late sixties, of medium height and slightly corpulent. He had a cheery red face and tonsured white hair. He wore an old-fashioned tail-coat and the points of his winged collar seemed for ever in danger of puncturing his dewlapped chin.

Charlton introduced himself and asked to hear Mr. Farquarson's story. As their talk proceeded, he noticed the secretary's disconcerting habit of changing his manner without warning from a proper solemnity to the frivolity of a mischievous schoolboy.

"I was upstairs in one of the back rooms this morning," he explained, "and I suddenly heard a sharp explosion. I looked out of the window, which overlooks the Paragon, and saw a van moving away from the monumental masons' on the other side of the road. I did not, at the time, give it a second thought, but took my hat and umbrella and strolled round into the Square, in the hope that something interesting was going on. There is so little excitement in a sleepy town like this, that one welcomes a little diversion now and again, even if it is only the grocer's boy falling off his bicycle!"

He shook with laughter and his chin bounced on his collar like a toy balloon on a spiked fence.

"You can imagine my surprise," he said, "when I discovered that I had narrowly missed witnessing the escape of a bull and the murder of a human being!"

"Did you notice anything about this van?" asked Charlton, not entirely agreeing with the secretary's idea of a little diversion.

"I fear not. I am not a particularly observant person and one van is more or less like any other van me. That is the trouble, Inspector, with most of us. If I had never seen a van before— by which I mean any van, of whatever kind or description—I should have been intrigued enough to take in and remember every detail of it; but as I have seen many hundreds of vans in my time, this particular vehicle was registered to my mind under the general heading of 'Vans, Mechanically Propelled.'"

He smiled impishly.

"Now *if* the van had been upside down, Inspector, I should certainly have noticed a few things about it. One doesn't often see a van upside down. I should have taken more note of the lettering on the side of it, if my curiosity had been whetted by seeing it written the wrong way up. Have you ever caught yourself taking an intense interest in anything written upside down?

'The boy hit the dog with a stick' or 'Why not own your house?' take on a new and tantalizing significance when they are inverted. I wonder that our advertisers—"

Charlton interrupted this amiable digression.

"So there *was* some lettering on the side of the van? It wasn't"—he smiled—"a plain van?"

"Oh, yes," agreed Mr. Farquarson decisively. "There was certainly something written on the side, but I can't, for the life of me, tell you what it was. Apart from fact that I wasn't sufficiently interested at the time, I doubt if I could have read even such big lettering. I am very short-sighted."

"Then it was *big* lettering," Charlton enquired, with the thought that Mr. Farquarson was being jollied along quite nicely.

"Yes," said the secretary with a nod, "I do recollect that."

"And the girl in the driving-seat—can you describe her at all?"

"There *was* no girl in the driving-seat," retorted the old gentleman. "You have been misinformed. The van was in charge of a man in a peaked cap."

"Several witnesses," Charlton lied without shame, "say that the van was blue."

"Nonsense! It was most definitely red. I thought, at first, that it was a Post Office van."

"Why did you change your mind?"

"It wasn't the same shape. It was larger and had a rounded white top."

"My other witnesses seem to be at fault!" said Charlton with a smile. "I hesitate to believe now that the van was driven away with one of the doors at the back hanging open."

"Doors?" ejaculated Mr. Farquarson. *"Doors?* There were no doors. The back of the van was covered by canvas flaps. Your informant was probably deceived by the draught bellying them out."

"Would you agree with another witness that the wording on the side of the van was, 'Charles Enterton, Jobmaster, Light Removals'?"

This time the trick failed.

"I can neither agree nor disagree," said Mr. Farquarson, "because I don't know. I heard the explosion and caught sight of the van, imagined that the engine had back-fired, dismissed the matter from my mind, and went out."

And that was about as far as he seemed prepared to go.

"While I am here," Charlton changed the subject, "perhaps you will answer a few questions about the Horticultural Hall. Was it occupied at twelve o'clock to-day?"

The secretary shook his head.

"It was locked up and empty," he said. "When I left the house, I took the keys with me, with the idea of going into the Hall, to make sure that everything was in order, but Sergeant Martin rather forestalled me!"

"I think I'm right in saying that there are no windows in the front of the Hall or on its eastern side?"

"That is quite correct," Mr. Farquarson agreed. "The passage between it and Mr. Beamish's shop is private property and the Society has no right of light over it. We have to get all our illumination from the Paragon."

Charlton thanked him for his assistance and went along to the monumental masons; but nobody there could recollect having seen a van standing outside. A certain Mrs. Jenkins, however, who lived next door but one to them, remembered having caught sight of it go by, when she was shaking a mop from a bedroom window. To the best of her belief, the lettering on the side of it said:

"Something about somebody's biscuits."

VII.

The Sweet-Toothed Irishman

THERE were eleven shops in Paulsfield where biscuits were sold. The next morning, Charlton visited them all, and his time was not entirely wasted. None of the shops had received a call the day before from any biscuit manufacturers, who avoided delivering stocks on market-days; but most of the proprietors and managers were able to associate the van with two firms: Henfrew, Ltd., who made their famous "Seaside" biscuits in their factory just outside Southmouth, and John Padgett & Co., Ltd., the big London people. Both these companies used red vans with rounded white tops and bearing the similar slogans, "Henfrew's Seaside Biscuits" and "Padgett's Biscuits." Mrs. Jenkins had remembered about the biscuits, but had failed to recall the name; and as everybody in Downshire knew Henfrew's, whose products had earned a well-deserved fame in the neighbourhood, it seemed likely that the van had belonged to Padgett's. But when Charlton went again to see Mrs. Jenkins, she told him that she had never heard of Henfrew's or of their "Seaside" biscuits. She and her husband had but recently moved from London and when, she said, she needed biscuits, she always bought Padgett's. If the van had belonged to them, she would certainly have noticed it. So it looked to Charlton as if a call upon Henfrew, Ltd. was indicated; but he deferred enquiries in that direction until he went home. Captain Harmon of Whitchester had first to be consulted about the bullet extracted from Earnshaw's head.

Whitchester was the County Town of Downshire and lay eight miles to the north-west of Paulsfield. Captain Peter

Harmon, D.S.O. (Royal Engineers, retired) was at home when he called. He was a man of fifty-four, whose brilliant achievements during the War were cut short in 1917 by a bomb that deprived him of his right leg. Since the Armistice, he had made a reputation for himself as an expert on firearms and his services were much in demand by Scotland Yard and the Home Office. It was he who produced in court the remarkable composite photograph of two bullets that proved they had both been fired from the same revolver, and brought the famous Belsize Park flat murderer to the gallows.

The Inspector unwrapped the bullet and handed it to Captain Harmon.

"What can you tell me about that?" he asked.

The Captain examined it and then said:

"It's a nickel-jacketed pistol bullet, slightly deformed, and has been fired from a weapon with Browning type rifling: six broad grooves and a right-hand twist. Calibre, 9mm."

"Revolver or automatic?"

"By automatic," smiled the other, "I take it you mean a self-loading pistol?"

"What's the difference?"

"An automatic pistol will keep on firing shot after shot, as long as you hold back the trigger. It is, in fact, a sub-machine gun. But a self-loading pistol must have the trigger pulled for each round. The recoil throws out the empty cartridge-case, automatically supplies a fresh round in the chamber and recocks the weapon, but the trigger has to be pulled for each shot."

"I didn't know *that*," Charlton admitted. "The ignorance of most of us on the question of firearms is simply astounding."

"And the two chief classes of offenders are the ones who should know better," smiled the Captain. "The police and writers of detective fiction. Even the great Edgar Wallace wasn't blameless. In one of his books, he made a character say, 'Will you please tell me what you did with the revolver . . .?

It was a Colt automatic.' You might just as well say, 'Will you please tell me what you did with the apple? It was an orange.'"

"I hasten to put my question in a different way!" laughed Charlton. "Was the bullet fired from a revolver or a self-loading pistol?"

"For the moment, I won't answer that. There are many firearms of 9mm. calibre—the celebrated *Le Français,* for instance, the only decent pistol the French ever turned out. The trouble is that there is no standardisation in pistols, particularly in the cheaper foreign makes. They buy up lengths of barrel from half a dozen different manufacturers and cut them up. So you'll get two foreign pistols of the same make with entirely different characteristics. You'll find that the rifling of one has a left-hand twist and the other a right-hand twist. And the widths of the lands differ enormously."

"What, if it is not an indelicate question, are lands? Something to do with the League of Nations?"

Harmon smiled at this joking enquiry.

"They are part of the rifling inside the barrel of a weapon—the metal that is left behind when the grooves have been cut out. The better-class English makes are consistent in the relative sizes of the lands and grooves, but the happy-go-lucky foreigner is not so careful."

"I don't seem to be getting much forwarder," said Charlton in a disappointed tone.

"If you had given me a cartridge-case, it would have been more helpful. A revolver cartridge has a rim to prevent it from sliding right through the chamber, but a self-loading pistol cartridge has not. It is, of course, possible to file down the rim of a revolver cartridge and use it in a self-loading pistol of the same calibre, but the marks left on the case by the ejector would tell their own tale."

"I was hoping," said Charlton, "that you would be able to say what make of weapon was used for that bullet, but now it looks as if I'm going to be unlucky."

"Just wait a moment, will you?" said the Captain, and limped out of the room.

"There's one little thing I can tell you," he said when he returned. "This bullet weighs a shade under 124 grains and, allowing for a slight loss in weight, it suggests to me a particular make of self-loading pistol."

"And what is that?"

"The 9 mm. Parabellum, the regulation self-loading pistol used by most of the German officers during the War. If you want a few more facts, it was designed by G. Luger and originally appeared in 1902 with a calibre of 7.65 mm., which was increased in 1908 to 9 mm."

"Now we're getting somewhere!" said Charlton.

"Wait!" was the hurried reply. "You mustn't take this evidence as completely conclusive. There are other pistols that will take that particular bullet, but the Parabellum is by far the most common make in which it is used."

"It will make a good starting-point, anyway," said Charlton contentedly.

From Captain Harmon's house, he drove to the police station in Whitchester and asked for a search to be made in the record of firearm certificates issued. An hour's investigation produced all the available data about Parabellums registered in Downshire. Fortunately, there were very few of them.

Under the Firearms Act, 1920, war trophies in the way of weapons were allowed to be held without firearm certificates, if the owners gave notice of the fact to the chief officers of police in their districts. These weapons were not to be used or carried and no ammunition was permitted. Amongst the trophies so registered at Whitchester were three Parabellum 9 mm. self-loading pistols; but as a result of a general appeal by the police in 1933, two of these had been given up. The third was still in the hands of a licensed victualler in Lulverton. Charlton made a note of his name.

Apart from these three pistols, there was another Parabellum figuring in the Whitchester records. This had not been registered as a trophy, but a firearm certificate had been taken out for it in 1921. A supply of eight rounds of ammunition was permitted by the certificate, which had been granted to a Mr. Percy Symes, of Effingham Street, Paulsfield.

The Inspector drove to Lulverton and interviewed Mr. Garnett, the licensee of the "Red Cow," who was delighted to produce, after fifteen minutes' search by the whole staff, his Parabellum souvenir.

"I'aven't got any ammunition, of course, Inspector," Mr. Garnett explained, "but even if I had, it wouldn't be no good, because the thing doesn't work. It never 'as done since I snitched it from a German dug-out in '18. Something's jammed inside it, so that the trigger won't pull. P'r'aps that's why Jerry left it behind. Young Bert Short up at the garage,'oo knows something about engineering, monkeyed with it some years ago, to try and get it to go, but 'e couldn't do nothing with it."

Charlton "couldn't do nothing with it" either. It did not look as if *that* was the weapon that killed Earnshaw.

It was then nearly lunch time and, as Lulverton lay about half-way between Paulsfield and Southmouth-by-the-Sea, Charlton thought it would be a nice idea to go home to lunch with Molly, then, after seeing Henfrew's, the biscuit people, return to Paulsfield for a word or two with Mr. Percy Symes, the holder of the only registered Parabellum in the district.

Mr. Leon Henfrew, the managing director of Henfrew, Ltd., greeted the Inspector effusively. He had a big nose and spoke a lot with his hands, from which Charlton drew his own conclusions. He pressed on his visitor a cigar whose quality proved that there was money in biscuits.

"I am anxious to trace a commercial van, Mr. Henfrew," Charlton explained, "and I believe it is one of yours."

"No trouble, I hope?" asked Mr. Henfrew apprehensively. "Our drivers have strict instructions to observe every rule of the road. What is it?"

"There's nothing wrong at all, as far as I know," said Charlton easily. "The position is this: I have been told that a red, white-topped van, belonging to some firm of biscuit manufacturers, was seen at midday yesterday in a road just off Paulsfield Square.

"When that man was shot?" asked Mr. Henfrew quickly.

"Yes. Everyone who was in the Square at the time has been questioned by the police, but the van drove away before it could be stopped and I am anxious to have a word with the man who drove it and with anybody else who may have been with him. I am not sure that it *was* one of your vans, but I think it was."

"Why, certainly," said Mr. Henfrew with an expansive smile. "I'll put through an enquiry."

He lifted the receiver of a house telephone on his desk and pressed down a lever.

"Please step into my office, Mr. Jessop," he said after a pause, then turned to Charlton as he replaced the receiver. "Our vans don't usually deliver in Paulsfield on market-days, but I expect the one that was seen yesterday was passing through the town, on its way to some other place."

The door opened and a man came in.

"Ah, Mr. Jessop! Inspector Charlton is trying to trace one of our vans that passed—or so he has been told—through Paulsfield yesterday. Can we help him at all? I have told him that we do not usually deliver in Paulsfield on market Tuesdays."

Mr. Jessop stroked his chin pensively and then said: "We did have one van out in that neighbourhood yesterday, sir. It went to Burgeston and Hazeloak villages, to the south of Paulsfield and then, I believe, to Meanhurst, which is another village slightly to the north-west of Paulsfield."

"Who was driving it?"

"Murphy, sir."

"Please fetch him, Mr. Jessop."

Murphy, a beefy uniformed Irishman holding a flabby peaked cap in his large red, uncared-for hands, was fetched.

"Murphy," said Mr. Henfrew, "Inspector Charlton wishes you to answer some questions. Please do so, to the best of your ability."

He leant back in his chair, placed the fingers of his hands together and looked at the ceiling.

"Did you drive one of your firm's vans through Paulsfield yesterday?" Charlton asked Murphy.

"Yes, sir," said Murphy, whose accent was a strange mixture of Downshire dialect and Irish brogue. "I drove from here to Lulverton, then along the new main road until I turned off to Burgeston village, where I called at the grocer's. Then I went to Hazeloak and stopped at the grocer's there. My next call was at Mean'urst, the other side of Paulsfield, so I drove along from Hazeloak and came up Paulsfield High Street and, seeing that the road was being repaired further along, took a turning to the left, which led me into Heather Street. Then I took the van along the west side of the Square into the Paragon, which connected me up with the Mean'urst road and—"

The Inspector arrested the description of Murphy's Odyssey with a question.

"Why did you stop the van in the entrance to the Paragon?"

Murphy looked awkward.

"I only slipped out for a jiff. I was back again and on the road in next to no time. It wasn't a dangerous place to leave it, either, being well in to the side of the road and I switched off the engine while—"

"Murphy!" said Mr. Henfrew sharply. "Answer the Inspector's question, *if* you please."

"Why did you stop the van?" Charlton repeated.

"I wanted to get out for something."

"And that was?"

Murphy looked at Mr. Jessop beseechingly, but Mr. Jessop

glanced another way, so Murphy turned his eyes to Mr. Henfrew. The managing director, however, was not to be besought.

"Have you lost your voice, Murphy?" he demanded.

"I got out to buy a toffee-apple," was the Irishman's hasty admission, with a blush like a discomfited schoolboy. "I like them," he added lamely.

"A very human weakness," Charlton agreed. "Had you anyone else with you in the van at the time?"

"No," replied Murphy, "I was alone by myself."

Charlton asked for the number of the van and Murphy told him.

"A man was shot dead in Paulsfield Square yesterday, Murphy. Did you see or hear anything of it?"

"Not a thing, sir," said Murphy definitely. "I must 'ave driven off just before it happened. The first word I had of it was when I got back 'ere."

That seemed to settle that. Murphy was dismissed, Mr. Jessop was told that that would be all and, with mutual expressions of goodwill and the promise of close collaboration in the future between the County Constabulary and Henfrew, Ltd. (makers of the celebrated "Seaside" biscuits), Charlton and Mr. Leon Henfrew bade each other a very good afternoon.

With a sigh of resignation, Charlton climbed into his car and drove off towards Paulsfield. For how many hours of his busy life, he pondered, had he absolutely nothing to show? He *had* to follow all these little things up, but seventy-five per cent of them led him nowhere. And then they wondered why one's expenses got a bit inflated! It was, he decided, a mug's game, the only consolation being the handsome allowance of £16 per annum granted by a munificent Secretary of State to those who wore their own natty gent's d.b. suiting on duty. From which austere meditation, it appeared that Charlton was unusually depressed. Then suddenly he remembered Murphy's toffee-apple and felt considerably cheered.

As he went along the High Street, on his way to see Mr. Percy Symes, he was hailed from the pavement in a way that can be briefly summarised as:

"Hoy!"

He turned his head, saw that the hoyer was Mr. Farquarson and brought the car to a standstill against the kerb. The secretary trotted along to him.

"Forgive my unconventional ejaculation!" he smiled. "But I wanted to attract your attention. It reminds me of the story of the small boy who was out walking with his mother and shouted out 'Hoy!' to a passing gentleman, who happened to be one of his schoolmasters, which prompted his mother to reprove him by saying, 'You shouldn't be so rude to your master, Tommy. 'Hoy, mister!' is what you ought to say.'"

Charlton hoped that he had not been stopped to hear that immensely funny little anecdote, but laughed politely.

"Will you take a cup of tea with me?" Mr. Farquarson invited, with a wave of his hand towards the shop outside which Charlton had stopped the car.

The Inspector's tongue was already hanging out like a tired dog's for a drink, so he said he would be delighted and followed Mr. Farquarson into the shop. When their order had been given, the old gentleman said: "I am very interested to know what progress you have made in the identification of that red van. I feel that in that lies the solution to the whole mystery."

"'There is no practice,'" Charlton quoted to himself from the book of words, as he passed Mr. Farquarson the sugar, "'more pernicious to the police service than gossiping to strangers about matters of duty.'"

But the paragraph, as he remembered it, went on, "Idle rumours are readily magnified into positive facts . . ." It was his business to see, he resolved, that one idle rumour did not spread.

"I'm afraid you are due for a disappointment, Mr. Farquarson," he smiled. "That van contained nothing more frightening than foodstuffs and was driven by a large Irish gentleman, with no more criminal tendencies than a leaning towards sickly sweetmeats."

"You have laid the van by the heels?" asked the secretary, impetuously mixing his metaphors.

"I have traced it without any trouble, thanks to your help, but I think you can safely dismiss from your mind any thought of its being concerned in the death of Earnshaw."

"You disappoint me," said Mr. Farquarson in a regretful tone, as he stirred his tea. "I saw, in my mind's eye, that van standing in the entrance to the Paragon, with the intending murderer crouched inside. I saw him taking advantage of the diversion created by the escaping bull and—well, it speaks for itself. Would it not be as well, if I may be allowed to give you a word of advice, to find out whether there existed any association between this Irishman you mention and the dead man? Something significant might emerge. I recommend you not to lose sight of the van, in spite of the fact that the driver had a penchant for lollipops."

He gave vent to such a hearty guffaw at his own little witticism, that one of the white-aproned girls dropped a tray and another spilt twice as much coffee in a saucer as the standard amount fixed by the Waitresses' Convention.

"I value your guidance, Mr. Farquarson," said the Inspector humbly, when the cachinnatory typhoon had spent itself.

"Here's another thing," said Mr. Farquarson handsomely. "Suppose that the driver of the van knew nothing at all of the crime, but stopped the vehicle in the entrance to the Paragon for some purpose or other; and suppose that some ill-disposed person took the opportunity to secrete himself in the van's dark interior, shot and killed Earnshaw just as the driver was starting up the engine and then, when the van had left the purlieus of Paulsfield behind unobtrusively dropped from the tail-board, without the driver being any the wiser. Consider that point, Inspector. Would you care for a fancy cake?"

VIII.

A Parabellum

WHEN Charlton called later at the house in Effingham Street, a woman opened the door.

"Are you Mrs. Symes?" he asked.

She nodded. She was a fat little person with straggling grey hair.

"I am Detective-inspector Charlton and I should like to speak to your husband."

"You can't do that, I'm afraid," replied Mrs. Symes. "My husband died in 1934."

"I'm sorry, Charlton apologised hurriedly. "I didn't know that."

"Is there anything I can do for you? My son, Ronald, has just gone off to play tennis."

She led him into the front room of the house.

"I think I am right in saying," Charlton opened the conversation, "that your husband owned an automat—a self-loading pistol?"

"Yes," she agreed, "he did have a pistol, but whether it was self-loading, I don't know. He brought it back from the War with him."

"May I see his firearm certificate, please?"

"Certainly," said the widow, "if I can lay my hands on it. I haven't seen it for years."

The booklet was discovered, after a long search, in the drawer of a tall-boy. Mrs. Symes handed it to Charlton, who opened it and jotted down in his notebook the particulars recorded therein: —

"Date of grant: 14th June, 1921.

"Possessed at date of grant: 1 Parabellum 9 mm. self-loading pistol.

"*Ammunition.*

"Possessed at date of grant: 8 rounds.

"Authority to possess: 8 rounds.

"Maximum amount to be possessed at one time: 8 rounds.

"Total amount authorised to be acquired in three years: Nil.

"Maximum amount authorised to be acquired at any one time: Nil."

It was evident that the late Percy Symes had no intention of using the weapon: he had merely obtained permission to keep it exactly as it had come into his possession. Eight rounds was probably the capacity of the magazine.

The "Variation of Certificate" pages were blank and the necessary renewals had been made in 1924, 1927, 1930 and 1933. Charlton noticed that the 1936 renewal had not been effected.

"Is this weapon still in your possession?" he asked. Mrs. Symes nodded assent.

"I'm afraid I shall have to ask you to hand it over to me. This certificate has expired."

She looked frightened.

"Why, of course!" she agreed fervently. "I'll give it to you at once, if I can only find it. I believe it's up in the loft. I haven't given the horrible thing a thought for years. Is there a penalty for holding loaded firearms without a licence?"

Mrs. Symes looked healthy enough, but he hardly liked to take the risk of telling her that the punishment was anything up to fifty pounds and/or three months. He contented himself with the assurance that he had no doubt that the police authorities would take a lenient view of her case.

"Did you say," he asked, "that the weapon is now in the loft?"

"Yes, I think so. It's a pity my son is not at home, as it's rather a performance getting up there. You have to pull yourself up from the top of a pair of steps and I'm afraid that I couldn't manage it."

Charlton repressed a smile at the thought of Mrs. Symes indulging in such undignified acrobatics and offered to make the ascent himself. The steps were therefore obtained from the cupboard under the stairs and taken up into the bathroom at the front of the house, in the ceiling of which was the trap-door to the loft. Mrs. Symes supplied him with an electric torch from her son's bedroom and he climbed the steps, pushed up the trap-door and, by placing one foot on top of the bathroom door, was able to get into the loft.

"I believe it's in the big black trunk," Mrs. Symes called up to him from below.

Balancing himself on the rafters and directing the beam of the torch around him, Charlton located the trunk. Cautiously, for fear his foot should slip and go through the ceiling of the best bedroom, he made his way towards it, circumventing the inevitable contents of nine lofts out of ten—a pile of old Venetian blinds. The top of the trunk had a heavy coating of dust on it. The tray inside was filled with odds and ends, but the Parabellum was not amongst them. He lifted out the tray and after rummaging about, found the pistol in its leather holster at the bottom of the trunk.

The dark loft was hardly the place to carry out an examination of the weapon, so, with all the care of Blondin pushing the wheel-barrow over Niagara Falls, he returned to the trap-door and, with the holster gripped in one hand, let himself down onto the top step of the ladder.

The lower half of the bathroom window was frosted, but the upper part was clear glass. As Charlton descended the steps, he glanced casually through the window and instantly paused at the thing that met his eye.

It was the statue in the Square.

There was no real cause for astonishment. Effingham Street ran more or less parallel with the northern side of the Square and number eight, Mrs. Symes's house, stood directly opposite the entrance to the passage that led between the Horticultural Hall and Mr. Beamish's second-hand shop. The thing that really surprised Charlton was that, up to that moment, he had entirely failed to consider the potentialities of that passage.

Mrs. Symes was waiting for him on the landing and, carrying the steps and the holster, he followed her down the stairs. When the steps had been returned to the cupboard, he said:

"I think I'd better be alone when I examine this, Mrs. Symes. I don't want to have a double tragedy with it!"

The old lady was clearly of the same mind and hurriedly ushered him into the front room and closed the door.

He took the pistol from its case and laid it carefully on the table, to enable him to master the general principles of its construction. Your brilliant amateur investigator, the owner of the insouciant voice that breathes o'er WHItehall 1212, whose keen intelligence runs the whole gamut of human knowledge, from Aachen to Zythum, would doubtless have taken the weapon with a gay laugh and a flippant epigram, and carelessly spun it round by the trigger-guard on a supple forefinger. But apart from the fact that the Parabellum weighed over two pounds and would have taken some spinning, even on such an out-of-the-ordinary finger, Charlton was not in the business for the fun of the thing and had not quite the same comforting foreknowledge that he would successfully survive eighty thousand words of excitement and derring-do.

The first thing he noticed about the weapon, as it lay on its starboard side, was a small button placed (to continue the nautical idiom) aft. An indentation below it suggested that it was then in its upper position; and as it had all the appearance of a safety-catch, Charlton pulled it down and uncovered a word that was printed in white letters on the side of the pistol: *Gesichert*. His languages were getting a bit rusty, but he still remembered that *gesichert* was the German for "made safe." This meant that the weapon had been cocked, which would have stopped him, had he known it sooner, from embarking on the perilous enterprise of carrying both pistol and step-ladder together down the stairs. So far, so good. The safety-catch was now doing its work. The next step was to remove the magazine. A little button let into the stock just behind the trigger seemed to control that. He pressed it and the magazine shot out sufficiently for him to remove it entirely. The sliding breech block could be operated by hand by means of two circular milled bosses that formed a part of it. He crooked his fingers over them, but found that it was not until the safety-catch was released that the breech block was allowed to slide past the ejector and thereby throw out the cartridge that had been in the chamber. He let the breech block slide back into place, then having pulled the trigger, with no more noisy result than a subdued click, heaved a thankful sigh. The Parabellum was now as harmless as an astigmatic poetry-reader who has arrived at the church hall without his spectacles.

Charlton removed the cartridges from the magazine and stood them in a row, together with the one from the chamber, on the table.

There were seven in all.

Mr. Percy Symes had registered eight rounds. Where was the other? Charlton examined the barrel for fouling and was able to detect signs of rust at the muzzle. But that might have been caused by anything. The best thing to do was to hand the self-loader and ammunition over to Captain Harmon, who might be able to say whether or not the bullet extracted from Earnshaw had been fired from that particular weapon. He pulled down the spring of the magazine, inserted the cartridges and slipped the magazine back into the stock. Then when he had adjusted the safety-catch and replaced the weapon in its holster, he opened the door and went out into the hall. Mrs. Symes appeared from another room.

"I think I'll take this away with me, Mrs. Symes," he said.

"I shall be very relieved if you do," she answered. "I think firearms are thoroughly nasty things. Why my dear husband insisted on having it in the house, I never could see. He might have injured somebody with it."

"Can you call to mind any occasion when he used it?"

"Fired it off, do you mean? No, I don't think I can. He sometimes had to have a lot of the firm's money in the house and the pistol used to be kept in a locked drawer in our dressing-table. When he was taken away from me, I put it upstairs in the loft."

"Thank you, Mrs. Symes. I think that is all."

As she moved to open the front door for him, he said conversationally:

"A beautiful evening for your son's tennis."

"Yes," she said fondly. "He does love it so."

"He belongs to a club?"

"No. He and three of his friends go and play on the public courts on the Common. He'll be twenty next month and he's growing to be the living image of his father."

Charlton left the proud mother and drove to Whitchester for the second time that day, but now he had a meditative frown on his face.

Captain Harmon was glad to see him again and asked what more he could do.

"I have here," explained Charlton, "what I believe is a Parabellum. I don't know that it is, because the only indication of manufacture is the word *Erfurt,* which I think is a town in Saxony, and the date 1917."

He took the pistol from its holster and handed it to the Captain.

"Yes," said Harmon, "that's a Parabellum. I take it you want me to try to 'marry' it with that bullet you showed me this morning?"

"That's the general idea, but I should like you, first of all, to tell me this: can you estimate, from the condition of the barrel, the time that has elapsed since a shot was fired?"

"No," replied Harmon decisively. "The corrosion inside a barrel is rust, and rust is one of the most uncertain things in this uncertain world. Would you like me to deliver a lecture on the topic?"

"I am not too young to learn," laughed Charlton.

"But not too fossilized to fling off epigrams!" the Captain retaliated. "This rust, then, is set up, in the first place, by the potassium chlorate that is a constituent of most cartridge caps. When the cap is fired, this potassium chlorate gives up its oxygen and becomes potassium chloride, which deposits itself in the bore of the weapon, and, having an affinity for water, attracts moisture to the barrel. Hence the rust. But apart from this potassium chloride, there are all sorts of other things that may hasten or retard corrosion. A damp atmosphere, for instance, might help the potassium chloride to do its work more swiftly or might itself be entirely responsible for rusting. Again, there might be no potassium chlorate in the cartridge cap—some types of cap don't contain it.

"So you see, Inspector," he smiled, "that the most we can hope to do is to hazard an intelligent guess, which is not of much value in criminal jurisprudence!"

"This Parabellum," said Charlton. "How many rounds does it hold?"

"Eight."

"So I thought. Is it convenient for you to have a look at that gun now? I don't want to put you out at all, but I should really like to know whether or not the bullet was fired from it."

"Delighted!" said Harmon. "My wife is away and you've saved me from being bored to tears. Ballistics are a hobby-horse of mine, I'm afraid! Are you going to wait? It may take me some time."

"I'd like to watch, if I may," said Charlton frankly. "By all means. Now, we must first find out how many bullets we have for the test . . . Seven. To make the thing conclusive, we shall need three of these. That will leave four for the use of the defence if there is a prosecution. The next thing is to fire the cartridges in such a way that the bullets don't get damaged. Some people catch them in oiled sawdust and others fire them through a hole in the side of a box stuffed with cotton waste. Personally I use an outsize in dustbins filled with water, but only for nickel-jacketed bullets. Shall we step into the garden?"

They went out together and Harmon climbed some rough steps by the side of a six-foot tank. He fired two rounds into the water, but the third shot misfired.

"That's not to be wondered at, I suppose," said Charlton, who was an interested spectator. "The pistol was brought back from the War and that makes the cartridges a good many years old."

"We won't try another," said the Captain, "but see if we can manage with a couple of samples."

He retrieved the bullets from the bottom of the tank with a small net on the end of a pole and they went indoors again.

"Now we have to compare the engraving left by the barrel on these two fellows," explained the expert, "and then try to pick out similar features on the one in your pill-box. You can see by the furrows made by the lands that the rifling of your self-loader has a right-hand twist and that the grooves are wider than the lands."

He handed the test bullets to the Inspector.

"If," he said, "the engraving on these two had shown a left-hand twist or the lands and grooves the same width, that would have been conclusive proof that your bullet was not fired by the same weapon. Unfortunately, the bullets are the same in those major characteristics, so we must take our trusty microscope and investigate the minor characteristics."

He produced an imposing piece of apparatus.

"This is a Comparison Microscope. We fix the two test bullets in these cups with a bit of Plasticene and examine each one separately through these eye-pieces. When we find on one of them certain striations—or lines—we'll look for the same combination of striations on the other bullet. It naturally follows that, like fingerprints, no two barrels are exactly alike. The scoring left in each one of them by the machining of the bore is absolutely peculiar to it."

For some time, Captain Harmon busied himself with the microscope. Then he fitted on the comparison eye-piece, which enabled the two test bullets to be viewed simultaneously, and invited Charlton to examine them.

"Do you see, he asked, those two parallel lines with a third line a little distance away from them? And that the same three lines are present in both bullets?"

"They occupy the same positions in the furrows left by the lands," added Charlton.

"Smart of you to notice that," approved Harmon.

"Now I'll rotate them and show you some more striations that are common to both bullets."

After he had pointed out other mutual characteristics, he removed one of the test bullets and fitted the Inspector's bullet in its place. For ten minutes, he peered through the eye-pieces. Then he turned to Charlton.

"Nothing doing," he said briefly; and produced his cigarette case.

"My bullet couldn't have been fired from that gun?"

"Definitely not. It's an odds-on chance that it was fired from a Parabellum, but not from this one."

"What do I do now?" asked Charlton, hiding his real disappointment by an exaggerated gesture of despair.

"I suggest you have a drink," smiled Captain Harmon, and rang the bell.

IX.

A Friend of Mr. Symes

ONLY one of the four hard courts on Paulsfield Common, which lay to the north of the town, was in use. Four young men in white flannels were playing an energetic game under the torrid evening sun, and it made Charlton quite hot even to look at them. He stopped the car by the side of the wired enclosure and watched the game. One of them he already knew: Arthur Ransome, the alert young photographer. Of the other three, he could only guess which was Ronald Symes.

As he sat following the play, that shockingly hackneyed quotation from Thomas Gray drifted into Charlton's mind:

> "Alas! regardless of their doom,
>   The little victims play;
> No sense they have of ills to come,
>   Nor care beyond the day."

Which, if he had given any credence at all to that sort of thing, he might afterwards have called a premonition.

Arthur Ransome came to retrieve a ball and caught sight of Charlton sitting in the car. He recognized him at once.

"Good evening, Mr. Ransome," smiled Charlton.

"Have you had any more scoops?"

"Not a single one!" Ransome smiled back. "Have you stopped to speak to me about yesterday's business?"

"No. I want to talk to Ronald Symes, but I'll wait till you've finished this set."

"Certainly not!" protested Ransome, clearly anxious to make up for his mistake of the day before. "Your time is more

85

important than ours. Ronald!"

He called to a good-looking, fair-haired, tall young man, who had been playing against him. Symes ran round the net and Ransome introduced him to the Inspector. While the three others filled the interval by lobbing a ball across the net, Symes came into the road through the iron gate to where Charlton was now standing by his car.

"I want to give you a word of warning, Mr. Symes," said Charlton with a disarming smile, "about leaving firearms lying around in a dangerous condition."

"I don't understand you, Inspector."

Charlton saw by his face that he understood completely.

"When a firearm is not in active use, the safety-catch should always be in position. When did you fire your father's pistol, Symes?"

Ronald swallowed hard and looked very uncomfortable. "I am investigating a murder," added Charlton chattily.

"About two years ago," said Ronald in a great hurry.

"Where?"

"In the garden. When my father was alive—he's dead now, you know—he used to keep it locked up in his bedroom. After he died, Mother put it upstairs in the loft. I'd always had a sort of itch to play about with it and when Mother was out one afternoon—I was only, of course, a kid at the time (one would have thought it was a quarter of a century and not twenty-four months that had passed)—I went up into the loft and got the thing out of the trunk where Mother had put it.

I took it downstairs to have a good look at it and after I'd got some idea of how it worked, suddenly took it into my head to have a pot at something with it. So I took it out into the garden, aimed at the fence at the bottom and pulled the trigger."

He smiled wryly.

"I wasn't ready for the terrible kick of the thing and didn't imagine that it was going to make such an infernal row. It nearly frightened me out of my skin. I leapt back indoors and had the pistol upstairs again in the trunk before you could have winked!"

"You were very foolish," Charlton reproved him.

"Firstly, you had no right to touch the weapon. Secondly, you might have killed somebody by firing at random like that. And thirdly, when you put the thing back in the trunk, it was cocked and a slight touch by your mother, as she rummaged through the trunk for something, might easily have sent it off."

Ronald accepted this rebuke with a humility that the Inspector liked.

"I've often thought what a silly young fool I was and I've never had the pluck to touch the pistol again! I was terrified at the time that the neighbours would tell Mother about the explosion and rushed out and bought one of those two-shilling things and a box of percussion-caps, so that I could tell Mother that it was that that had made the shindy."

It was a great effort for Charlton not to smile at this little piece of strategy.

"Did the bullet hit the fence?" he asked.

"Yes. When I got over my dithers, I went and had a look and found it imbedded in one of the thick uprights."

"Did you prise it out?"

"No. As far as I know, it is still there."

"Right. That's all, I think, Symes. You'd better get back to your game. And don't be such a damned fool another time, will you?"

Symes said fervently that he most certainly wouldn't and Charlton allowed him to go.

Before he went home to Southmouth, Charlton called in at the police station, to see if Sergeant Martin had any news.

"I'm glad you've dropped in, sir," said Martin. "A Mrs. Symes of Effingham Street came round earlier on and wanted to speak to you. I told 'er that if I saw you, I'd ask you to go and see 'er."

"Right."

"Old man Farquarson buttonholed me in the 'Igh Street this afternoon," said Martin, "and 'e was full of the blasted van. Told me that I mustn't let you lose sight of it: that the whole investigation 'inged on it."

"That seems to be the old fellow's theme-song."

"And who should I walk into after shaking 'im off but Miss Beamish. She pushed a list into my hand and before you could say, 'Kiss me, Sergeant,' she'd prised a couple of bob out of me. Said 'er sister, Mrs. Archer, was getting up a subscription to help Earnshaw's widow and kids."

"Put me down when you see the list again, will you?" said the Inspector, and felt in his pocket.

"Martin," he went on seriously, "this thing has got me guessing. Bring that sound common-sense of yours to bear on the problem. I'll give you a brief account of my investigation so far. We've been over some of the ground before, but I'll start again at the beginning. See if you can spot anything that I've missed.

"At midday yesterday Earnshaw was shot dead in an isolated position in the middle of the Square. We have questioned, with some possible omissions, everybody who was present in the Square at the time; and it is a perfectly sound assumption that Earnshaw was not shot by anyone standing in the Square.

"That photograph in yesterday's paper was taken a split second before Earnshaw was shot, so we know exactly how he was standing and in which direction he was facing when the sniper got him. The bullet went through his right temple and Dr. Weston has said that it did not enter at a very acute angle. I don't quite know how much latitude that allows us for our theories, but I *do* think that all the buildings on the east side of the High Street can be ruled out. That leaves us with the monumental masons', the Horticultural Hall, Beamish's, Pope's, the Bank and the Post Office.

"There are no windows or openings of any kind in the

portion of the masons' frontage that overlooks the statue. The same with the Hall, with the exception, of course, of the front entrance, which was locked at noon yesterday."

He paused and lighted a cigarette.

"Have you a large scale map of this town?" he then asked.

Martin went and fetched an Ordnance Survey sheet and they fixed it to the desk with some drawing-pins that the Sergeant produced with a proud flourish. When his superior asked for a compass, however, he had to admit defeat and suggested a piece of string. He had, he said, a piece of string.

"I don't know much about firearms, Martin," confessed Charlton, "but I do know this: revolvers and pistols are only accurate up to a certain limited distance, which is from twenty-five to thirty yards, although a crack shot might get his man at fifty. Beyond that, scoring a hit would be a miracle."

"Or an accident."

"Yes, we mustn't forget that. A pistol bullet would kill a man at a much greater range than fifty yards, but I'll measure off the distances that a premeditated killing would be limited to."

He tied one end of the string to a pencil and measured off seventy-five feet by the scale. Then, with his thumbnail holding the string on the point where Earnshaw had stood, he described a section of a circle. He followed this with two more arcs, one with a radius of ninety feet and the other with a radius of one hundred and fifty feet.

"There you are, Martin," he said, standing back.

"From all the evidence at our disposal, Earnshaw was *most* likely shot from anywhere inside that smallest sector, *quite* likely from anywhere inside the next sector and *not at all* likely, but *possibly,* from anywhere inside the largest sector. Beyond that, it was either an accident or a miracle.

"Actually, the fifty-yard sector doesn't include many more buildings than the thirty-yard one. Only the stonemasons', the Post Office and that empty block of shops in the High Street, and I don't think any of those need concern us tremendously."

"The twenty-five yard what's-its-name," said Martin, "just misses the Bank. That leaves us the Hall, which's got no windows, and the two shops. Why don't you take out a search warrant? The Firearms Act, 1920, would cover you."

"It would cover me in certain circumstances. I should have to swear that I have—what's the wording?

'. . . reasonable belief that firearms are held in contravention to the Act.' Would *you* be prepared to swear that, Martin?"

"Not likely!" was two-thirds of Martin's reply.

"And neither am I. The interpretation placed by the powers that be on 'reasonable belief' depends entirely on results. There's something else we must take into account before we consider a search warrant."

"What's that?"

"That passage between the Hall and Beamish's shop."

"Well, I never! I'd forgotten that."

"Do you know that it's possible to see the statue in the Square from the bathroom of Mrs. Symes's house in Effingham Street?"

"No, I didn't. Mrs. Symes' as never asked me round."

Charlton went out to his car and brought back the Parabellum.

"Where do you think I found that?" he asked, as he took the weapon from its holster. "I found it this afternoon in Mrs. Symes's loft."

"Would it be likely to 'ave done it?" said Martin in a hushed voice.

"According to Captain Harmon, the chances are in favour of the bullet having been fired from a Parabellum self-loader, and this is the only registered Parabellum in the whole of Downshire."

"Don't tease me!" complained Martin. "Could the Captain say if it was the one that fired the shot?"

"He said it most definitely wasn't."

"What a pity," said the Sergeant dismally.

"So we must look for another Parabellum."

"Talking about looking for things, did you trace that van old Farquarson was shouting the odds about?"

"Yes. It belonged to Henfrew's, the biscuit people of Southmouth, and it was driven by an Irishman named Murphy, who pulled it up for the frivolous purpose of buying a toffee-apple. We must enquire, by the way, from the stall-holders whether a toffee-apple was bought by a big uniformed man. He had nobody else in the van at the time—or so he says."

"Old man Farquarson suggested to me," observed Martin, "that somebody might 'ave nipped in when the driver wasn't looking."

"He might have been able to do that without Murphy seeing him, but I'll wager he couldn't have done it without someone in the Square seeing him. He wouldn't have dared to take the risk."

"P'r'aps he slipped in when this Murphy fellow stopped somewhere where it was a bit quieter."

"In the hope that Murphy would pull up to buy a toffee-apple and give him the chance to shoot Earnshaw in comfort? It was only a last minute decision that took Murphy into the Paragon. Don't forget that. No, Martin, I'm reluctantly forced to discard the van theory." Martin scratched his head.

"So what?" he enquired hopelessly.

"If you can't think of anything more helpful than a confoundedly silly question," said Charlton, "I'm going to seek inspiration in the company of Mrs. Symes."

"She *is* a widow," Martin called after his respected superior as he left the station.

Left by himself, Martin carefully measured on the Ordnance Survey map the distance from the statue to number eight, Effingham Street.

"A miracle," he murmured, rubbing his chin, "or an accident."

Mrs. Symes was all of a twitter when Charlton arrived.

"Oh, Inspector!" she said excitedly, "I'm *so* glad you've come. I've got something to tell you and it may turn out to be a Clue! I didn't realize when you came round earlier to-day exactly why you wanted to see my husband's pistol. I thought it was because the licence had expired. But just after you'd gone, it suddenly came to me. You're trying to find out how that poor man was shot in the Square yesterday and you're going round looking at all the pistols in the neighbourhood!"

Charlton bowed his head non-committally.

"Well, *that's* where I can help you! You can only go to see people you *know* have pistols—people who have taken out a permit for them. But I can tell you about *one* pistol that I don't believe has ever been registered!"

"Please tell me about it."

"When my husband came back from the War, he brought two pistols with him, both the same make. What was the name on the certificate? Parabellum—that was it. Two Parabellums. They were both loaded and for some years my husband kept them together in the dressing-table drawer. Then, some time in 1921, he told me that he wasn't going to take the risk any longer of having loaded firearms in the house without proper authority. This was a long time ago, of course, and my memory's not as good as it might be, but I do remember asking my husband whether he was going to get a certificate for both the Parabellums. He said he wasn't going to *keep* both of them; that he was going to give one away or, if he couldn't get anybody to take it, surrender it to the police. It didn't really matter much which he did."

It may not have mattered much to the late Percy Symes, but it mattered a very great deal to a good many other people, for if he had given up that Parabellum, this story might never have been written.

"Afterwards—it may have been the same day or a month

later—he showed me the certificate and said he had got rid of the other pistol, but the man he had given it to wasn't going to take out a certificate because it was too much bother."

"Can you recall the name of the other man, Mrs. Symes?"

"That's the awkward part, Inspector. Ever since I remembered about that second pistol, I've been racking my brains for that man's name; and I don't believe now that I ever heard his surname. My husband used to mix a lot in the social life of Paulsfield. When I say social life, I mean that he was a Bullfinch, belonged to the bowls club and all that sort of thing. A good many of his friends I knew, of course, but there were others I didn't know and only heard about now and then— and I think this man was one of those."

"Can't you remember anything about him? Perhaps he was a Bullfinch or a fellow member of the bowls club. He may have been a business friend or—"

"I *think* I can remember something," she said slowly, "but I'm not quite sure. I've got a sort of feeling in the back of my mind that my husband did mention a name when he told me about giving the pistol away, but he may have used it about something entirely different. He probably came home late and told me when I was in bed and three-quarters asleep. I hardly like to tell you what I think the name was, for fear of giving you wrong information. Anyway, I don't know which way it's spelt."

"I think you had better tell me," said Charlton.

Mrs. Symes looked doubtful: then she said:

"It was Jeff."

X.

Act Two

THE church clock struck three times. It was a quarter to six on the Thursday morning and the Square was deserted. In the High Street the night-watchman sat hunched in his shelter, gazing sadly at his coke fire, blind to the hazy blue of the sky and deaf to the early songs of the birds. The sun had started on its day's journey, but the High Street shops still cast long shadows across the market-place.

But the Square was not to be empty for long, for a man turned out of Effingham Street and strode along the passage, gently whistling a gay dance tune. He emerged from between the Horticultural Hall and Beamish's shop and made straight across the Square towards Heather Street; but before he had walked twenty-five yards, a deafening report shattered the silence and, as the whistle died on his lips, he fell forward on to his face.

For fifteen seconds it was quiet in the Square, except for the anxious twittering of the sparrows. Then the old night watchman slowly rose to his feet and went round the front of the shelter, to see what had happened. Windows were pushed up, pyjama-clad shoulders leant out and sleepy eyes under tousled hair blinked in the morning brightness. The watchman walked along until the statue allowed him to see the body lying on the ground, ducked under the barrier and broke into a shambling run towards it. As he bent over the still form, Mrs. Archer, with a bright wrap flung over her nightdress, called down to him. He straightened his back and turned to her with a look of blank astonishment on his face.

"'E's bin shot through the back. What are we going to do?"

Alexander Pope, the tobacconist, was at his window.

"Get the police, of course!" he shouted. "Mrs. Archer, you've a telephone. Will you ring for them?"

Mrs. Archer's head disappeared and a voice came across from the other side of the Square. It was the harness-maker from over his shop.

"What's happened to him, Mr. Pope?"

"He's been shot through the back."

"Who is it?" asked the grocer next door.

"I don't know," Mr. Pope called back, "but he seems to be a young fellow."

Hastily dressed men and women began to come into the Square and, before many minutes had gone by, an awed and whispering crowd had formed around the body.

"No one's got to touch 'im," said the night-watchman authoritatively, "till the p'lice come."

★ ★ ★

The maid knocked on Inspector Charlton's door, but he was sound asleep. She knocked again more insistently and he stirred.

"Yes, what is it?" he asked drowsily.

"The Paulsfield police are on the 'phone, sir."

"Wass time?"

"Just after six, sir."

"Give my compliments to the Paulsfield police and tell them to go to the devil."

This long, clearly delivered speech exhausted him and he was just drifting off again when the maid said:

"Someone else has been shot in Paulsfield Square, sir."

"*What?*"

Before she had time to open her mouth again, he was out of bed and running down the stairs in his pyjamas. He grabbed at the receiver.

"Charlton here. . . . Yes, Harwood. ... Is he dead? . . . Have you got Dr. Weston? . . . I'll come over now. Hold everything till I get to you. Goodbye." He hung up the receiver. His usual urbane manner had deserted him and his face was hard.

"Get me a cup of coffee and some biscuits," he said brusquely to the maid, as he passed her on the landing.

When he got back into his room, he plumped down on the side of the bed and ran his fingers through his hair. "Arthur Ransome," he muttered. "My God!" Then he began hurriedly to dress.

By the time he had driven through the clean morning air to Paulsfield, he had got a grip on himself. There was still a crowd round Ransome's body and, when he had pushed his way through, he found P.C. Harwood and Dr. Weston waiting for him.

"Get these people away from here," he murmured to Harwood and, as the constable was persuading the curious townsfolk to go back to bed, said to the doctor, "Was the poor devil dead when you got to him?"

"Yes. Shot through the back. The bullet entered the heart— or so I should imagine. You can see the hole in his coat. I haven't disturbed him at all and the night-watchman, who was sitting over there in his shelter when it happened, kept close guard over him until Harwood came."

"Intelligent fellow. I must have a word with him."

He turned to Harwood, who had successfully cleared their immediate vicinity.

"Was anybody besides the watchman in the Square when this happened?" he asked.

"Not as far as I know, sir."

"Has his mother been told?"

"Yes, sir."

"How did she take it?"

"Badly, sir. The lady from next door's in with 'er now. Shall I get the ambulance, sir?"

Charlton nodded and, as Harwood left them, felt in his pocket for his camera. As he was folding it up after taking his photographs, a dignified figure emerged from the passage and walked across towards them. It was Mr. Farquarson in his long black overcoat and high-crowned boxer hat; and he was carrying his tightly rolled umbrella and a white paper bag.

"Another disaster, Inspector?" he asked as he drew near. "What shocking times we live in. Young Arthur Ransome, so they tell me. A death as unaccountable as Earnshaw's. From the hole in his coat, I see he was shot?"

He ended on a questioning note.

"Good morning, Mr. Farquarson," said Charlton civilly.

"Have you found any trace of a van in the Square this morning?" the secretary prattled on. "You know, I still feel—"

But that morning Charlton had no patience with the amiable old gentleman.

"I am bearing your theories in mind, Mr. Farquarson," he said with admirable courtesy, "but now, if you'll forgive my rudeness, I am rather busy. Perhaps we can have a chat some other time?"

Mr. Farquarson accepted his dismissal with great docility and made a majestic departure, after blandly informing Charlton and the doctor that he was off to feed the ducks on the lake. The two of them were left alone in the Square, although interested spectators still peered between curtains. Mrs. Archer was sitting at her open window dividing her attention between the Inspector and a crossword puzzle. The ambulance came and took away Ransome's body; and Dr. Weston went off to get some breakfast.

"Contrary to popular belief, Charlton," he said as he left, "we medicos do sometimes sleep and eat."

"Don't forget I want that bullet," Charlton called after him.

"You'll get the bullet all right," said the doctor morbidly, "when the Chief Constable hears about this."

Charlton went over to speak to the watchman, who had returned to his fire. The old fellow could tell him very little. He had heard a shot, gone round the side of the shelter and seen Ransome's body. He had heard nothing else and had seen nobody in or near the Square. Charlton nodded his thanks and strolled back to the spot where Ransome had fallen, to consider its position. It has not been thought in the best interests of this story to mark it on the plan with the wonted cross, but it was just by the back off-side wing of the motor car that our draughtsman, with no thought of the crime in his mind, has drawn in.

The first thing Charlton noticed was that this spot was not in alignment with the passage. The Horticultural Hall prevented it from being seen from Mrs. Symes's bathroom. Secondly, although it was not protected from so large a portion of the Square as the place where Earnshaw met his death, it was within range of all the buildings that fell inside the sectors he had drawn on Martin's map. The shots that had killed both men, therefore, could have been fired from the same point, but—and it was an important but—whereas Earnshaw had been vulnerable from the whole length of the passage, Ransome's danger from that direction had been limited to a few yards. Thirdly, Ransome had fallen towards Heather Street and it was a rational premise that he had been making for it when the shot arrested his steps.

Charlton pondered the question of the boy's starting-point. Had he come via the High Street or the passage? The passage seemed the more feasible. If he had come from the High Street, he would have passed nearer to the statue, perhaps to the other side of it.

The Inspector crossed over to the passage, which was about six feet wide and paved with asphalt. About five yards along it, his roving glance caught something that lay close to the right-hand wall. With a grunt of satisfaction, he bent down and picked it up: a small rimless cartridge-case.

He took out his notebook and made a sketch of that part of the passage; and, after careful measurements with the flexible steel rule from the bakelite case in his pocket, marked on the sketch the exact position of his find.

Mr. Beamish's plot and the Effingham Street garden that backed on to it were protected from curious eyes by a fence fully six feet in height, as were, on the other side of the passage, the yard of the Horticultural Hall and the garden of Mr. Farquarson. Because of the narrowness of the passage, the statue in the Square was not visible from the windows of the houses on either side of Effingham Street, with the single exception of number eight.

Having absorbed these facts, Charlton looked up at the high side wall of the Horticultural Hall and stood for a while abstractedly shaking the cartridge-case in his cupped hand. Then he threw away his cigarette, put the cartridge-case in his waistcoat pocket and walked briskly along the passage towards Effingham Street.

When he knocked at the door of number seven, it was answered by a charwoman.

"Good morning," he said. "I'm afraid it's rather early, but is Mr. Farquarson able to see me?"

At that particular moment, Mr. Farquarson was probably distributing tasty snacks to the ducks, but it was as good an opening remark as any.

"'E's hout," said the woman, whose speech was as plain as her face, but fortunately not so smutty. "Always hout this time of a morning. Wet or fine,'e goes and feeds the ducks on the Common."

"When do you expect him back?"

"Eight o'clock to the tick. I'm getting 'is breakfast now."

"That's a pity. I rather wanted to get into the Horticultural Hall."

"Then you'll 'ave to wait till 'e comes back."

"Has he the keys with him?"

"No, they're kep' in a drawer of 'is desk."

"Perhaps I could borrow them?"

"Not till Mr. Farquarson says so."

"I am an Inspector of Police."

99

"If you were the Harchbishop of Canterbury, it wouldn't make no difference. Come back at eight."

So Charlton came back at eight and Mr. Farquarson expressed himself delighted to see him again. Charlton explained that he wanted to have a look round the Hall, but that the secretary had been out when he had called earlier.

"You should have stated your requirements to Mrs. Grabbery. She knows where the keys are kept."

"I did tentatively broach the subject," admitted Charlton, "but it was suggested that I came back later."

"I'll speak to Mrs. Grabbery," said Mr. Farquarson with a magnificent wave of his arm and went out into the kitchen, from where his loud admonitions to his help came clearly to Charlton's ears.

"'E ought to 'ave a search warrant," was Mrs. Grabbery's shrill retort.

"Search warrant? You silly old woman, if you impede the police again, I'll give you a week's notice. Go at once and wash your face. At the moment, it looks more like bad news than a human visage. And I don't like the way you grill bacon, anyway."

"I'll hand in my notice *now*!" screeched the woman. "Accepted!" said Mr. Farquarson and came back to the Inspector with all the swagger of Caesar returning in triumph from Hither Gaul.

"I'm sorry to cause all this upset," said Charlton regretfully.

"Don't let that worry you! We give each other notice four or five times a week. It keeps one's powers of invective from becoming rusty. Now, I'll get the keys and we'll go straight to the Hall."

"What about your breakfast?"

"That can wait," said Mr. Farquarson; then raising his voice, "It's always half cold, so it doesn't really matter."

As a strangled cry came from the kitchen, Mr. Farquarson collected the keys from his desk and led Charlton through the french windows into the garden.

"My little pleasance," he said with modest pride, as they walked down the crazy path, past the trim flowerbeds and the pedestal bird-bath.

At the bottom of the garden was a padlocked door, which Mr. Farquarson unlocked and then, with a polite gesture, invited Charlton to precede him into the cemented yard at the back of the Hall.

"Now, Inspector," he said, as he pushed the door to behind him, "which part of the Hall can I show you first? It strikes me as a little strange that you want to see it at all, but I am not the one to interfere with your investigation."

On this point, Charlton was in entire agreement, but he merely said:

"I should like to get on the roof, if it is possible?"

"The roof? Yes, that is perfectly simple, although the route is fraught with peril."

Mr. Farquarson grossly exaggerated the danger. The Hall's lavatory accommodation was in the form of a one-storeyed annexe at the rear. Fixed to the top of this was an iron ladder that led up to the roof. Access to the ladder was gained from inside the Hall through a gallery window.

The old gentleman led the way up to the gallery and threw up the sash.

"' Taste your legs, sir,'" he quoted; "'put them in motion.' That," he added kindly, for the guidance of the Inspector, "is a bit from Shakespeare's *Twelfth Night.*"

"Act three, scene one, to be precise," said Charlton and climbed through the window, leaving the secretary with the sensation of having been hit when he wasn't looking.

The roof of the Hall was flat and a three-foot parapet ran round it. In the middle was a large domed top-light, several of the sections of which could be opened for ventilating purposes. Charlton clambered over the parapet and made his way past an accumulation of empty paint tins and long planks, to the front. Down below him, the Square was showing signs of human activity, as the townspeople began to go about the business of the day. None of them glanced up at the roof of the Hall, but he saw them pointing out to each other the spot where young Ransome had fallen; and nobody seemed to fancy walking too near.

But Charlton had not gone up to meditate alone on the tragedy of it, but to have a look at the other roofs in the Square. In the passage, he had thought suddenly that he had been paying too much attention to windows and too little to roofs, particularly roofs with useful parapets round them. It was all very well for him to say that Earnshaw and Ransome could have been shot only from certain buildings in the Square. It was true, as far as it went, but he must not lose sight of the possibility that the roofs of those buildings might be easily accessible from other roofs. The Horticultural Hall stood on an island site, but, with the exception of Mr. Beamish's shop, all the other buildings along that side of the Square had not even the distinction, beloved by estate agents, of semi-detachedness; and the unbroken line of commanding business premises continued right round into the High Street, until Effingham Street intervened.

The Horticultural Hall had been chosen by Charlton for his survey, because it was sufficiently higher than the other buildings to enable him to scan their roofs. He crossed over to the eastern side and stood by the parapet with a hand shielding his eyes from the sun, which already promised another scorching day.

The roofs of the buildings were, for the most part, flat. They were not all the same height, but an active man could have made his way with ease from one to the other. He studied them for a few minutes, then a far-away look came into his eyes and speculation filled his mind. . . .

When he climbed back through the window into the gallery, Mr. Farquarson was standing in front of an extending step-ladder that leant against the wall.

"I don't think I need trouble you any more, Mr. Farquarson," he smiled.

"As long as you don't want me to climb that suicidal ladder," said the secretary with a wriggle of his shoulders. "Heights terrify me. Now, before you go, just step along here."

Charlton followed him to the other end of the gallery, where a corner window looked out on to the Paragon.

"That," said Mr. Farquarson with a wave of his hand, "was where that van was standing. Just outside the masons'."

Charlton politely studied the spot indicated by the secretary's pointing finger. He felt called upon to say something, but was gripped by that peculiar inarticulateness that is the terror of those who are shown holiday snaps by their friends. He hardly thought that "How nice!" did justice to the old gentleman's dramatic posture and eventually contented himself with a comprehending grunt, which seemed to satisfy Mr. Farquarson, who turned and led the way downstairs and out into the yard.

"Is that kept locked?" Charlton enquired, pointing to a gate in the fence that bordered the Paragon side of the yard.

"Always, except, naturally, when there is any sort of show taking place in the Hall. The key is kept on this bunch with the others."

"So that if one wanted to get into the yard, one would have to climb the fence?"

"Precisely so. Are you contemplating breaking into the place, Inspector?"

They both laughed at this sally and Charlton left the secretary to his breakfast, which was probably stone-cold by then.

XI.

The Literary Brother

MR. JOSEPH BEAMISH was engaged, with every appearance of immense activity, upon more or less nothing at all. He was an odd little man, whose character was best illustrated by his habit of carrying two empty fountain-pens in his waistcoat pocket and calling it System. His idea of clearing away the dinner things was to move the plates and dishes from one part of the table to another. "Just," as he would explain, "getting them sorted out."

It was not necessary for Charlton to bellow his opening question, for, as soon as he saw him, Mr. Beamish laid down a china soap-dish and said:

"Oh, good morning, Inspector! I suppose you have come in about this new tragedy? It was only when my sister, Miss Beamish, aroused me that I knew anything about it. I expect you would like to speak to her?" The Inspector nodded and Mr. Beamish went to the bottom of the stairs and called, "Ruth!"

When his sister came down, she smiled on seeing Charlton standing in the shop. He took off his hat and was just about to bid her good morning when her brother forestalled him.

"My dear," he said, as if the two of them had never met before, "this is Inspector Carton." Mrs. Archer's voice floated down from the top of the stairs.

"Joseph, the Inspector may be going to do some far, far better thing, but his name is not Carton."

She came down carrying a card in her hand.

"What a shocking thing it is," said Miss Beamish, " about Arthur Ransome. His poor, dear mother must be prostrated."

"Can you tell me anything about it? I suppose it's too much to hope that either of you ladies was awake?"

"I was roused by the shot," said Miss Beamish. "I sleep at the back of the house, but it was quite loud enough to wake me up. Erica came out on to the landing and called up to me that somebody else had been killed in the Square; and then I went in and woke my brother, who sleeps on the same floor, only in the front."

"*I* heard the report, too," said Mrs. Archer. "I was only really half asleep at the time and immediately guessed that it was a pistol shot. I'm getting quite accustomed to the Square being turned into a shooting-range, Inspector! I jumped out of bed and went to the window. Arthur Ransome's body was lying on the ground and the old night-watchman was running across from his shelter. I called out something to him—asked him what had happened. Mr. Pope, next door, was leaning out of his window and it was he who suggested that I 'phoned for the police, but before I did that, I told Ruth what had happened."

"Did you see anybody else in the Square?"

"No. Except for the night-watchman and the body, it was absolutely empty. That, I think, is all I can tell you about the actual shooting, Inspector, but I've brought down Arthur Ransome's card. It may help you." Miss Beamish was beginning to fidget.

"If you'll excuse me," she said, "I'll run into the kitchen. There's something on the gas-stove."

"Arthur Ransome," said Mrs. Archer with unction, when her sister had left them, "was born in 1914. He was educated at Paulsfield College and on leaving school, took up press photography as a career. He won a prize in the *Daily Star* snapshot competition in 1932. He lived in Effingham Street—number one—with his widowed mother and elder brother."

"A brother? I didn't know he had a brother."

"John, known as Jack. He is two years older than Arthur and a brilliant young man. Not a bit like Arthur, who never did anything much at school, but a real genius. Matriculated at an almost unheard of age and afterwards became quite a well-known botanist. He's written several Nature books, although I'm afraid not many people buy them. Surely you've heard of John Ransome?" Charlton admitted that he had not.

"He'll be very cut up about his brother. Arthur used to help him with the photographs for his books and I believe they were very attached to each other. In a quiet way, of course, like most brothers are, especially when they're that age."

Mrs. Archer was plainly prepared to settle down to a nice long chat, but Charlton excused himself at this point and went in next door to see Alexander Pope, whose story was that the report had roused him and he had gone into the front room to investigate.

The Bank and the Post Office had, of course, been locked up and deserted when the shooting happened. He passed them by and crossed the High Street to interview the outfitter, Mr. Harbottle, and his family; but neither they nor any of the other residents round the Square could throw fresh light on the crime.

He walked along the High Street and stood irresolute on the corner of Effingham Street, wanting to see Mrs. Ransome and Jack, yet hesitant to cause her more pain than she suffered already. Then he noticed the wires that ran to the house and decided to ring up Jack from the police station and ask him to step round the corner.

Sergeant Martin looked up from his desk as Charlton came into the charge-room and flung his hat on a chair.

"Morning, sir," he said. "Things are not looking so good."

"And I've a nasty feeling they're going to look worse, Martin," was the grave answer. "There's a homicidal maniac running round loose and God knows what he'll be doing next."

"D'you mean he's goofy?"

"It looks like it to me. Of course, I don't know yet that

Earnshaw and Ransome were killed by the same person and with the same gun, but I'm willing to bet they were. Earnshaw's death was easy to understand—at least, I *thought* it was easy. Somebody formed an acute dislike for him and shot him. On the face of it, one couldn't quite see why anybody should hate him enough to kill him, but it was a straightforward case of murder. Now, with this Ransome business . . . Just a moment— that reminds me."

He reached across Martin and pulled the telephone towards him. Martin found the number for him and he was put through.

"Are you Mr. John Ransome? . . . This is Inspector Charlton here. Can you give me a few moments at the police station? . . . Yes, now . . . Thank you."

He turned to Martin and resumed.

"This Ransome business puts a different complexion on things. Why should he suffer the same fate as Earnshaw? Surely there was no connection between them?"

"Ransome took them photographs," said Martin slowly. "They were a bit dangerous for 'is nibs."

"But that was over and finished. If Ransome had been shot before he could send the photos to London, I could have understood it, but he was killed after the damage was done."

"What about revenge?"

"Hardly, Martin. A possibility, of course, but highly unlikely. A sane man would hesitate to double the risk of detection, just to satisfy a grudge. Personally, I don't think he *was* sane; and there's no knowing where he'll crop up next. Look at that impudent killing of Earnshaw. Right at midday, with a couple of hundred witnesses looking on."

"Looking on," said Martin, "but not seeing much. If my old razor was as sharp as their eyes, I'd be tripping over me whiskers with every step I took!"

The door swung open and a slim young man came in. He was neatly dressed in grey and his dark hair was smooth.

Although his nose was too sharp for him to be really handsome, he was a very personable young man and a couple of inches taller than his brother's five-feet-eight.

"I'm Jack Ransome," he said in a well modulated voice. "You want to see me?"

"Thank you for coming round, Mr. Ransome. I am Inspector Charlton. I didn't call on you for fear of disturbing your mother."

"That's very kind of you," said Jack with a grateful smile. "The shock has been rather too much for her. *I* can't believe yet that my brother is dead."

"Did you see him before he went out this morning?"

"No. The last time was last night. He was playing tennis with some friends and went home to supper at one of their houses. I saw him for a minute or two at about ten o'clock."

"Did you know that he was going to leave home so early this morning?"

"No. He said nothing to me about it. He sometimes used to go out early to get photographs, but I had no idea that he intended to this morning."

"Whether he proposed to take photographs or not, he usually carried his camera about with him, didn't he?"

"Yes," answered Jack, smiling slightly, "they were inseparable."

"Does your mother know why he went out this morning?"

"When she first heard that someone else had been shot, she thought he was still upstairs in bed. It wasn't until the police told us that we knew who it was."

"You and your brother sleep in different rooms?"

"Yes, although they are on the same landing. I didn't hear him go out."

"He left no note to say where he was going?"

"I didn't see one, but I'll have a good look round when I get back home."

"Would he be likely to have made an appointment with a friend at that early hour? A day's walking, or something like that?"

"It's quite likely. He did go off on hikes sometimes. He may have said something about it to the fellows he was playing tennis with yesterday evening. I can give you their names and addresses."

He mentioned Ronald Symes and the other two players and Charlton made a a note of them.

"That is all, thank you," Charlton said as he closed the book. "I'm afraid I shall have to speak to your mother later on, but I won't trouble her now. You both have my deepest sympathy, Mr. Ransome."

"And mine," agreed Martin.

When their visitor had gone, the Sergeant said that they had not got much out of that.

"A certain amount of negative evidence which may be useful," said the Inspector. "Neither Jack nor Mrs. Ransome knew that Arthur was going out or even that he *had* gone out. If he proposed to spend the day away from home, surely he would have told them or left a note?"

"Young Jack said Arthur used to go out early sometimes to get photos."

"For which purpose, Martin, a camera is indispensable — and he hadn't one with him this morning. Jack has told us that his camera was Arthur's constant companion. It is significant that he was not carrying it when he was shot this morning."

"'E must've been going off on some other errand."

"That's what I must find out, Martin: whether anyone knew he was going out so early. I think that somebody *did* and that the meeting was only to be a short one. Had Ransome gone out for a quick morning stroll, he would have taken his camera; and had he planned a long excursion, he would have warned his mother beforehand. It all boils down to this, Martin: If somebody knew in advance that Ransome proposed to go out soon after daybreak, plans could have been laid to shoot him as he crossed the Square; but if he had said not a word about it to anyone, but acted entirely on an impulse of the moment or carried out a private idea that only he knew, the murderer either had his intended victim playing, by a stroke of luck, right into his hands, or—and this is a most unpleasant and disquieting possibility, Martin—was waiting there like a watchful, blood-lusting spider for some innocent sacrifice to come along."

"You're giving me the willies!" said Martin plaintively.

"I'm giving myself the willies, too. I don't like the look of things at all. I've two unexplained murders on my hands and if I don't put a jerk in finding out who did them and seeing that's he's safely put away in Broadmoor, we're going to have more widows and bereaved mothers in this town.

"The trouble is, Martin, that I don't quite know what to do next. I have narrowed down the area from which Earnshaw could have been shot. This morning, Ransome was killed at a point accessible from the whole of the Earnshaw sector. There is every chance that Earnshaw and Ransome were killed by means of a Parabellum self-loader; and I have reason to think that there is such a gun held without a certificate by a man in Paulsfield called Jeff."

"That's news to me," said Martin. "What we've got to do, then, is to comb out the population for Jeffs."

"Bearing in mind," added Charlton, "that it might be either a surname or a Christian name and that it might be spelt J-E-F-F or G-E-O-F-F and that more than one name can be contracted to Jeff or Geoff—if," he smiled, "you can detect from my intonation the two different spellings! The one thing that we do know is that this Jeff person was a grown man in 1921, so we needn't look for any adolescent or stripling Jeffs. The weapon was given to him by a responsible member of the public. That, in itself, was an illegal act, but I feel sure that the giver would not aggravate the offence by handing over a loaded pistol to a young boy. That would make the the present age of the recipient not less than forty."

"Would you like me to see to that for you?" asked Martin obligingly. "Get out a list of all the men living in this town who are over forty and who've got names with J-E-F-F or G-E-O-F-F in'em?"

"I should be glad if you would, Martin," said Charlton gratefully. "Better be on the safe side and make the minimum present age thirty-five. And don't forget that when a man dies, he leaves his firearms behind. Include any man who would have been thirty-five or over now if he had lived."

"Right, sir," said the Sergeant smartly. "I'll do that."

"I was up on the roof of the Horticultural Hall this morning," Charlton began another topic, "having a look round."

"See anything interesting?"

"I saw that the roofs of the buildings in the Square and the ones that carry on round in the High Street are all comparatively flat and that it would be child's play to get from one end to the other without attracting too much attention. I think our suspicions must not be restricted to the buildings coming inside the sectors that I drew on your map: we must also consider all the buildings in that *block* and all the means of access to their roofs.

"Another thing I noticed was that it is a simple matter for any active person to get on the roof of the Horticultural Hall, although it would be rather conspicuous. He could climb over the fence from the Paragon or the passage, reach the roof of the lavatory annexe at the back of the Hall via one of the barred windows, and then get up the iron ladder that leads to the roof of the Hall, which is a delightful centre for a happy day's sniping. Of course, the means of getting up there are noticeable in broad daylight. This morning it might have been done, because the town was wrapped in childlike slumber when it happened and too taken up afterwards with what was going on in the Square to pay much heed to the Hall, although that ladder must be visible from a good many windows. But Earnshaw was killed when all Paulsfield was wide awake and surely nobody could have climbed that ladder without *someone* seeing?"

"'E might'ave got up there fine and early in the morning and stayed there till nightfall. You didn't 'ave a look round there on Tuesday, I suppose?"

"I scent a reproach, Martin!"

"I didn't mean one," said the Sergeant hastily. "I was just putting the question."

"Frankly, I didn't. I entirely overlooked the importance of roofs. When you come to write the story of my life, Martin, it will be as well to omit any reference to that carelessly misplaced footprint on the sands of time."

He picked up his hat.

"And now I think I'll go and see those tennis-players."

Ronald Symes and his two friends, whose names need not concern us, could not recall any mention by Arthur Ransome of an intended early rising. They knew of no one else who might be able to help.

The Inspector sought out Albert Earnshaw and afterwards the widow. To each of them he put the same question: Did Thomas Earnshaw know an Irishman named Murphy? In both cases the answer was No. As he was driving back, Dr. Weston's car caught him up and they both stopped.

"I've got your second bullet, Charlton," said the doctor and handed him another pill-box. "It looks the twin of the first one."

Charlton thanked him and decided to take it straight over to Captain Harmon.

The Captain, who was becoming more than interested in the investigation, fixed the two bullets in position under the Comparison Microscope and eventually delivered the verdict that Charlton would have gambled heavily upon: both bullets had been fired from the same gun.

As Charlton drove back to Paulsfield, after an early lunch in the "Bell and Three Tuns" in Whitchester High Street, the brilliance of the morning faded and the storm clouds began to gather.

"We're in for it," was his thought.

He was right.

XII.

The Co-Respondent

Those who live in the never-ceasing bustle of London will hardly credit the hush that falls on a country town between the hours of one and two in the afternoon. The shops close and the whole population sits down to dinner. Some of them call it lunch, some of them even call it luncheon, but as the same butcher serves them all, that is mere pedantry. And while these simultaneous meals are in progress, the streets have all the emptiness of the lone and level sands of Ozymandias.

So it was not a remarkable thing that, when the storm broke over Paulsfield, the Square and High Street were as deserted as they had been when young Arthur Ransome died. It is true that the road-menders were working, for they had been to their dinners at twelve; but when the rain came down as if the drops had merged into one solid and continuous cascade, and the thunder no longer rolled distantly, but followed the lightning instantly, like the crack of a mighty whip, they retired into their shelter and, with the thought that Nature was wonderful, contentedly lighted their pipes.

For five minutes the storm roared vengeance, while the townsfolk munched their food, sometimes looking at each other and saying, "That was close." Then it turned like a disgruntled bully and drifted away across the countryside, until all that could be heard were its far-off complaints that the people of Paulsfield had been too busy feeding their faces to tremble at its rantings.

The rain stopped, the watercourses in the gutters ebbed, steam began to rise from the pavements, the sun shone again as if there had been no storm, and the silence of the dinner

113

hour descended once more on Paulsfield. But the quiet in the Square was not complete: it was broken by a continuous throbbing noise—a familiar, everyday sound that would normally pass unnoticed, but now commanded attention by its subdued persistency.

The Square was used, as a rule, for parking cars, and on that Thursday afternoon there were five or six of them scattered here and there. Paulsfield Square is not Finsbury Circus and there was nothing systematic about their disposal. One of them—a four-seater saloon—was standing to the west of the statue, with its bonnet facing the churchyard. It will be found on the plan and has been mentioned in an earlier chapter. There was nobody sitting in the driving-seat and the engine was gently turning over, as if its owner had slipped across to Pope's for some cigarettes.

P.C. Johnson was walking along the High Street when his attention was attracted by this car left unattended with the engine running. He strolled round the barricade, behind which the workmen were now again taking up their tools, and went towards the car. The off-side windows were down and, after looking round to see if the driver was coming back, he reached through the front window. But as his hand sought the switch on the dashboard, he suddenly paused and stiffened.

Lying sideways across the front seats was the body of a man, with his head a mess of blood.

Johnson turned off the engine, stood upright and glanced about him. A man was walking past the Hall and the constable beckoned to him.

"Anything wrong?" the man asked as he approached.

"I don't know, sir," Johnson replied cautiously, "but would you mind going round to the police station and asking the Sergeant to ring for Dr. Weston to come to the Square at once? I can't leave here."

The man wasted no time in further questions, but hurried off. The ambulance was the first to arrive and was followed almost immediately by the doctor, who opened the door of the car and bent over the body.

"He isn't dead," he said to Johnson; and then to the ambulance men, "Take him round to the hospital."

As the doctor's car followed the ambulance along the Paragon, on their way to the hospital, Inspector Charlton's big six-cylinder saloon swung round into the Square.

"What's happened, Johnson?" he asked apprehensively, as he jumped out.

"Another man's been shot, sir. Dr. Weston says he's still alive and they've rushed him off to hospital."

"Thank God for that! Where was he?"

"Lying across the front seat of this car, sir. The engine was running when I found him."

"You haven't moved the car?"

"The only thing we've done is to open the door and lift him into the ambulance."

"Where did the bullet get him?"

"In the head. It seems to have torn most of his right ear off."

"If it had perforated his skull, it would have killed him. It must still be here somewhere."

He leant inside the car and searched the floor, where he found a badly deformed bullet.

"The front off-side window was down, as it is now?" he asked, as he put the bullet in his pocket.

Johnson nodded and said that the hand-brake had been off, as if the driver was about to start when the shot got him.

"How long did the storm last here?"

"It was *really* bad for about five minutes—I should say from 1.15 to 1.20."

"D'you know the man?"

"I know him by sight, but I don't know his name. I believe he lives at Burgeston."

Charlton searched the pockets of the car and found the certificate of insurance. The name recorded on it was "Anthony Humphries."

"What was he like?"

"Medium height—five feet seven or eight. About fifty. Dark hair, bald on top. Small moustache. Wearing a plus-four suit, a fawn sports shirt and a tie made of the same material. No hat. Gold signet-ring on the little finger of his left hand and a round-dialled watch fixed to his wrist by a silver bracelet."

Johnson was eager for promotion.

"What time did you find him?"

"Just before half-past one."

"The shops were closed then. He'd probably just come from the Bank. I'll try them." The cashier at the counter had not been present when Charlton had called the previous Tuesday, but Bloar, the young ledger-clerk, glanced over the screen and wished him a cheery good afternoon. It seemed from the deportment of the staff that they knew nothing about the most recent shooting. Charlton asked them if a Mr. Anthony Humphries had been in that morning, and the cashier agreed that he had.

"He came in at about five-past one," he said, "to cash a cheque."

"What time did he leave?"

"We chatted for a minute or two and then the storm started. He hadn't a hat or a mackintosh, so I suggested that he should wait in here until it blew over; but he laughed and went out to his car. I should say he left here at a quarter past one."

"Can you give me his address?"

"He lives just outside Burgeston. Normanhurst is the name of the house."

"Is he married, can you tell me?"

"No, he's a bachelor — a gentleman of private means."

Charlton thanked him for this information and left the Bank. As he came out into the Square, he narrowly avoided a collision with Mr. Farquarson.

"Ah, Inspector!" said the secretary. "I was looking for you."

Charlton would have dearly liked to express his deep regret that the quest had met with so much success, but a police officer had to be above such human weaknesses.

"What can I do for you?" he asked, as they stood together on the pavement.

"I had an idea when I was eating my lunch to-day and I want to pass it on to you. I noticed, by the way, that there was an ambulance in the Square a little earlier. No more unpleasantness, I hope?"

"Somebody was taken ill," said Charlton shortly.

"I have been told by three or four people," Mr. Farquarson went on chattily, "that a man was shot while sitting in his car. They say his face and head were covered with blood when he was taken away. Tell me, Inspector," he asked anxiously, "was he dead?"

"I am glad to say that he was not," said Charlton even more abruptly.

Mr. Farquarson would have been a good enough companion with whom to while away ten minutes' wait for a train on a wet night at Norwood Junction, but on occasions such as this he was pestilent.

"What a merciful escape!" said the secretary with a great sigh of relief. "It would have been too terrible to have three murders in one week in the district under your care, and two of them on the same day."

Charlton, who was restless with anxiety, turned to leave him, but the other caught his arm.

"But I wanted to tell you about the idea that occurred to me this morning, Inspector. It was your climbing on to the roof of the Hall that put it into my mind. I have finally discarded my theory about the van—the weight of evidence seems to be against it. But might it not be that these luckless men were shot down in cold blood from the roof of a building? A man lying on a flat roof with a parapet running round it, would be invisible to those walking in the Square below."

"That is a very helpful suggestion," said Charlton with a praiseworthy show of interest. "I will keep it before me. And now I must be—"

"What gives a certain point to this supposition," Mr. Farquarson serenely interrupted these leavetakings, "is the fact that this morning I saw a man on the roof of Mr. Pope's premises."

"What time was this?" Charlton asked casually.

"Soon after one o'clock. I was sitting in a deckchair in my garden, enjoying the comic strip in my newspaper. It's wonderful, isn't it, how these cartoonists manage to think up a fresh joke every day?"

There was very nearly another brutal murder in Paulsfield Square, but Charlton's iron self-control averted it.

"And I happened to look up and saw the silhouette of a man outlined against the sky. He may not have been on Mr. Pope's roof, but that was how it appeared to me."

"Did you recognize him?"

"I fear not. I was some little distance away and he was standing against the bright sky. The only thing I can say is that, if the outline was anything to go by, it was a man."

"What was he doing?"

"I haven't the least notion. He was moving about—first standing upright and then bending down, and I decided that he was some workman or other, who was repairing the roof or cleaning the gutters. Then I felt a spot of rain and hurried indoors before the storm began. It wasn't until I had sat down to my luncheon that the thought came to me that there may have been some sinister purpose behind this man's activities."

"May I urge you to keep your own counsel about this?" asked Charlton earnestly. "I am faced with a difficult task and discretion is imperative."

"Cross my heart, wish I may die!" said Mr. Farquarson solemnly—and then laughed with such sudden gusto that every bird in the Square took flight.

One of the chief difficulties foreseen, when starting upon this account of the most disasterous case that Inspector Charlton ever tackled, was the "damnable iteration" of the events. After each crime, the Inspector interviewed the residents in the Square and the form that his questions took did not vary much. An attempt has been made to lighten the tedium of these visits by recording in detail only those conversations that either had some bearing on the business in hand or afforded sufficient incidental entertainment to be included.

The reader will learn, in due course, of the two other deaths that occurred in Paulsfield before the sniper's reign of terror came to an end; but as, by the very nature of things, the Inspector was prevented from carrying out his house-to-house enquiries after the later shootings, the reader will, perhaps, forgive the setting down of the Inspector's talks that Thursday afternoon with Mr. Beamish, his sisters and Mr. Pope. This forgiveness will doubtless be readily granted when it is realized that Charlton's questions to the fine old English tobacconist were far more pertinent than those he had asked after Earnshaw and Ransome died, and that had it not been for the information supplied by Mrs. Archer from her unique card-index records, he might not have hit upon the solution to one of the most fantastic riddle-me-rees that ever vexed a poor "busy-fellow."

When Mr. Farquarson had taken himself off on some private errand, Charlton went in to see Mr. Pope. He came straight to the point.

"I am told," he said, "that a man was seen on the roof of this building earlier to-day. Have you any knowledge of him?"

Mr. Pope removed his pince-nez glasses and replaced them at precisely the same coquettish angle.

"It was I," he said.

"What time did you go up there, Mr. Pope?"

"A little after one o'clock, at which time I closed the shop for the lunch interval."

"And when did you come down?"

"I descended in some haste, just as the first drops of rain began to fall. When would that be, now? Ten-past? Yes, I should say ten-past. I was carrying out some work to my wireless aerial and had scarcely begun before the storm brought me scampering down the ladder."

Charlton nearly smiled: he would have loved to see Mr. Pope scamper.

"I was afraid it was some unauthorised person," he said, as if dismissing the matter, and went on conversationally: "Isn't your radio functioning properly?"

"Not as well as I should like," confessed Mr. Pope. "For some time, I have thought it to be the fault of the crystal."

"The—er—what?"

"The crystal. I haven't yet invested in one of those modern, new-fangled valve sets. But the other day, I read an advertisement in a newspaper of a special aerial wire that is guaranteed to bring in signals at remarkably increased strength. So I purchased a hundred-foot length yesterday and began, as I say, to instal it to-day. In the intervals between customers this morning, I secured the new lead-in to what I estimated was the right point on the aerial and all that was required then was to fix the aerial to the insulators."

"How did you get on the roof? Isn't it rather hazardous?"

"It is," Mr. Pope agreed. "I reached it by means of a ladder. As you possibly know, my kitchen juts out from the main building. The roof of it is flat, so by placing my ladder upon it I was able to attain the upper roof. The aerial is fixed by insulators to the chimney-stack."

"From your remarks," smiled Charlton, "I gather that the aerial is *not* fixed to the chimney-stack! Not the new one, at any rate."

Mr. Pope tut-tutted.

"That's the annoying part," he said. "There is no aerial at all, at the moment. I had already released the old wire and allowed it to fall into the garden when I had to come down. If it had not been for that untimely thunder-storm, I should have the new wire in position by this time. As it is, I am tied for the rest of the day to this counter—and there is a Bach concert at eight this evening."

Charlton's opinion of Bach, coupled with his affection for Mr. Pope, prompted him to leave things at that; but duty had to come first.

"I hope," he said, hoping just the opposite, "that you'll take my offer in the spirit in which it is meant. I don't want to thrust unwanted assistance upon you, but if you like, *I'll* fix that wire to the chimney insulator for you. Forgive me for being personal, but such an undertaking is dangerous for a man of your years."

"I know it is," agreed Mr. Pope, "but I can ill afford to pay to have done anything that I can do myself."

He smiled rather pathetically.

"There is little profit to be made, Inspector, from selling tobacco and toffee-apples."

There leapt into Charlton's mind the thought of a large, sweet-loving Irishman.

"Toffee-apples?" he said, raising his eyebrows. "Do you still stock such things. I thought toffee-apples went out with Dundrearys."

"Oh, yes!" replied Mr. Pope. "There is a regular, though not large, sale for them among the young people of the town. Their great virtue is that they combine toothsomeness with nourishment."

"It is a pity," said Charlton with a regretful smile, "that, when we grow up, we lose the taste for them."

"Not *all* of us," dissented Mr. Pope. "The other day—last Tuesday, to be exact—a full-grown man came into this shop and asked for one." He smiled. "He stated his requirements so sheepishly that I had much ado to maintain the serious demeanour required for such an important transaction!"

"I should hardly have thought that a local man would have cared to be seen—"

"He wasn't a Paulsfield resident," Mr. Pope interrupted, as Charlton intended he should. "He was only passing through the town. Some sort of lorry-driver, I should imagine from his peaked cap and general appearance. A big man with a suggestion of Irish brogue in his voice."

"I should never have credited it!" said Charlton; then, having learnt what he wanted, "What about this aerial of yours?"

"Won't it be taking too much of your valuable time?"

"Not a bit. I've nothing important on hand. Only," he added to himself, "a couple of murders, an attempted murder and probably a sticky interview with the Superintendent."

Mr. Pope looked so grateful that if Charlton had had a conscience, it would have smitten him a shrewd buffet.

"Then if you would be so kind . . .?" he said. "I left the new wire on my dressing-table and the ladder is still in position. It is merely a question of securing the new aerial to the existing insulator that is attached to the chimney-stack. With that done, it will be a small task for me to fix the other end to the pole at the bottom of the garden.

"Will you follow me upstairs?"

XIII.

A Case of Agoraphobia

MR. POPE'S bedroom was a model of neatness. The bed was made as if deft feminine hands had shaken and patted it into shape. A clean folded towel was laid over the mouth of the jug that stood in the basin on the washstand. Two old-fashioned, hollow-ground razors lay on the shelf with a shaving-brush and a bakelite case for the soap. Over the mantelpiece was a photograph of the late Mrs. Pope—or so Charlton assumed; and on the dressing-table was none of the accumulation of small sundries that usually encumbers the dressing-table of a man who lives by himself. To say *none* is not strictly true: Mr. Pope had fallen from grace by allowing a coil of covered wire to share the top of it with his hair brushes.

Let it not be supposed that the reader is invited to guffaw at Mr. Alexander Pope. Among those who knew him, only unimaginative clods did that: the others hid smiles in which there was no derision, but something that an Englishman is more anxious to conceal. He was such a confoundedly nice old chap.

He went to a cupboard and produced a suit of overalls.

"This is not a very presentable garment," he said apologetically. "I wear it during the periodical creosoting of my fence and shed. But I insist upon your donning it for your work. If that excellent suit of yours were soiled, I should never forgive myself."

With his mind on that sixteen pounds per annum, Charlton agreed that it was a good idea and got into the overalls. He swung his leg over the sill and, as Mr. Pope handed him the coil of wire, they both heard the shop bell ring.

"I must leave you," said the old gentleman. "Some small child probably wants an empty box or two halfpennies for a penny. Such are the majority of my clientele."

Charlton mounted the ladder, but before climbing over the parapet, examined the surface of the roof. There were no footmarks visible. It had been dry when Mr. Pope had been up there and whatever prints his boots may have made in the dust had been washed away by the rain.

The shot had been fired, he felt certain, when the storm had been at its height—the thunder's heavy artillery would have made such an excellent cover for the pistol-shot. But the thunder had not got really going over Paulsfield until a quarter past one, so that as Mr. Pope had fled from the approaching storm at ten-past one, there would have been at least five minutes available for anyone to reach the tobacconist's roof for the purpose of sniping Humphries. But if he had left any footprints, they too had disappeared.

The insulators were hanging against the chimney-stack at the back of the building and, after clambering over the parapet, he released one end of the coil of wire and secured it to one of the insulators with a thoroughness that made amends for his deception of the lover of Bach. Then he dropped the wire down into the back garden.

This left him at liberty to have what is colloquially known as a "nose round" and every inch of Mr. Pope's roof was examined for discarded cartridge-cases, of which, apart from the one in Charlton's pocket, there were two in existence. The search, however, was fruitless.

He walked to the front parapet and looked down at Humphries' car. The head of a man sitting in the driving seat would have been plainly visible from Mr. Pope's roof and Charlton decided, after glancing to his right at the roof of the Hall, that a marksman could have hit Humphries from there. It would have been a close thing, but it was possible.

The ejector of a self-loading pistol will sometimes fling empty cases surprisingly long distances. This made it quite possible that the case of the bullet that killed Ransome had been thrown across the top of Mr. Beamish's premises. Its position in the passage, close against the wall, might easily have resulted from its bouncing back from the side of the Horticultural Hall. But the aim of an ejector is as uncertain as its range: the other two cases might have been thrown out in any direction. If the word can be used in such a context, Charlton had the *entrée* to Mr. Pope's roof, but he had no right to go beyond it. This, however, did not cause him any acute distress, for he stepped on to Mr. Beamish's property without hesitation. If anyone saw him, his overalls would suggest that he was up there to clear a gutter or investigate a leaking roof.

No cartridge case lurked in any cranny of Mr. Beamish's roof, which could be reached from the flat roof of the kitchen, in the same way as next door. Charlton went back across Mr. Pope's premises and clambered on to the roof of the Bank, which was slightly higher than its western neighbour, carefully searching for signs of any other person having passed that way.

By slow degrees, keeping his body bent to avoid notice, he worked his way across the Post Office and round into the High Street, until he reached the building on the corner of Effingham Street, which housed the Paulsfield branch of a multiple store that sold articles of all descriptions at a small maximum cost. Because of the limited area, the building occupied nearly all the available space, so that a part of the back wall came within eight feet of the side wall of Mrs. Ransome's residence and obscured, with its unbroken brickwork, the view from a side window of the house.

This excursion yielded nothing in the way of a clue. Crouched on top of the corner building, Charlton looked at his watch, then as quickly and as cautiously as possible, made his way back to Mr. Pope's roof. The journey took him just two minutes and he was panting from the exertion by the time he arrived. A scorching summer's afternoon was not the time for such strenuous athletics.

Mr. Pope turned from serving a brace of diminutive urchins with two "sepritaporths" of pear-drops, as Charlton came into the shop, after having discarded the overalls upstairs.

"That was quick work!" said the tobacconist admiringly.

"I haven't moved so fast for years, Mr. Pope," was the ambiguous reply. "There's no need for you to go on the roof again. I've left the aerial and the lead-in hanging over the back wall, so you'll be able to hear that Bach concert after all."

"I am more than obliged to you, Inspector. The exercise has made you rather hot. May I offer you a cooling drink?"

Charlton thought longingly of a pint tankard of Southmouth brew, but felt that Mr. Pope's hospitality would not rise to such heights as that. He said, however, that it was extremely kind of Mr. Pope and was shepherded round into the public space and urged to take a seat at the marble-topped table.

"What will you have?" asked Mr. Pope, the light of liberality shining in his eyes, and mentioned three or four fizzy abominations.

"I'm afraid," smiled Charlton, "that aerated drinks play havoc with my good manners! Their repercussions are so unexpected."

"What about a still-lemon?" suggested his host; and a still-lemon it was.

Revived by the glass that cheered but not, alas, inebriated, Charlton wished Mr. Pope a good afternoon and went out into the Square. He was wondering whether to go and see Joseph Beamish and his womenfolk, when a voice called his name. He looked up and saw Mrs. Archer leaning over her window-sill.

"Will you come up, Inspector?" she asked. "I have something to tell you."

Charlton said he would certainly go up and went into the shop, which was empty. He walked up the stairs past the assegais and tennis-rackets. Mrs. Archer was sitting in her usual place by the window when he knocked on the door and went in.

"Sit down, Inspector," she invited him, "and smoke if you want to. Try one of those in the box on the table. No, not for me, thank you. I only keep them for visitors."

As Charlton helped himself to a cigarette and lighted it, Mrs. Archer went on:

"So Mr. Humphries of Normanhurst, Burgeston, has met with an accident?"

"Yes," he acknowledged, "I'm sorry to say that he has."

"He wasn't killed?"

"No. Did you see anything of the—accident?"

"I'll tell you everything I saw," was her answer. "I am not a temperamental or nervous sort of woman, Inspector, but I *do not like* thunderstorms. I had been sitting near the window and when it burst upon us, I moved away and having, as I say, a horror of storms, put an extra loud record on the gramophone, to try and drown the noise of the thunder. It didn't, of course, but it helped to distract my attention."

"Where were Miss Beamish and your brother?"

"Downstairs. Ruth was preparing lunch and Joseph—well, you know what Joseph is like! He was probably taking the opportunity of the shop being closed to tidy everything up into a bigger mess than it was in before. One of the funniest things I have ever seen, Inspector, is my brother unravelling a tangled ball of string!

"When the storm had passed over, I went back to the window and saw P.C. Johnson looking across from the High Street at a motor-car that was standing with its engine running just by the statue. Johnson walked across and looked inside the car. Then he beckoned to Mr. Merridew, who happened to be passing. He's the father, you know, of Miss Southmouth (1935) and—"

"Forgive my interrupting you, Mrs. Archer, but I was hoping that you could tell me something important about this tragedy. What you are telling me now, I know already. Did you hear the sound of a shot anywhere between 1.15 and 1.20 to-day?"

"I heard nothing but the thunder and my noisy gramophone record," said Mrs. Archer sharply, obviously put out by the Inspector's remarks. "And," she went on exultantly, "neither did Ruth. She came upstairs while I was watching Mr. Merridew hurrying away, to ask me if I would like lunch in here or have it with them; and I made a point of asking her if she had heard a pistol-shot." Her bad temper evaporated and she smiled brightly at Charlton.

"But I am being unreasonable!" she said. "Of course you don't want me to tell you something you know already. What you are in search of is fresh information—something that will give you a new angle—as the Americans say—on these distressing crimes. *That* is why I asked you to come up here and see me."

She leant towards him.

"You are looking for a person, Inspector, who has killed two men and wounded another so badly that he may also die. You know, as well as I do, that all the shots were fired from this side of the Square. Earnshaw was protected by the statue from the other three sides, poor young Arthur Ransome was shot through the back as he walked towards Heather Street and Mr. Humphries was shot through the open window of his car, which could only have been possible from this side of the Square. It isn't conceivable to me that these three could have been fired upon from anywhere but one of these buildings along here and I think you are right to concentrate your attention upon them.

"But have you done this, Inspector: have you tried to associate the three crimes with each other? I feel that you are considering each one separately—believing that they have all been done by the same hand, but not trying to identify them with each other. Earnshaw was killed, then Arthur Ransome—

and now Mr. Humphries is shot. Were they chosen at random, or does each shooting form part of some larger prearranged plan? Are there any *links?*"

Charlton was not prepared to discuss the case with Mrs. Archer, but he did not mind listening to her. He disregarded her questions, although his face showed amiable interest.

"I'm not going to give you any advice, Inspector," she continued. "You are too intelligent a man to need it. But if you are thinking of establishing the contacts between these men, I can tell you something that may assist you. My card-index has come in useful again! Don't imagine that I am going to tell you that Arthur Ransome was the natural son of Mr. Humphries or that Earnshaw was the first husband of Mrs. Ransome, because there's nothing so sensational about it!"

He smiled and patiently waited.

"Do you remember about eleven years ago, when the papers used to publish divorce court proceedings in far greater detail than they do now, a case that created a big stir at the time? The husband was a well-known figure in the diplomatic world—a Permanent Under-Secretary of State or something?"

"Yes, but I don't remember his name."

"Sir Waldo Stevenage. His wife became involved with a man named Ibbotson and Sir Waldo eventually began divorce proceedings. Ibbotson came out of it without a shred of reputation left. The judge told him exactly what he thought of him and every door was closed against him—every respectable door, that is."

"Yes," Charlton agreed, "I remember the case very well. Ibbotson disappeared soon afterwards, didn't he? Went to America or somewhere?"

"Not as far as that," smiled Mrs. Archer. "He went to Burgeston and was shot this afternoon outside this house."

He guessed that she had been working up to that, but now expressed the necessary surprise.

"His photograph was in all the papers and when he came here, I immediately recognized him, in spite of his having grown a moustache and parted his hair differently. He had more hair to part than he has now! I've all the details down on his card, if you would like to see it?"

As she felt for the key, Charlton urged her not to trouble. She had given him enough information, he said, for his purpose.

"But I had better make a note of the husband. What was his name?"

"Sir Waldo Stevenage."

He wrote it down in his notebook.

"And Ibbotson's Christian name or names—can you tell me those?"

"Geoffrey Alan," was the ready reply.

"*Geoffrey* Alan?"

"Yes," said Mrs. Archer, "Geoffrey."

When Charlton had politely declined the offer of a cup of tea, he left Mrs. Archer and went downstairs. Mr. Beamish was then in his shop and Charlton asked him bluntly where he had been between 1.15 and 1.20 that day. He was told that Mr. Beamish had been busying himself in the shop—the phrase was Mr. Beamish's—until his sister came to announce that lunch was ready. As it was the dinner-hour, the shop door was locked and the blind pulled down.

Miss Beamish, when her brother called her in, said that between 1.15 and 1.20—in fact, until half-past one, she had been in the kitchen preparing lunch, which was rather late that day. On the stroke of the half-hour—she had looked at the clock and congratulated herself on not being so late as she might have been—she had gone into the shop to tell her brother that the meal was ready and had then gone up to inform Mrs. Archer.

Charlton left the Beamish establishment and walked round the corner into the High Street. The shops between the Post Office and Effingham Street, he felt, had waited overlong for his attention.

Next door to the Post Office was an ironmonger's lock-up shop, the upper floors of which were used for storage. To the north of that, a chemist plied his business and between him and the big store on the corner were the offices of the *Paulsfield Weekly News,* the circulation of which seemed sufficiently satisfactory to warrant the additional use of the first and second floors for its publication.

Charlton had already decided that, for all these premises, with the exception of the chemist's shop, the murder of Arthur Ransome was the "key" crime. Like the Post Office and the Bank, they would have been shut at 5.45 a.m. His questions, therefore, were confined to one point; had there been any person on the premises at a quarter to six that morning? In each case, the answer was an unequivocal No. Caretakers and night-watchmen were not employed and the buildings would have been deserted at that early hour.

There remained the chemist. He was a bald, self-effacing little man, whose every gesture seemed to express an apology. Charlton asked if he was addressing Mr. Muttigen. The question was put with a certain diffidence, for at the last moment he had the sudden fear that he had confused the name over the shop with one of the proprietary medicines in the window.

Mr. Muttigen smiled deprecatingly.

"The 'g' is hard, as in 'tiger'," he said, as if the phonetic anomaly was entirely his fault. "What can I do for you?"

Charlton explained who he was and Mr. Muttigen mentioned that he had been standing in the doorway of his shop when the Inspector hurried by on the previous Tuesday.

"And I was rude enough," said Charlton, "to take no notice of a question you put to me. I'm very sorry, but I was rather bothered."

"The fault was entirely mine," said the chemist. "My wife was out shopping at the time and I was afraid that some accident might have happened to her. You know how it is, don't you?"

The Inspector said he understood exactly and added that he would be grateful if Mr. Muttigen would answer a few purely routine questions. Mr. Muttigen waited with the pleased alertness of one about to be asked a conundrum. Charlton resisted the urge to enquire why a mouse was when it wasn't, and said:

"Do you live over this shop?"

"Yes, with my wife and only son."

"You had no visitors sleeping here last night?"

"No."

"Were you awake at a quarter to six this morning?" Mr. Muttigen shook his head.

"My wife and I," he said, "both slept soundly until roused by the alarm at the side of our bed at seven o'clock."

"And your son?"

"I don't know," confessed the chemist. "He is a sound sleeper and my wife usually has to go in and shake his shoulder."

"Was he asleep when she went to him this morning?"

"Yes. I remember hearing her efforts to wake him, as I was dressing. He sleeps in the back room and this morning seemed to be even more difficult than usual."

"May I have a word with Mrs. Muttigen?"

"I'm sorry you can't," regretted her husband. "She has gone to Southmouth for the day."

"Is your son in?"

Mr. Muttigen hesitated and then said that he was. "I should like to speak to him, if you don't mind."

"*I* don't mind at all," was the reply, "but I am afraid that I couldn't persuade Harold to come down. He is of an intensely retiring disposition and spends most of his life in his room with his books and Meccano, which, although he is nearly eighteen, still pleases him. Because of this—and I'm afraid Harold is slowly getting worse, instead of better—we very seldom entertain, but even when we are visited by close relations, Harold refuses to leave his room and, if pressed too much to come down and say how-do-you-do to them, locks himself in the lavatory and nothing can get him out until they go."

"That is very sad," said Charlton sympathetically. "Does he go out at all?"

"Very seldom. Sometimes he ventures into the garden and I *have* been able to get him to take a short walk with me, but not often."

"Only when it is dark and quiet, I suppose?" asked Charlton. "I should scarcely imagine, for instance, that he would stray far from the house on market-days, with all the commotion in the Square."

"Good heavens, no!" said Mr. Muttigen. "I have found that nothing in the whole world would ever tempt him to cross the Square."

A morbid fear of the market-place, thought Charlton. The Greeks had a word for it. Agoraphobia. It was useless to make the suggestion, but he said:

"In spite of that, perhaps you can induce him to see me?"

Mr. Muttigen gave a sigh and shrugged his shoulders hopelessly.

"I don't want to stand in the way of the police," he said, "but it would be an impossible task."

"I am still young enough to talk enthusiastically about Meccano," smiled Charlton. "It has always been my ambition to own a No. 6. Say that I am keen to see his latest model."

Mr. Muttigen's answering smile was piteous, but he went upstairs. When he came down again in three minutes, he said apologetically:

"He has locked himself in the lavatory."

And that was that. When Charlton left the shop, he walked straight across the road, then turning suddenly, caught a glimpse of a white young face staring at him from a top window.

XIV.

Intermission

LET US pause awhile to consider the problem that confronted Charlton. His chief trouble, of course, was that each crime was carried out at what is erroneously called and, with inexcusable slovenliness, is described here as, the psychological moment. With Earnshaw, the crowded Square, the excitement of the escaping bull and the clatter of the pneumatic drills; with Ransome, the empty Square, with no one awake but a nodding night-watchman: and with Humphries, again the empty Square, with a thunderstorm raging overhead. No witness had seen the flash of any of the three shots; no witness had been able to say that the report had come from a certain point. There was not a single person whom Charlton had so far met, who had any apparent reason for shooting the first two men, which left him with the conviction that the murderer was mad—and madmen need no other motive for murder than the stimulus of their own diseased imaginations.

If he had to look for a homicidal maniac, from whom had he to choose? Somebody, naturally, who had access to a roof or window of any of the three suspected buildings: the Horticultural Hall, Beamish's secondhand shop and Pope's tobacco and confectionery shop. All the other properties—the monumental masons', the Bank, the Post Office, the empty shops in the High Street, Harbottle's, Highman's, Burnside's, the two shops to the south of Burnside's and those along the southern side—were out of it. The weight of evidence was against them.

A roof or a window. Let us take the roofs first. The roof of the Hall could be reached from the ground by means of the iron ladder on top of the lavatories, but the manoeuvre would have been almost sure to attract notice. The two other suspected roofs were approachable from all the buildings round as far as the corner of Effingham Street and a man who moved warily might have made his way from one end to the other without inviting attention. His chief difficulty would have been to get on to the roof in the first place and down again when the job had been done. Everybody, then, who was in that block at the time of the second crime was suspect, unless he or she could produce evidence to prove the contrary.

Certain buildings were locked up and empty: the Bank with its unoccupied flat, the Post Office, the ironmonger's, the offices of the *Paulsfield Weekly News,* and the multiple store. Therefore, apart from those in the suspected buildings, the only persons in the block when Arthur Ransome was murdered were Mr. and Mrs. Muttigen and their agoraphobic son, Harold.

On the evidence of her husband, Mrs. Muttigen was out shopping when Earnshaw was killed and at Southmouth-by-the-Sea when Humphries was shot. At the time of the first and third crimes, then, the Muttigen father and son were alone together in the house.

We will take the father's case first.

When Ransome was killed, Mr. Muttigen was in bed with his wife. That they did not sleep in single beds or separate rooms was proved by the chemist s remark to Charlton about the alarm clock by the side of their bed. It was possible that he could have slipped out of the room, climbed to the roof, shot Ransome and gone back to bed without rousing her, but the risk of detectionwould have been enormous.

When Humphries was shot, Mr. Muttigen was alone, but in order to get on to the roof, he would have had to pass near the window of the room where his son was. The reader does not know that Harold did *not* see him or, for that matter, that Harold's agoraphobia was not an invention of his father's to prevent Charlton from questioning the boy. But neither did Charlton.

A very few minutes after Earnshaw had died, Charlton himself had seen Mr. Muttigen standing in the doorway of his shop. The chemist had spoken to him, but that might have been merely to establish an alibi, after a spectacular scramble (in the sense rather of a miraculous achievement than a public exhibition) back from a suspected roof.

We have not yet heard Mrs. Muttigen's evidence, but the reader is told in advance that, when Charlton had a later opportunity to interrogate her, she agreed with her husband's story.

Then there was Harold's case:

When Ransome was killed, Harold's parents, so his father had said, were asleep, which would have enabled him to leave the house and return in due course without their knowledge.

When Humphries was shot, Mr. Muttigen was, so he had told the Inspector, having his lunch. Harold had refused any food, preferring to play with his Meccano—or to slip out and shoot Humphries.

When Earnshaw was killed, Mrs. Muttigen was out. A short while after the crime, her husband was seen by the Inspector, standing in the doorway of his shop. The upper part of the house, therefore, had been free to Harold.

There were certain practical difficulties as to how he got on to the roof and from where he had procured the weapon, but that was the general position.

Now we turn to windows. These can be confined to the suspected buildings in the block. The reader can rest assured that the only opening of any description whatsoever in the south and east elevations of the Horticultural Hall was the front entrance. In the suspected buildings in the block, there had been, at the times of the murders, a maximum of four persons; Mr. Beamish, Mrs. Archer, Miss Beamish and Mr. Pope. We will consider each one separately.

Firstly, Mr. Beamish:

When Earnshaw was killed, Mr. Beamish was in his shop. The premises were open for business, but there were no customers in at the time. He might have fired through the open door at Earnshaw, but Mrs. Archer was in the room just above and, although she had said that the sound of the shot was very loud, she had added that such an explosion was very elusive and seemed to come from everywhere at once. Whether she would have said that if the shot had been fired within a few feet of her, with only the ceiling and floor boards between, is a debatable point.

As to the Ransome crime, when Mrs. Archer came out on the landing, she told Miss Beamish what had happened and her sister went in and roused their brother. That was some time after the shot was fired, because Mrs. Archer did not speak to her sister until she had got out of bed, gone to the window, seen Ransome's body lying on the ground, watched the night-watchman come across the Square, enquired of him what had happened and then been asked by Mr. Pope to ring for the police. During that period, Mr. Beamish would have been able to slip back into bed and adopt an appearance of deep and innocent repose.

When Humphries was shot, Mr. Beamish was again alone in his shop, but this time it was closed. The door was locked and the blind down. To shoot Humphries, he would have had to open the door and step outside. Humphries' car, as will be remembered, was standing opposite the Horticultural Hall and the man in the driving-seat could not have been shot, as was the case with Earnshaw, from the interior of the shop, because the door was set back between the side windows. For all that, Mr. Beamish would have had the time and opportunity to undo the door, shoot Humphries and refasten the door before his sister appeared from the kitchen to say that lunch was ready.

Secondly, Mrs. Archer.

When Earnshaw was killed, she was alone in her room. Her brother was down in the room below and told the Inspector afterwards that he had noticed no sound of an explosion. But Mr. Beamish was very deaf and, as he had explained, although he might have heard the shot, it had not impressed itself on his mind. Miss Beamish was out at the time and could, therefore, express no opinion about that particular report.

When Ransome was killed, Mrs. Archer was again alone in her room, as a widowed lady very properly should be at 5.45 a.m. The first person to see her was the night-watchman, who looked up to her window when she called to him. The shot had not aroused her brother, who slept in the room over her head, but Miss Beamish, who slept at the back of the house, had been awakened by it.

When Humphries was shot, Mrs. Archer was once more alone in her room. Miss Beamish was the first person to see her after the crime, when she went upstairs to announce lunch.

Mrs. Archer, then, had on each occasion an opportunity to commit the crime, although the danger of being seen at or near the open window with a pistol in her hand would have been great.

Thirdly, Miss Beamish.

This amiable lady was relieved of suspicion about Earnshaw by her absence from the house when he was shot; and as the three crimes may safely be assumed to have been the work of one perpetrator, her absence on that occasion automatically dispersed any doubt about her concernment with Ransome and Humphries. That she really *was* out shopping at the time was testified by her brother.

Fourthly, Mr. Pope.

He admitted to Charlton that when Earnshaw was shot, he himself was upstairs. Murphy, the Irish lorry-driver, had been in the shop a very short time before midday, for Mr. Farquarson had seen the van begin to move just as the explosion sounded, which was, as near as makes no matter, on the stroke of noon.

It would not have taken Murphy long to leave the sweet-shop, walk past the Horticultural Hall and start up his engine. He might have spent an ecstatic moment or two sampling the delights of the toffee-apple, but that was hardly likely. The driving-cabin of his van was a snugger place for such orgies.

A very little while after Ransome was killed, Mr. Pope called out to the watchman from his window. That was the first time he was seen by a witness that morning.

Soon after one o'clock that day, Mr. Farquarson saw a man on the roof of Pope's premises. The tobacconist freely admitted to having been on the roof at that time, but said that he had descended at ten minutes past one, some time before the thunder was loud enough to mask the sound of a shot. No evidence of this descent was forthcoming from Mr. Farquarson. Mr. Pope might have lingered longer on the roof than he afterwards said, but even if he had come down at the time he stated, would have had the whole house to himself. Which raises this question: why did he climb on the roof to shoot Humphries, if his front room window had proved very satisfactory to polish off young Ransome? It might have been, of course, that the window was a rather conspicious spot at the time of the day when Humphries had been so gravely wounded.

There is one last word to add before the case for windows is concluded. After the death of Ransome, Inspector Charlton picked up a rimless cartridge-case in the passage between Beamish's shop and the Horticultural Hall.

XV.

The Girl at Normanhurst

WITH his thoughts turning on Harold Muttigen, Charlton walked back to the Square, where he had left his car. He drove to the hospital to enquire about Humphries, but the only information he could obtain about the wounded man's condition was: "He's not dead yet."

He turned the car in the direction of Burgeston. Normanhurst, Humphries' home, was a handsome house standing by itself in a lane just outside the village. He drove up the gravelled drive to the front door and, when a smart little maid answered his ring, enquired if Mrs. Humphries was at home. According to the cashier at the Bank, there was no Mrs. Humphries, but it was the easiest question. The maid was plainly perturbed and he guessed that the news about their employer had already reached the household.

"Mr. Humphries is not married," she said. "Would you like to speak to Miss Steward, his secretary?" Charlton said that he would, handed the maid his card and was shown into a large room at the back of the house, whose open french windows allowed a view of the large well-kept garden and grass tennis-court. Under a tree on the lawn outside were a few deck-chairs and an iron green-painted table with a gaily coloured awning over it. He was thinking grimly of their owner lying in Paulsfield hospital, when Miss Steward came into the room.

She was a most attractive young person, little more than twenty-one. Her dark hair was shingled—if the word is not out-of-date—and her large eyes were brown. In happier moments, she would have had a healthy colour, but now her cheeks were pale.

"Good afternoon, Inspector," she said. "I am Miss Steward. We have heard—about Mr. Humphries. I suppose you have come to ask me some questions? Won't you sit down?"

Charlton took a chair by the fireplace and Miss Steward sat down on a settee near the windows.

"He was shot, wasn't he?" she asked with forced calmness.

"Yes, through the head, but I'm glad to say that, by some miracle, he is still alive and under the care of Dr. Weston, the finest surgeon in the district."

This was a pleasanter description of the patient's situation than that used at the hospital.

"How did it hap—" began the girl, then interrupted herself with a slight smile: "But it is you who must ask the questions."

"He went to the branch of the Southern Counties Bank in Paulsfield Square," Charlton explained, "drew some money, went out and got into his car. He started the engine, but before he had time to drive away, was shot through the open window of the car. I am now trying to find out who did it, Miss Steward."

"I'll do everything I can to help you," she said readily.

"Does Mr. Humphries go regularly to the Bank?"

"Yes. The staff here get their wages and I receive my salary"—Charlton noticed the delicate distinction—"every Thursday afternoon. Mr. Humphries makes a practice of driving in to Paulsfield just before lunch."

"Which is served at a fixed time?"

"Exactly half-past one. Mr. Humphries is very keen on punctuality. That's why we couldn't understand it when he didn't turn up to-day."

"Have his relations been told?"

"I don't think he has any," said Miss Steward doubtfully. "Well, I suppose he must have *some,* but I've never heard of them. He gets private letters now and again, but I don't know where they come from. I only deal with his business correspondence, not that there's really enough to keep me very busy."

"I understand that Mr. Humphries has lived here for some years. Have you any knowledge of him before that? Where he lived and so on?"

"None at all. He's never spoken of it to me. Of course, I've only been with him for eighteen months. Mrs. Simmonds, the housekeeper, has been here much longer than I have. Perhaps she will be able to help you."

"Do you live here?"

"Yes. My mother and father live at Whitchester, but"—with a smile—"the salary Mr. Humphries offered me was tempting enough to lure me away from home. Daddy is not very rich, you know."

"Does Mr. Humphries entertain much?"

"Not a great deal, but he's anything but a hermit. We have tennis parties here and he sometimes has people in for an evening's bridge."

"Miss Steward," said Charlton seriously, "Mr. Humphries has been shot. It was not an accident, but a deliberate attempt on his life. Do you know of anybody who might do that?"

"No, I don't think so. Not anybody who would shoot him."

"But he *has* enemies?"

"Not enemies. There are some people he doesn't like and some people who don't like him. It's the same with all of us, isn't it?"

"You can't recall anybody he has quarrelled with?"

"He's generally very even-tempered and I don't think I've ever heard of him falling out with anybody. Before he had our new gardener, he used to have arguments with Frank Baggs, the man who was here before, about the proper way to prune roses and the right kind of soil for this, that and the other. But Baggs wasn't a *real* gardener. He could just about cut the grass and use a hose. Mr. Humphries does most of the work. He's very keen on it."

"Did he discharge this man?"

"Yes. There was quite a scene, according to Cook," smiled Miss Steward, and Charlton took an entirely academic pleasure in the phenomenon. "One day Baggs got huffy and asked Mr. Humphries who was doing the job. Mr. Humphries said that Baggs was doing it for *him* and he was jolly well going to do it his way—and Cook says Mr. Humphries didn't say 'jolly' either! Then Baggs said that, in that case, he could jolly well do it himself—and Mr. Humphries sacked him on the spot."

"How jolly!" smiled Charlton.

Miss Steward forgot about her unfortunate employer and laughed. This quiet, whimsical man seemed no more like a policeman than the Commissioner himself.

"Yes," she agreed, "but it's *too* silly to imagine anything in that. I can't think of anyone else."

"Did Mr. Humphries know Arthur Ransome?"

"That poor boy who was shot in the Square early this morning? No, he didn't know *him,* but he knew his brother Jack. He's been here."

"Often?"

"Quite a lot. Mr. Humphries was very interested in his work. He writes books about Nature, you know—birds and plants and all that kind of thing. He comes over here now and again to have a chat with Mr. Humphries. They got some wonderful photographs of baby birds down at the bottom of the garden this Spring and Jack is going to put them into his new book."

"A nice young fellow," observed Charlton. "I met him this morning."

"He is," agreed Miss Steward. "Quite nice. Of course, when he comes here, Mr. Humphries usually monopolizes him, so I haven't really had very much to do with him."

"He must be very cut up about his brother. I'm told they were great friends."

"Oh, they were! It's a terrible thing about Arthur. I've been thinking about it all day. He was so full of life, so enthusiastic

143

about his photography, that it's horrible to think he's dead. And then poor Mr. Humphries shot on the same day. Do you think they were done by one man?"

"You knew Arthur Ransome, Miss Steward?"

"Yes, but not very well. I've met him at dances and places. He was so different from Jack. You'd hardly think they were brothers. I don't mean that Jack isn't keen on his job, but he's quieter—more restrained. And that *adorable* American accent Arthur used to talk in! He did it for fun at first and then it gradually got a habit."

"Can you call to mind whether Mr. Humphries had any dealings with a man called Earnshaw?"

"That workman who was shot? No, I don't think so. He was one of the District Council's men, wasn't he?"

"Yes, but what I mean is, did Mr. Humphries have dealings with *any* man called Earnshaw?"

"Not as far as I can remember."

"Have you ever heard him mention anyone whose name was an expanded version of J-E-F-F or G-E-O-F-F?"

"There's Mr. Jefferson, who lives on the edge of Paulsfield Common. They play golf together sometimes. . . . And Mr. Geoffrey Somers, who comes with his wife to dinner. . . . They're the only ones I can think of off-hand."

"You have never heard anybody call Mr. Humphries 'Geoffrey' or 'Geoff'?"

The girl gave Charlton a sharp glance.

"Yes," she said, after a slight pause, "I have, but only once. About six weeks ago, Mr. Humphries was visited by a friend from London. While I was busy pouring out the tea—it's one of my jobs to act as a sort of unofficial hostess—this man said something to Mr. Humphries and did actually call him 'Geoff'. I was rather surprised, because his name is really Anthony, and when I looked at him, I saw that he was frowning a bit. He must have guessed that I was a little—intrigued, because then he smiled and said it was funny to hear his old school nickname used after so many years."

"Can you recall the name of this friend?"

"Mr. Humphries introduced him as 'Mr. Smith'."

"And probably addressed him as 'Jack?'"

"He did, as a matter of fact," said Miss Steward. "Do you know him?"

Charlton thought that Mr. Humphries' powers of invention were not very highly developed. He answered the girl's question by asking another.

"What was this Mr. Smith like?"

"About forty-five. Tall, with a small moustache and ordinary sort of hair, parted down the side. He was wearing horn-rimmed glasses, but they weren't just ordinary circular ones—they had one, two, three, four . . . eight sides. Four long sides and four short sides, like a square with the corners cut off."

"What kind of clothes was he wearing?"

"A black coat and striped trousers with no turn-ups, with a white collar and a dark tie. He came down in a black felt hat and was carrying a portfolio of the same colour."

"Sounds like a prosperous City gent!" smiled Charlton. "Was it just a friendly call, or did he come on business?"

"Business, but I don't know any details. After tea, Mr. Humphries took him into his study and he went back to London about an hour later."

Charlton changed the subject.

"Does Mr. Humphries possess any firearms?" he asked.

"He has a shot-gun for rabbits and things."

"No revolver or pistol?"

"I've never seen one about the place, but he might have one tucked away somewhere, of course."

"How many are employed here?"

"Besides myself, there are two maids, a cook and Mrs. Simmonds, the housekeeper. Then there's the gardener, of course."

"Quite an extensive establishment for a bachelor gentleman?"

"It's a big house," explained Miss Steward, "and Mr. Humphries has oodles of money."

"Does he treat you well?"

"He is very generous. You can see that by the way he pays me a jolly good salary for doing practically nothing."

"What you might call a model employer?" smiled Charlton, and the girl nodded.

His quick ears caught the sound of hurrying feet and the girl evidently heard it as well. Somebody came running round the side of the house and called out, on catching sight of Miss Steward just inside the window:

"Diana, darling!"

Charlton saw that it was Jack Ransome.

XVI.

The Leopard's Spots

CHARLTON was the first to break a difficult silence.

"Good afternoon, Mr. Ransome," he said.

"I'm sorry to burst in like that," Jack replied with an awkward smile, "but I thought Miss Steward was alone." It seemed from her expression that the secretary was not too pleased with him. She suggested rather testily that he came inside, instead of standing there like, to use her own phrase, that.

"Miss Steward has been telling me," said Charlton, "that you are often here, Mr. Ransome."

"Yes," agreed Jack, sitting down as if the chair plotted some trick against him, "I come to see Mr. Humphries. He's been fearfully decent about my work, you know. I've just popped over now on my bicycle to ask Miss Steward how he is."

"The Inspector's told me," said Diana, "that he's—still alive."

"That doesn't sound too good," said Jack seriously. "Lord, what a ghastly day it's been! Poor old Arthur this morning and now Mr. Humphries."

"I very much want to see your mother, Mr. Ransome," said the Inspector. "Is she recovered enough for me to visit her this evening?"

"She's still pretty knocked, but I've told her that you want to see her as soon as possible, so she's expecting you." Charlton thanked him and turned to Diana, to catch her looking resentfully at Jack.

"Before I go, Miss Steward," he said, "I should like a word with the servants. Can you arrange that for me? I think you mentioned a Mrs. Simmonds."

147

Diana jumped up and left the room. The two men were silent for a little time. Then, when Jack was giving a final polish to a remark about the weather, Charlton said: "Did you see anything of Mr. Humphries' mishap?" The carefully selected word made Jack forget his embarrassment.

"*Mishap?*" he said spiritedly. "That wasn't a mishap! It was an attempted murder. Somebody tried to get Mr. Humphries in the same way as they got Arthur and that workman, Earnshaw. There's some stark staring potty lunatic running about killing people off like flies for the fun of the thing; and if *you* don't find him soon, he'll get somebody else and he'll go on getting them as long as his ammunition lasts!"

"You describe the situation with admirable fluency, Mr. Ransome," said Charlton smoothly, "but you have omitted to answer my question."

"To say it was a mishap," went on Jack bravely, in the face of the Inspector's remark, "is just playing with words. I believe in calling a thing by its name!"

"So I have noticed," was the quiet reply, and Jack blushed violently.

"I'm sorry to fly off the handle like that," he said ruefully, "but I expect you understand that I feel a bit strongly about the whole thing. This time yesterday evening, my brother was playing tennis on Paulsfield Common and now, because of some maniac's twisted idea of a joke. . . ."

"I told you this morning that I sympathize with you very much and I meant it. Your brother was shot through the back without a chance to defend himself, in the same was as Earnshaw made target-practice and Humphries was treacherously sniped as he sat in his car. If I call these things mishaps, Mr. Ransome, instead of coldblooded murder, it does not interfere with my purpose to discover who did them. To attain that end, I expect the full support of everyone but the assassin."

He paused to allow this to sink in, then continued:

"I think you were going to tell me whether you saw anything of what happened to Mr. Humphries?"

"Nothing, I'm afraid," answered Jack. "I was upstairs working in my room—or trying to work."

"I suppose you *didn't* find any note from your brother this morning? You'll remember that you said you'd make another search."

"Not a sign of anything. He went out without either mother or me being any the wiser."

"Was there any indication that he had any breakfast before he started out?"

"I thought of that, but he definitely didn't, not even a cup of tea."

Diana came back, followed by an elderly woman dressed in black.

"This is Mrs. Simmonds, Inspector," she said. "Jack, you and I will go for a walk round the garden."

As the two young things walked across the lawn, Mrs. Simmonds gazed fondly after them. She was a motherly, white-haired old body and the action suited her.

"A most attractive couple," said Charlton.

"Yes," Mrs. Simmonds agreed, turning her eyes to him. "Mr. Ransome comes here quite a lot to see Mr. Humphries."

It seemed, thought Charlton, to be quite a convention that Jack visited the house with no other end in view than a chat with Mr. Humphries.

"*And* to see Miss Steward, I'll wager!" he said with a waggishness that made him ashamed of himself.

"Oh, no!" said Mrs. Simmonds. "It's only that Miss Steward happens to be here. Mr. Humphries is very interested in Mr. Ransome and they have long talks together."

Charlton left things at that. There was obviously a conspiracy afoot.

"I think you know," he said, "that Mr. Humphries was shot in Paulsfield Square to-day and is now lying in hospital, gravely wounded?"

Mrs. Simmonds nodded, adding that it was very sad and had come as a great shock to them all.

"How long have you been employed by Mr. Humphries?"

"Eight years next month."

"I expect you know most of his friends by this time?"

"Yes, I think so."

"And his enemies?"

"I really don't believe he has any, Inspector. He has his funny little ways, but most people like him."

"I'm told that he has lived in Burgeston for a good many years. Do you know anything of him before he came here?"

"No, I don't. Mr. Humphries never spoke to anyone about the past, which I've always somehow had the feeling was a very sad one."

"A few weeks ago, a gentleman named Smith visited here. Had you ever seen him before?"

Mrs. Simmonds shook her head.

"I remember Mr. Smith coming," she said, "but that's the only time I've seen him, before or since."

"Is Mr. Humphries all that can be desired as an employer, Mrs. Simmonds? I'm not asking you to tell me something you would rather not, but I am interested in the possibility of disgruntled servants."

"Mr. Humphries," said Mrs. Simmonds definitely, "is a good master. He's very open-handed and we get our proper time off—*and* more. The only servant who didn't get on with him was Frank Baggs, who used to come three times a week to do the garden. According to Mr. Humphries—and, after all, *he* was the best judge—Baggs didn't do it just so. He wasn't a proper gardener, you know—only a sort of odd-job man. Mr. Humphries got tired of him and discharged him about six weeks ago."

"A man's usually more likely to fall out with his secretary than anyone else," said Charlton, well knowing that this was a tricky topic. "How does Mr. Humphries get on with Miss Steward?"

He sensed a sudden tension in Mrs. Simmonds.

"He is always the gentleman," was all she said.

"And Miss Steward is perfectly happy to stay here?"

"And why not?" she said, bridling. "She has a pretty easy time, the pay's good and everything's found."

"Thank you, Mrs. Simmonds. And now, if you please. I should like a word with the cook."

"I don't think she can tell you much," said Mrs. Simmonds doubtfully.

"Nevertheless, I should like to speak to her."

The housekeeper shrugged her shoulders almost imperceptibly and left the room. In a couple of minutes, Charlton heard the unmistakable accent of the Old Kent Road raised in strident protest.

"I shall tell 'im just what I think, Mrs. Simmonds, and if you don't like it, you can do the other thing."

The door opened and a fat little woman in a large white apron marched in.

"You was wanting me?" she asked. "Iggens is the name— Miss Evangeline Iggens."

"Thank you, Miss Higgins," smiled Charlton.

"Iggens is the name," repeated the cook with an impatient flounce, "and Iggens is what I said. There's no haitch."

"I beg your pardon," said Charlton hurriedly, for Miss Iggens would plainly stand no hanky-panky. "It's a most unusual name. I want to speak to you, Miss Iggens, about Mr. Humphries—"

"You've come up the right street," Miss Iggens interrupted with an anticipatory smack of her lips. "That Mrs. Simmonds is all right as far as she goes, which is no great distance, if the truth must be told; but she shuts er eyes to the facks. To give the devil'is jew, Mr. Rumphries is open-'anded to a fault. 'A very nice steak, Cook,"'e says, 'and the apple-pie was a beautiful dream.'Ere! Buy yerself something with this.' But I'll tell you, Inspector, that 'e'd got 'is blinkers on Miss Steward. Not being the kind to throw mud at them at death's door, so to speak, I ain't going to let me tongue wag, but I *should* like to say—and it's me duty to say—that Mr. Rumphries made overchures *and* what's more, the young party didn't take it so amiss as she might ve done."

"What makes you think that, Miss Iggens?"

"Well, she's still 'ere, ain't she? A burnt child fears the fire, all the world over. If 'e'd tried 'is little games on me, I'd 'ave given in me notice and packed me trunk before you could say—"

"But surely," threw in Charlton, who was sick of the gentleman she was about to mention.

"Jack Robinson," said Miss Iggens triumphantly.

"But isn't a gentleman's offer of marriage . . ."

Miss Iggens took the bait.

"*Marriage?*" she said, and there was such a mixture of derision, amazement, disbelief and cynical amusement in her tone that Charlton did not pursue the subject.

"Do you remember Frank Baggs?" he asked.

"That lazy, good-for-nothing, shifty shirk-work? Yes, I remember 'im all right."

If there still remained in Miss Iggens's nature any of the milk of human kindness, it would have made excellent scones.

"Do you know where he lives?"

"With'is mother and sister in Paulsfield—and *they* pay the rent. I don't know the street."

After Charlton had suggested on four different occasions that their chat should be brought to a close, Miss Iggens retired to her kitchen with the comforting knowledge that she had said just what she thought. But for all that, she had told the Inspector no more about her employer than had Mrs. Simmonds.

He questioned the other servants, but they could tell him

very little. Mr. Smith, the mysterious visitor, had given one of the maids half-a-crown and she was able to confirm that he was tall and middle-aged, with a closely trimmed moustache. He was, she said, a real gent, but that impression may have been heightened by the handsome gratuity that she had received.

On his way back to Paulsfield, Charlton stopped his car outside the hospital. As he was about to get out, Mr. Farquarson came down the path. He was looking unusually austere.

"I have been to inquire about the patient," he explained.

"How is he?" asked Charlton anxiously. Humphries' condition meant a good deal to him.

"Serious," said Mr. Farquarson. "I managed to get a word with the matron and she said that he's in a very bad way. Whether he will survive is a debatable point. Who's going to be the next, Inspector?"

"God knows," said Charlton and, with a nod, drove on into the town.

Mrs. Ransome opened the door to him and, when he had apologized for having to trouble her, told him, with an attempt at a smile, that she felt quite able to answer his questions and led him into the front room.

"There are very few of them, Mrs. Ransome," he said "First of all, did you know beforehand, or have you found out since, why your son left home at such an early hour this morning?"

"I didn't know he was going out," she replied. "He was always running off, of course, on little errands of his own, usually to take photographs; but when he had the intention of staying away for very long at a time, he always told me in advance. I should think that he went out this morning without any idea of being very long."

"Can you think of anybody he may have had an appointment with? He obviously wasn't going on a photographic excursion, because he left his camera behind."

"I can't think of anyone at all," Mrs. Ransome admitted.

"Did he receive any letter yesterday?"

She shook her head.

"I hesitate to ask you, Mrs. Ransome, but is there anybody, to your knowledge, who might wish to do—what was done this morning?"

"Nobody at all," was the positive answer. "Arthur hadn't an enemy in the world—and that's what makes it so hard to bear. The only thing I can think of is that he was shot by a maniac."

"Had he a"—Charlton felt for the right phrase—"girl friend?"

"No. Both my sons are too young to think seriously of marriage. They go to dances, but I have always been against them striking up close friendships. Even Jack is only twenty-four."

Only twenty-four, thought Charlton. What blind fools some mothers were!

"I take it that he, too, has not yet formed an attachment?"

"No. In five or six years time, perhaps, when he has established himself with his books, he will probably start looking round for a wife. Jack is a dear boy and I'm sure he won't do anything without consulting me. He had a brilliant career at school, you know, in both examinations and sports. All those are his."

She pointed to a low table laden with cups of all sizes. "He's good at tennis and played for the 1st XV. The last year he was at school, he was first in the mile race, first in the 220 yards, second in the hurdles and he broke the school record with a long jump of twenty-eight feet."

"A remarkable achievement," said Charlton, hardly caring to tell the pathetically proud mother that the *world* record for the long jump was considerably less than that.

"Arthur was quite different. He wasn't a bit successful at school and the only thing he was at all clever at was photography. But he was a sticker. He kept at a thing until it was finished . . . Do you want to ask me anything else, Inspector, because I'm afraid . . ."

He stayed no longer, but went round to see Sergeant Martin,

in the hope that that sturdy Cockney would cheer him up. He was beginning to admit frankly to himself that he was getting rattled and the humorous philosophy of Martin might restore his self-confidence.

"What about those Jeffs, Martin?" was his first question. "Have you any statistics for me?"

"Lummy!" said Martin, in defiance of all the rules of seniority. "You don't expect much, do you? Johnson comes back and tells me that there's been another bit of frightfulness in the Square and then, before I've 'ad time to pull meself together, I'm expected to do my celebrated Registrar of Births and Deaths turn!"

"Keep on talking, Martin," said Charlton. "It does me a world of good. You're the only person in this town that I don't suspect of murderous insanity."

"Which makes it all the more likely," grinned Martin, "that I'm the man you're after!"

The grin faded and something more than sympathy showed on his face.

"Taking it out of you a bit?" he asked. "Brace yourself up! You and me'll get the swine before we've finished!"

"I shudder to think who'll be next," said Charlton wearily. "All those kids running about the Square—it might be any of them, even that young Ted of yours, Martin. I simply can't think that there's any other motive behind it all than a mad desire to take human life. This afternoon, I've been trying to find out things about this man, Humphries; trying to discover some reason for attempted murder: and in spite of the fact that there is at least one man who had reason to dislike him, and the added fact that Humphries is a man with a past, I'm sure in my own mind that if Jack Jones or Tom Smith had been sitting in that car at that particular time, he wouldn't have been any luckier than Humphries was." Which was not, as it turned out, true.

"How the devil he gets away with it," he went on

despairingly, "is beyond my comprehension."

He lighted a cigarette and drew hard at it.

"I'm behaving like an hysterical old woman, Martin!" he said with a lugubrious smile. "Let's get on with the job. When are you going to let me have that list of Jeffs?"

"I've got a great big surprise for you!" Martin replied and produced a piece of paper from his desk. "Old man Farrows thought I was cracked, but he got out the partic'lars for me."

He held up the sheet in the best "Be it known to All Men by These Presents" attitude and declaimed importantly:

"There are twenty-three Geoffrey Somebodies, who are, or would have been, thirty-five or over. When it comes to surnames, there are seven J-E-F-F-E-R-I-E-S, four J—E—F—F—R—I—E—S, one Jeffcoat, one Jeffcott, one G-E-O-F-F, one J-E-F-F-S and a couple of J-E-F-F-E-R-S-O-N's. There isn't anyone with J-E-F-F or G-E-O-F-F anywhere else than at the beginning. That," he added helpfully, "is forty altogether."

Charlton sighed.

"It'll probably be a shocking waste of time," he said, "but we'll try and weed them out tomorrow. Do any of them strike you as significant?"

"No," admitted Martin.

"Do you know that Humphries' Christian name is Geoffrey?"

"That it isn't!" contradicted the Sergeant. "It's Anthony."

"That it isn't!" retorted Charlton. "I have every reason to believe that his real name is Geoffrey Ibbotson."

"Then 'e's been living under a false name?"

"Your grip on the situation wins my admiration, Martin. Yes, I am almost sure he was the co-respondent in that big divorce case some years ago. What was the name of the husband? Sir Waldo Something-or-other ... I made a note of it this afternoon." He felt in his pocket for the book. On the first page he glanced at were the family-trees that he had scribbled down to please Mrs. Archer. One of the names caught his eye and he whistled.

"That's a coincidence, Martin," he said slowly. "Frank Baggs, a gardener who was discharged by Humphries, is the brother-in-law of Thomas Earnshaw."

XVII.

The Inspector at the Breakfast Table

PAULSFIELD SNIPER
TERROR SPREADS

"THE appalling series of tragedies that have taken place during the last few days in the little Downshire market town of Paulsfield have at last created a feeling of general alarm. The killing in the Square last Tuesday of Thomas Earnshaw, a workman engaged upon cleaning the central statue, was regarded as an isolated crime, aimed particularly against Earnshaw; but the shooting early yesterday morning of Arthur Ransome, a young photographer, and the grave wounding, later in the day, of Mr. Anthony Humphries, a local gentleman, whose home is in Burgeston, a small adjacent village, have now brought it home to Paulsfield residents that a homicidal maniac is abroad in the town.

"Yesterday afternoon, after it was learnt that a third tragedy had occurred during a thunderstorm which broke over the district soon after one o'clock, the Square took on a deserted appearance. The positions in which the three shot men were found preclude the possibility that they were fired upon from the west, east and south sides of the Square; and it is believed that the suspicions of the police are directed against certain buildings on the north side. Besides the Horticultural Hall, the Post Office is situated on that side, together with the local branch of the Southern Counties Bank, Ltd. and two shops.

"Mr. James E. Farquarson, the secretary of the Paulsfield Horticultural Society, whose home is close to the Horticultural Hall, told our representative that, on the occasion of the shooting of Thomas Earnshaw, he saw, through a back window of his house, a commercial van standing in a side street. This van was driven away just as the fatal shot was fired. Mr. Farquarson said that he was under the impression that the police have since satisfied themselves that the van was in no way concerned with the crime and went on to tell our representative that at a few minutes after one o'clock yesterday, he had seen from his garden the figure of a man standing on the roof of one of the suspected buildings in the Square. The identity of this man has not yet been established.

"Mrs. Archer, the widow of Captain Richard Archer, D.S.O., who died in 1923 as a result of wounds received in the Great War, said, when interviewed by our representative, that she was in her room when all three shots were fired. She is the sister-in-law of Mr. Joseph Beamish, a curio dealer, whose shop is on the north side of the Square, and, from her window on the first floor, actually saw Thomas Earnshaw fall from the plinth of the statue.

"Arthur Ransome, the second victim, procured the two wonderful photographs of the statue in the Square that appeared exclusively in the *Evening Messenger* and it is an ironic stroke of fate that the young photographer was destined to be the Sniper's next human sacrifice.

"It is understood that there is a growing dissatisfaction in the town at the alleged dilatory methods of the police. Three shocking crimes emanating from a common source have been perpetrated within a few days of each other and it is the general feeling locally that the arrest of the person or persons responsible is overdue. It is felt that the shooting in broad daylight of these unfortunate men should not be a problem whose solution presents any insuperable difficulties.

"Parents who fear for the lives of their children are forbidding them to venture near the Square and the customary coming and going across the open space was noticeably absent yesterday afternoon and evening. Shopkeepers, not only in the

Square, but also in that part of the High Street that borders its eastern side, are complaining already of a marked falling off in their business. The residents have obviously decided to do their shopping henceforth in those parts of the town that are free, as yet, from the murderous attentions of the Sniper.

"The investigations are in the hands of Detective-inspector Charlton, whose record as a police officer is a fine one. It is the earnest hope of everyone, not only in afflicted Paulsfield, but also all over the rest of the country, that Inspector Charlton will bring the criminal to justice before other innocent men, women and children come to their deaths at the Sniper's merciless hands.

"Pictures on Page Seven."

Charlton threw the paper on the floor and turned with a grunt to his bacon and egg. Molly Arnold, his niece, looked across at him from the other side of the breakfast table.

"A bad press, Uncle Harry?" she asked.

"Very bad, my dear," replied Charlton with a wry smile. "In effect, Detective-inspector Charlton may have done some good work in the past, but now he's gone right off the rails. That transcendent old idiot, Farquarson, has been opening his heart to the Fleet Street boys, in spite of having assured me that he would keep quiet about the man he saw on the roof. But I notice that Mrs. Archer hasn't passed on her suspicions about Humphries being the notorious Geoffrey Ibbotson not that it really matters, as far as I can see."

"What are you going to do next?" asked Molly. She took a keen interest in her uncle's cases and enjoyed his full confidence. She was the only woman he had ever met, he used to say, who never betrayed a secret and that, he would add, was why he was still a bachelor. As John Rutherford was to say, she had dark shingled hair, an incontrovertibly tip-tilted nose, big brown eyes and a voice like the sweet sound that breathes upon a bank of violets. He was madly in love with the girl, of course, but then, if it comes to that, so are we.

But, "What are you going to do next?" she asked.

"First of all," her uncle Harry replied, "get Captain Harmon to confirm that the third bullet was fired from the same pistol as the other two. He may not be able to, as it's badly knocked about. Secondly, see what I can do to prevent further accidents. The population is already fighting shy of the Square, which I hope will cramp our friend's style a good deal, unless it forces him to seek elsewhere for his pistol fodder."

He passed his cup across to Molly.

"The only pleasant aspect of the whole affair," he said, "is that the killer's ammunition is rapidly becoming exhausted— if, that is, a certain assumption of mine is correct. Captain Harmon has told me that the bullets taken from Earnshaw and Ransome are of such calibre and weight as to be identified with a Parabellum selfloader."

"That's the one you told me about," said Molly. "A Mrs. Symes said that her husband had given one to a man called Jeff, didn't she?"

"I'm not gambling on that one being the weapon used for the murders," said Charlton, "but what I *am* gambling on is that a Parabellum pistol is the weapon I am looking for. Thousands of men must have brought them back as souvenirs from France and an unpleasantly large percentage of them were probably loaded. Every Tom, Dick and Harry can't go into a shop and buy a gun like a pound of sausages. There are too many restrictions. But there's no knowing how many deadly weapons, ostensibly trophies, were smuggled back after the War.

"The Parabellum I found in Mrs. Symes's loft still had seven rounds left in it and, according to her, her husband's charming little gift to this man Jeff had its full complement of eight rounds. Three rounds of this 9 mm. German ammunition have already been used on Earnshaw, Ransome and Humphries. That leaves a maximum residue of five cartridges. *If* the weapon I'm after was a wartime souvenir, the cartridges are a good many years old and it's more likely than not that some of the caps—they're the little fellows in the bases of cartridges that are exploded by the hammers and catch the main charges of powder alight—some of the caps have lost their old-time exuberance. So the sniper has five more lives at his mercy—probably less."

"And if those five more lives are taken?" asked Molly seriously.

"Don't let's think about that, my dear," was the hurried answer.

As a matter of fact, he was thinking about it quite a lot and, even at that very moment—that sacrosanct time when an Englishman takes his breakfast—was waiting for the telephone to summon him to yet another tragedy.

"I've circularized all the suppliers within a large radius to let me know if anyone tries to buy 9 mm. ammunition."

He helped himself to a piece of toast.

"There was a time," he continued, "when I cast suspicious glances at that passage between the Hall and Beamish's shop; and when I found that Parabellum in Mrs. Symes's loft, I evolved a very beautiful theory, which it really grieved me eventually to discard, that Master Ronald had allowed curiosity to get the better of prudence—as every decently constituted boy should—and accidentally fired the weapon through the open window of the bathroom, which allows a clear view of the statue. But Captain Harmon has proved that that particular Parabellum was not the one used to kill Earnshaw and it certainly wasn't the one used against Ransome and Humphries, because it passed into my possession before they were shot.

"Turning to another thing, I've been toying with the idea of applying for a warrant to search Beamish's, Pope's and Muttigen's, but it's a definitely tricky business. When you start nosing round people's houses, the only thing you are likely to find is that they play bridge every Tuesday with the Chief Constable's aunt Anastasia."

"You could say," suggested Molly, "that it's all a matter of police routine and that no personal reflections are intended."

"I could say it," her uncle agreed, "but it wouldn't get me very far. No, I think the best plan is to give the people concerned the idea that the police have decided to apply for search warrants and then keep a close watch on their reactions. I'll ask the Super about it this morning."

"Didn't I hear you ringing Paulsfield hospital just now?" asked Molly.

"Yes, I wanted the latest bulletin about Humphries. They don't seem very enthusiastic about his chances of recovery, but it's nice to know that he's still hanging on. Which reminds me that I must go and see that Baggs person."

"I can't see," said Molly, "how he could have been mixed up in it. Mr. Humphries certainly gave him the sack, but that kind of thing's going on every day and, however much they'd like to, I don't think many 'sackees' would shoot the men who discharged them. Besides, if he tried to take his revenge on Mr. Humphries, what was the sense in first of all killing Arthur Ransome and his own brother-in-law? A couple of rehearsals, to make sure the pistol was working nicely?"

"Quite true, but, for all that, I must hear his story."

"What about the boy with the complex? He seems interesting."

"Harold Muttigen? He had, as far as I can tell, every opportunity. I hesitated to ask his father whether there were any firearms on the premises, but one would hardly imagine any normal parent leaving things like that about the home, especially when his offspring had such a marked mental kink."

"And Pope, the tobacconist man?"

"He seems a particularly harmless old gentleman. If he turns out to be a homicidal maniac, I shall be extremely surprised. The same with the people next door to him. Beamish is a deaf old fiddle-faddler, his unmarried sister is a contented, domesticated woman, with no thought beyond how the dinner's getting on, and his widowed sister, Mrs. Archer, although a bit eccentric, is wrapped up in her little hobbies— her crossword puzzles and her Paulsfield Who's Who and What's What."

He sipped his tea and then, as it was nearly cold, drained it at a draught.

"Tea's not as hot as it might be, my dear," he said reprovingly, as he put down his cup.

Molly maintained a dignified silence, which was all a part of the game. Her uncle's insistence on his tea being given to him boiling hot, because that was how tea should be taken, and then allowing it to reach tepidity before drinking it, was an old and valued controversy between them.

"In spite of my conviction," he said, unmoved by her disregard of his complaint, "that these three shootings were just random craziness, it is an indisputable fact that there *are* certain connections—fragile, I'll grant, but still connections— that can be traced. Frank Baggs, the brother-in-law of Thomas Earnshaw, was recently sacked by Humphries. Arthur Ransome was responsible for those photographs at the time that Earnshaw died. Jack Ransome, Arthur's elder brother, is carrying on a clandestine affair with the charming secretary of Humphries, who himself has certain ideas in that direction. Weighed against that, of course, is the consideration that, in a small community like Paulsfield, there are not many people who are not connected, in some way, with most of the other residents. If a butcher had been the first victim, more likely than not the second man to die would have been the uncle of a man he had discharged for using the captive bolt humane killer for driving in tin-tacks or a man to whose wife he had sold some worst end of the neck."

"I hate people who are funny at breakfast," said Molly.

"If the Sniper (with a capital 's')," said Charlton, "said to himself in the first place, 'I will kill Thomas Earnshaw first, then I will kill Arthur Ransome and after that I will kill

Anthony Humphries,' or if he planned the crimes separately, with no connection whatever between them, or if the second crime was necessitated by the first or the third necessitated by the second—"

"What is the size in acres of field B?" finished Molly, when Charlton paused for breath.

"Two pounds, three shillings and sevenpence," was the ready answer. "But you see what I'm driving at, don't you?" he went on. "If the Sniper *plotted,* for any reason at all, to kill these three men, he had to choose his moment in each case. Earnshaw was easy: he had been cleaning the statue on Monday and had left it in an unfinished condition. It was therefore a justifiable assumption that on Tuesday morning he would resume work. This made it easy for plans to be made. The would-be murderer had only to wait until Earnshaw worked his way round to the best position and pop went the homicidally inclined little weasel."

"But Arthur Ransome . . ." began Molly.

"The situation then was very different. Nobody I have questioned as yet had any idea beforehand that Ransome was going to leave home at 5.45 a.m. yesterday. I have asked his mother, his brother and the lads of the village he consorted with the previous evening, and not one of them could supply any reason. So if the murder of Ransome *was* premeditated, the Sniper must have known in advance that Ransome would be up with the lark—*and,* further, that he would be walking across the Square; or, alternatively, the Sniper must have *seen* Ransome leave the house, guess that he was going to get to the Square via the passage, and transported himself to some point that would enable him to shoot Ransome as he made his way across the Square. The only other hypothesis is the Sniper was waiting like—to repeat the phrase I used to Martin yesterday—a bloodthirsty spider, for some unsuspecting victim to come within his ken.

"Humphries' case was the same as Earnshaw's. His

presence could be depended upon. He drove to Paulsfield every Thursday and arrived back at Burgeston in time for an invariably punctual lunch at one-thirty. It was fortunate for the Sniper that a thunderstorm coincided with Humphries' departure from the Bank, but anyone who was aware of Humphries' habits could have been ready to deliver the goods, storm or no storm.

"So you see, my dear, the shooting of Ransome, just as it was when alibis had to be considered, is again the 'key' crime. If I can discover who knew in advance about Ransome's expedition, I shall feel keenly interested in that person's activities at midday last Tuesday and at one-fifteen yesterday!"

He munched his toast for a while and then shrugged his shoulders hopelessly.

"But these are not natural crimes. They can't be dealt with by ordinary police methods. There was probably no planning, no honest-to-goodness or honest-to-badness motive behind them. It's just a madman with a gun. It is an axiom in the police force that murder with robbery as its motive gives the investigator the stiffest task, because there is usually no connection at all between the killer and the killed, as there is when the cause of the crime is jealousy, blackmail or gain through wills, insurances and so forth. But even with robbery, the police are helped by finger-prints and the murderer's attempts to dispose of the booty. When, though, the only motive is an insane blood-lust, it's the very devil.

"Earnshaw died, Ransome died, Humphries is dying and the Sniper is chuckling to himself and plotting to play Old Harry."

"And if I know him," said Molly stoutly, "Old Harry will win the set, in spite of having lost the first three games!"

"Your staunch championship," said Charlton pompously, "will send me off to face with a lighter heart whatever troubles and disappointments the day may bring."

"I don't want to dictate to the County Constabulary," Molly

said with a smile, "but I think you ought to pay more attention to the Horticultural Hall. From what you tell me, anyone can climb on the roof without much trouble and it seems far more likely to this innocent child that *if* the shots were fired from a roof and not a window, they were fired from the Hall rather than the shops. It's so much easier to get at."

"But the approach is impossibly public!" protested Charlton. "An iron ladder running up the wall, in full view of the back windows in Effingham Street and numerous houses in the Paragon and elsewhere.

"Have you made sure that the iron ladder is the only means of getting on to the roof?"

"I know of no other way."

"What about from inside? Isn't there a sort of gallery running round?"

"Yes," said Charlton rubbing his chin doubtfully, "but that doesn't help much."

"Are there any windows in the roof?"

"There's a large domed top-light."

"Does any part of it open?"

"Yes, but it would be a bit of a job to get up there from inside."

"Ladders are handy things."

"It would have to be a devilishly long ladder," smiled Charlton. "I didn't see how you could possibly stand it on the gallery, so you'd have to start from the ground floor, which is a matter of thirty feet from the roof."

"But it must be done," persisted Molly. "Windows have to be cleaned from time to time. Did you see a ladder inside the Hall?"

"Yes, an extending step-ladder."

"Well, then."

"It's certainly an idea," said Charlton pensively.

"It's wonderful the way I fling them off, don't you think?" said Molly with a saucy smile. But the faces of both of them straightened as the telephone bell rang. They heard the maid hurry along the hall. Presently she knocked at the door.

"Sergeant Martin wants to speak to you, sir," she said.

XVIII.

Gin for the Woodcock

CHARLTON lifted the receiver.

"Hullo, Martin" he said. "Yes . . . Frank Baggs? . . . I'll come over."

The maid had gone back to the kitchen. As he replaced the receiver, Molly, who was standing in the doorway, asked apprehensively:

"Another?"

"Luckily, no," her uncle smiled and she sighed with relief. "Frank Baggs, the gardener Humphries discharged, has something he wants to tell me; but that, I think, can wait until I've seen the Superintendent."

Ten minutes later, he got out his car and drove to Lulverton, where were situated the headquarters of a division of the County Police, under which Paulsfield, in charge of Sergeant Martin, was a sub-division. Superintendent Kingsley saw Charlton in his office behind the police station. He was a big, bluff man and a thoroughly good fellow. That morning, however, he was a little fretful.

"The Chief Constable," he said, "is not too pleased with the way things are going at Paulsfield, Charlton. I gave you a free hand when that man Earnshaw was killed on the statue and the only thing that's happened so far is that two more men have been shot. Can't you speed things up a bit?"

"Nobody is more keen on speeding things up a bit than I am, sir," was Charlton's reply. "I've done everything possible to find out who fired the shots. I've questioned everybody who might be in any way concerned with the crimes; made sure that two of the bullets were fired from the same weapon and that the weapon was probably a Parabellum self-loader; checked every Parabellum that is registered at Whitchester; localized the area from which the three shots could have been fired; investigated each crime separately and also in relation to the others; considered all the windows in the suspected area and the neighbouring roofs—"

The Superintendent waved his hand impatiently.

"I know you're doing your best," he said, "but we want *results.* People are beginning to talk and the papers are getting sarcastic. What's the exact position now? Can't we do something to clear the whole thing up?"

"The exact position is this, sir: Although I have no witnesses as to the place from which the shots were fired, everything points to three particular buildings—the Horticultural Hall and the two adjoining shops. If the shots were fired from a window, the suspects are Joseph Beamish, a curio dealer, and Mrs. Archer, his widowed sister, in one shop and Alexander Pope, a tobacconist, in the other shop. If the shots were fired from a roof, the suspects are firstly, anyone who had access to the roof of the Hall, and secondly all those who were in the block of shops. These last I have reduced to five: Joseph Beamish, Mrs. Archer, Alexander Pope, a chemist round in the High Street named Muttigen and his seventeen-year-old son, who is suffering from a species of mental trouble—agoraphobia or something of that kind. It is safe to rule out the rest of the buildings in the block."

The Superintendent played with the lobe of his ear.

"Is it possible," he asked, "to reach the roofs of the block from any other buildings?"

"It's *possible*," was the dubious reply. "There's a multiple store at the High Street end of the block and the back wall of it is about eight feet from the wall of the first house in Effingham Street, the side road."

"Could an active person jump from one building to the other?"

"I should hardly like to try it myself, sir. The roof of number one Effingham Street is not flat, but gabled, and the only way to get from the house to the roof of the shop is through a side window, and from there it would be necessary to leap upwards and get a hold on the parapet of the shop roof, which is some distance above the level of the window."

"Who occupies the house?"

"A Mrs. Ransome, the widowed mother of Arthur Ransome, the second victim, and Jack, her elder son."

"What sort of man is he?"

"A young fellow of about twenty-four, who writes books about Nature."

"A studious type? Likely to be an introvert?"

"Just the opposite. He was something of an athlete at school, with running and jumping records."

"On friendly terms with his brother?"

"Very, if what I'm told is true."

"Is there anything to connect him with the other two shootings?"

"In a sense, yes. He's carrying on a clandestine love affair with the pretty young secretary of Humphries, who's now in Paulsfield Hospital."

"What was the association between Humphries and this girl?"

"She herself—her name's Diana Steward—says that he has always treated her as an employer should, and that is confirmed by Mrs. Simmonds, the housekeeper. The cook, however, expresses the definite opinion that Humphries has—importuned Miss Steward."

"What's *your* opinion?"

"The cook is a backbiter, only too ready to run others down, but I think she was speaking the truth. Mrs. Simmonds seemed rather too anxious to stress the gentlemanly qualities of Humphries, and Miss Steward seemed over keen to give the same impression."

"D'you think there *is* something between Humphries and the girl?"

"She doesn't seem that sort."

"Yet, for all that, she still stayed on."

"The salary was good and I don't think her parents are too well off."

"And this affair between Miss Steward and Jack Ransome?"

"They're obviously very much in love with each other, but the boy's mother knows nothing about it. She's definitely against him forming an attachment too early."

"Then if he's in love with the girl and Humphries tried any monkey business with her . . .?"

"You mean it gives him a motive for shooting Humphries? But if, as I think, the same gun was used to do the three crimes, why should Ransome want to kill his own brother?"

"Because he got to know about Diana Steward and threatened to spill the beans. How about that? No, it's not strong enough."

"And even if he did shoot the other two," added Charlton, "there seems absolutely no reason at all why he should shoot Earnshaw, the workman."

"Was there any connection between Earnshaw and Humphries?" asked Kingsley.

"A very slight one. Earnshaw's brother-in-law—a man called Frank Baggs—was once gardener to Humphries and was sacked by him. Sergeant Martin rang me this morning to say that Baggs wants a word with me."

"What about getting search warrants for the buildings in the block and Mrs. Ransome's house?" suggested the Superintendent.

"I *have* been thinking of suggesting it."

"It's a good idea. Even if the searching doesn't produce the gun, it'll clarify the position."

"I venture to suggest another course first. Let the people concerned know in a roundabout way that the police have applied for search warrants and then watch their reactions. It may make our man break cover."

"Good," said the Superintendent briefly.

"If you can let me have Bradfield or Emerson, sir, I'll see what we can do. There's another thing: I think we ought to police the Square. If I can have a couple of plain-clothes men to keep an eye on things, they may catch him in the act."

"Where do you propose to station them? If they kick their heels in the Square all day, somebody will smell a rat."

"I think I can avoid that, sir."

"Well, I'll leave it to you, Charlton," said Kingsley.

"Take whatever men you want, do whatever you think fit, but for God's sake get this blasted business cleared up. If the threat of a search warrant doesn't produce anything by Sunday evening, we'll go through that block with a small-tooth comb!"

Charlton left the Superintendent's office and went to look for Bradfield or Emerson, two energetic constables at that time on plain-clothes duty. He found Bradfield first.

"The Super wants you to give me a hand with this Paulsfield affair," he explained.

"Certainly, sir," said Bradfield promptly. "What would you like me to do?"

"There are two shops in the Square, another in the High Street and a private house in a side street that I wish to search. Before I get the warrant, I want to try frightening the person I'm after into doing something hasty. Will you go to these places—I'll give you the addresses—and warn the people concerned that their homes are likely to be searched. Drop the hint casually, in the course of your chat. I'll leave you to work out the details."

He took a piece of paper and wrote down the names and addresses of Beamish, Pope, Muttigen and Mrs. Ransome.

"The first three are easy," he said. "All you have to do is to go in and buy something. But the last one is a private house and the information must be passed on to a young man called Jack Ransome. . . . Just a moment, though. I've a better idea than that. Don't tell the Ransomes, but try to get a word with a Miss Steward, who lives at Normanhurst, a big house just outside Burgeston. She's secretary to Humphries, the man who was shot in his car. Find out Humphries' telephone number and go first of all to the Paulsfield Exchange. See the supervisor, tell her who you are and ask her to tell the girls to look out for a call from Humphries' extension to Paulsfield 381, which is Mrs. Ransome's number. The supervisor will probably go all haughty, but there's no need for them to break the rules and listen in. All you want to know is whether a call is put through. Diana Steward probably won't trust to the 'phone to warn Ransome, but I expect she'll ring him as soon as you've left her, to fix an urgent appointment. So hang about outside for half-an-hour or so and see whether she leaves the house. If she does, tail her—and don't forget that Humphries' car is back in its garage now."

"I'll see to it," said Bradfield confidently.

"When you've done that, stand by in the reading-room of the Paulsfield Public Library until you hear from me. If you'll take my advice, you won't walk across the Square. Keep close to the buildings."

Bradfield nodded and his superior asked where he could find Emerson. The young detective-constable was found in the guard-room and Bradfield went off to sow the seeds of panic in at least one guilty heart.

Charlton outlined his plan to Emerson and then went off alone to Paulsfield. Frank Baggs was still patiently waiting for him when he got there. He was a man of about thirty-five, with a down-at-heel appearance and badly in need of a shave. Charlton took him into the back office and asked what he had to say.

"I don't think you know 'oo I am," began Baggs.

"Only that you are Thomas Earnshaw's brother-in-law and were until recently employed as a gardener by Mr. Humphries," said Charlton.

Baggs's mouth fell open.

"I have been given to understand, Mr. Baggs," Charlton went on, "that Mr. Humphries dispensed with your services rather hurriedly. Have you come to talk to me about that?"

"You don't mean—you don't think . . ." said Baggs and then lost his voice.

"I am merely telling you what I know," said Charlton with an amiable smile, "and now I'm waiting for you to tell *me* something—probably that Mr. Humphries didn't fire you because you were a rotten gardener."

It was a shot in the dark, but it hit the target.

"That's right," Baggs agreed dazedly, "but how did you know?"

"We won't go into that now. What were you doing at a quarter past one yesterday?"

"Gardening."

"Where?"

"14, Chesapeake Road. I was generally tidying things up in the front—clippin' the yedge, trimmin' the borders and suchlike."

"Name?"

"Mr. Marling."

"Where do you live?"

"17, The Paragon."

"Now, what is it you want to tell me?"

"Mr. 'Umphries and me was always 'aving rows about the way things ought to be done in the garden, but 'e used to enjoy them. If 'e couldn't find fault with what I did, 'e thought 'is day was wasted. I didn't mind much, 'cos I gave as good as I got. 'E didn't give me the push for that, though 'e pretended that that's what it was. I'll tell you what 'e did give it me for."

His voice sank to a confidential murmur.

"I 'ope what I'm saying won't go no further?" he asked.

"You are at liberty to hope, Mr. Baggs."

"Well, it's me duty to tell you, whatever use you make of it. Mr. 'Umphries was sweet on Miss Steward, 'is seckertary."

He allowed a moment or two for this portentous news to sink in and then went on:

"I was working quietly by a nedge, a matter of six weeks ago, when the two of them came along and stopped just the other side. I needn't tell you everything they said, but he put the proposition to 'er what you might call blunt and she upped and did the 'ow-dare-you stuff and went off in a fine temper. I 'appened to make a bit of noise and 'e saw me on the other side of the yedge. Nothing was said then, but the next day 'e comes up to me and goes for me 'ammer and tongs about some delphiniums—all much ado about nothing, you understand. Then when I'd done me stuff, as was customary, 'e suddenly whips out 'is wallet, gives me a week's wages and tells me to get out and stay out, you impertinent so-and-so."

"And you think the real reason was because you overheard his conversation?"

"Sure of it," said Baggs. "But that wasn't what I really came to see you about. What's more important is that young Mr. Ransome was after Miss Steward as well and *he* knew what Mr. 'Umphries was up to. What I 'eard in the garden wasn't the first time 'e'd tried it on, if me information is correct. Some days before that, I'd over'eard the two young people talking in the garden. 'E was saying, 'If I catch the swine at it, I'll murder 'im! Why can't you get out of 'ere?' Then Miss Steward said, 'I know 'ow to look after meself, Jack, and we've got to put up with it for a little while—just until 'e's done what 'e promised about your new book.'"

Baggs paused.

"Is that all?" asked Charlton.

"*All?*" demanded Baggs. "Isn't it enough? Mr. 'Umphries is shot down in cold blood and 'ere was a young fellow 'oo'd sworn to murder 'im. What more do you want?"

"Thank you, Mr. Baggs," said Charlton evenly. "I won't keep you any longer. This passage will lead you to the street. Good morning."

When the abashed man had left him alone, Charlton sat thinking for a few minutes, then went and opened the window. It was entirely his imagination, but he felt that the room needed ventilation.

★ ★ ★

Soon after half-past ten that morning, the men who still worked in the Square behind their trestled barrier—though now the noisy, chattering drills had given place to quieter tools and the morning air was heavy with the breath-catching smell of boiling tar—were joined by another man in labourer's clothes, who, when the moment was propitious, dissolved into the gloomiest recess of the shelter, where a useful little hole in the tarpaulin gave a splendid view of the north side of the Square. As a task, this unexciting peeking might not have been to everybody's taste, but as this watcher received seven shillings and sixpence a week more than his uniformed colleagues on street duty, he was inclined to be philosophic. After his term of duty, his place would be taken by a man as roughly clad and unremarked as he; and each would be furtively supplied with tit-bits from the frying-pan above the brazier by the conniving foreman and his men.

At about the same time, another quietly dressed young man climbed the narrow stairs of the church tower and settled himself down by the narrow central window in the dusty room below the clock. From there, he and those who relieved him would be able to keep a watchful eye on the roofs of the Horticultural Hall and all the buildings in the suspected block.

Meanwhile, Bradfield had motor-cycled to Normanhurst. He asked the maid if he could speak to Mr. Humphries' secretary. When Diana Steward came down, he explained that he represented a news agency and would be glad to have a few words from her about the great tragedy that had overtaken the household.

"What *can* I tell you?" asked Diana with a helpless little gesture. "I can only say that I and all the others here are terribly sorry that it's happened and we can't possibly understand why anybody should want to do such a frightful thing as shoot Mr. Humphries."

Bradfield conscientiously wrote this down in a notebook.

"That's fine!" he said, as he closed the book. "The human touch, you know. They'll fairly lap that up. What is your name, please?"

"Steward. Miss Diana Steward. Is that really all you want me to say?"

"I can't think of anything else," said Bradfield quite truthfully. "I expect you're tired of answering questions, what with the police and everybody?"

"They've all been very kind," Diana replied. "The Inspector who came here didn't seem a bit like a policeman. He was more like a . . ."

"Doctor?" suggested Bradfield innocently and Diana nodded eagerly.

"The police," went on Bradfield, "are certainly doing all they can to clear the matter up. I learnt this morning through our Central Confidential Intelligence Department"—he felt rather pleased with that—"that the police have applied for a search warrant."

Diana swallowed hard.

"Where for?" she asked indifferently.

"My people believe they've got their eyes on someone in a side street that's quite near the Square. They did tell me, but I've forgotten the name of it."

"Effingham Street is close. Is it that?"

"Yes, I remember now you mention it," he agreed. "Well, I mustn't keep you any longer, Miss Steward. Thanks for the"— he sought feverishly round in his mind for the right word— "dope."

The short lane in which Normanhurst stood was a *cul-de-sac* and the entrance to it was visible from Burgeston High Street. Bradfield saw a small shop that advertised "TEAS" and brought his machine to a standstill outside it. At a table in the window, he was able to drink his cup of coffee and watch, at the same time, the entrance to the lane. In a little over ten minutes, Diana Steward emerged from the lane, went past the tea-shop and walked briskly off in the direction of Paulsfield.

XIX.

A Question of Window Cleaning

INSPECTOR CHARLTON called at Trevona in Hill Road, Paulsfield, but Dr. Weston was just starting out on his morning round.

"Did you find that third bullet, Charlton?" he asked at his gate. "You did? Good. I'd like to have a chat with you about it, but if you don't mind, we'll leave it for the moment. There are now anxiously waiting for me a large assortment of ailing ladies, who have been at death's door for so many years that I really don't think there's anyone at home!"

"Shall I come back about one o'clock?" suggested Charlton and the doctor agreed.

With the three bullets in his pocket, Charlton drove to Whitchester to see Captain Harmon. The firearms expert was at home, but, as Charlton had feared, the bullet he had picked up from the floor of Humphries' car was too deformed for the Captain to do more than confirm that it was of the same type as the other two. He was not prepared to say that it was fired from the same gun as the others.

By the time the Inspector walked into the reading-room of the Paulsfield Public Library, Bradfield had worked through most of the available light reading and was running a lack-lustre eye over the pages of *Our Feathered Friends.* Charlton went over to where he sat, reached rather rudely across for *Punch,* and murmured as he did so:

"Walk out towards Burgeston. I'll catch you up."

A minute or two later, Bradfield left the Library and, after enjoying the cartoons and an article by "Evoe," Charlton followed him. He picked Bradfield up some way outside Paulsfield and drove into a quiet lane.

"We're being rather conspiratorial, Bradfield," he smiled as he stopped the car, "but I don't want it to be known in Paulsfield that you are attached to the police. Anything to report?"

"I saw Miss Steward, sir, and tipped her the wink that the police were going to search the Ransomes' house. After I left her, I hung about just round the corner and in something like ten minutes, she came out and made off at a pretty sharp pace. I guessed that she was making for Paulsfield and gave her plenty of time before I went after her. I had a motor-bike, which I've garaged, for the time being, in the town. When I caught her up, she was talking to a young fellow with a bicycle. Tall and dark, with a bit of a sharp nose on him. I rode on in to Paulsfield and saw the supervisor at the Exchange. She said that a call was put through from the Normanhurst number to Ransome's house a couple of minutes after I left Miss Steward."

"Good work!" said Charlton. "What about Beamish and the others?"

"I picked a book from the box outside Beamish's shop and took it in. A little man of sixty-five or thereabouts, with hair like a shaving-brush, told me that it would be fourpence. I gave him a shilling and while he was collecting the change from all round the shop——"

"You'll go a long way, Bradfield," said Charlton approvingly. "You have a certain descriptive faculty."

Bradfield grinned and went on:

"I said casually that they must be having a pretty anxious time in Paulsfield. He looked at me as if he didn't understand and I said it again. Then I realized that he was as deaf as a post and that it wasn't going to be easy to drop him a hint. So I asked him in my ordinary voice if he'd got a copy of *The Thirty-Nine Steps* by John Buchan. He said he was hard of hearing and would I please speak up a bit. I pretended to shout, but made the words a bit blurry and after we'd got into a fine old mess, he did what I wanted him to do—went and fetched his wife."

"Was she short and plump?"

"Yes, a homely old soul with pince-nez glasses."

"That's his sister; but go on."

"I asked her about the Buchan book and gradually turned the conversation round to the murders. I told her that I had a sister who does all the Chief Constable's confidential correspondence——"

"Magnificent mendacity!" applauded his superior.

"I said my sister had told me that the police had their eyes on a building in Paulsfield Square and were going to search it for weapons. Then, when Miss Beamish said she was sorry they hadn't the book I wanted, I went in next door and told the same tale to Pope, the tobacconist."

He smirked like a schoolboy.

"I thought of a fine yarn for him, but decided I'd better not vary the details, in case they compared notes afterwards. Then I went round to see Muttigen."

"Thanks very much," said Charlton. "Emerson is looking after the other arrangements. You'd better get back to Lulverton and mark time."

He dropped the detective on the way back to Paulsfield and drove on into the town. When he saw the Square, he glanced instinctively at his watch. It was only just after midday, yet over it was the dinner-hour peace. There were no hurrying housewives with full baskets on their arms, no whistling errand-boys cycling madly in all directions and none of the usual loungers against the railings outside the Post Office. Even the customary half-dozen parked cars were absent. In the adjacent parts of the High Street, the pedestrians were few and they walked as if death were at their heels. Only the open doors of the shops showed that it was a Friday noon and not a Sunday dawn.

Charlton was not prone to the jitters, but the sight of the empty market-place slumbering serenely under the midsummer sun sent a ripple of apprehension through him. Everything seemed so ideally peaceful: yet in the roadmenders' shelter and the church tower keen eyes watched, and somewhere there was a lurking lunatic with an itching finger curled ready round the trigger of a gun. . . .

He pressed his foot on the accelerator and drove further along the High Street, where, out of sight of the Square, business was more or less as usual.

As he ran up the steps of the police station, he saw through the open door that the charge-room was full of solemn men, who turned towards him as he entered. Sergeant Martin, looking hot and flurried, was standing at his desk and Charlton looked enquiringly at him.

"These gentlemen, Inspector," said Martin, "'ave formed a deputation. This is Mr. Cooper, the manager of the Southern Counties Bank and——"

"Mr. Cooper and I have met before," said Charlton with a polite smile, "and I think I know all the other gentlemen." A bank manager in a country town is something of a nabob and Mr. Cooper was naturally the spokesman of the party. He was a tall, earnest man, secretary of the Paulsfield Golf Club and a prominent figure in other local activities. The rest of the men Charlton recognized as shopkeepers from the Square: the greengrocer, the chemist, the harness-maker, the manager of Highman's and little Mr. Harbottle, the complete outfitter of gents and boys. The notable absentees were Messrs. Beamish and Pope, and John Rutherford, who kept "Voslivres" and who would have run like a hare if asked to join a deputation.

"We have come to ask, Inspector," said Mr. Cooper in his best Annual General Meeting voice, "whether something cannot be done about the terrible crimes that are becoming a daily occurrence in the town. The business of these gentlemen is at a standstill and the few of my customers who have entered the Bank to-day have confessed that only the urgent need of money has persuaded them to face the dangers of the Square."

"I assure you, Mr. Cooper," Charlton answered, "that we are doing all we can and that whatever inconvenience and loss of trade you are suffering is only of a temporary nature."

"And so are my cabbages," grumbled the greengrocer.

"I know that it is a great hardship to you," Charlton went on, "but I feel sure that you will be the first to appreciate the difficulty of our position. The results of one false step by the police are incalculable. However, I am glad to say that my Superintendent has granted me special powers to deal with the situation and I hope it will not be long before your customers can walk with safety across the Square." He paused for effect, then continued:

"I know it is worse for some of you gentlemen than others——"

"Precisely so," said Mr. Cooper promptly. "It will not be very long before my Head Office——"

"If this goes on," said the chemist, "I shall be facing bankruptcy. I feel——"

"The Inspector's right," said the greengrocer. "*My* stuff doesn't keep. If I don't sell it at once——"

"Anyone 'd think you were the only one who was suffering," said the saddler hotly. "As far as I can see, it doesn't make much difference if your goods are perishable or not, if you can't sell them. In my case——"

"Take my bacon and butter," interrupted the grocer.

"Do you mean to tell me that, in a situation like this, it's no worse for me to have bacon and butter and eggs left on my hands than it is for you with your bridles and stirrup-leathers and straps and——"

"*I* sell eggs," said the greengrocer, "and *my* peas are fresh—not sold in tins."

"Tinned peas are as good as fresh ones any day," said the grocer angrily, "and while we're on the subject of eggs, I don't think a greengrocer has any right to sell——"

"The position of banks is unique," said Mr. Cooper in sedate tones. "They are the heart of commerce. If there were no banks, there would be no——"

"Iniquitous rates of interest," said the chemist sharply. "If a bank lends money, it charges five per cent., but when it borrows money from its customers, it only allows them two per——"

"A Bank Holiday," went on Mr. Cooper, regardless of this tirade, "is so called because on that day even the banks close. If customers cannot go to their banks on account of the danger to their lives, the whole social system is imperilled. They can seek elsewhere for their potatoes, their cheese and their——"

"I represent," said the manager of Highman's to Mr. Cooper, "a firm that has a large account with your Bank. If, through loss of business, our handsome balance is reduced——"

"What about the boys of Paulsfield College?" broke in Mr. Harbottle. "I am the officially appointed agent for the school caps, and if the mothers dare not bring their sons——"

"I still think that I'm in the worst position," said the greengrocer, as if delivering his last word on the topic.

Charlton looked across at the Sergeant and Martin winked. The storm centre had shifted. The disputants drifted out of the police station and carried their arguments down the High Street. Mr. Cooper, who was the last to go, said to Charlton:

"I look forward to a swift conclusion to your investigation, Inspector."

"Everything that can be done," replied Charlton, "shall be done. Good morning, sir."

Mr. Cooper ran to catch up the others, for fear they should lose sight of the singular importance of the Bank.

Martin mopped his brow with his handkerchief.

"Phew!" he said. "Wasn't I glad to see you come in. I was at my wits' end how to get rid of them. It was a bit of luck when you said it was worse for some of them than others!"

"There was no luck about it," grinned Charlton.

"If you'll forgive a certain lack of modesty, the remark was prompted by a profound knowledge of human nature."

He wagged his finger at the chuckling Sergeant.

"When you find yourself cornered, Martin, always create a diversion: and while I'm on the subject of diversion, do you know whether Arthur Ransome had a sweetheart?"

Martin shook his head.

"See if you can find out for me, will you? Mrs. Ransome told me that he was unattached, but she said that about Jack as well, and *he's* far from heart-whole. I'm beginning to wonder if Arthur had a rendezvous yesterday with a girl, although a quarter to six in the morning seems a silly time to go courting."

"Any time's a silly time to go courting," said Martin sardonically.

"Cynic!" rebuked Charlton. "By the way, I think we'll jettison those Jeffs. There are too many of them to be of any real use."

"That's good," said Martin with satisfaction. "I never did imagine there'd be anything much in that idea, if you don't mind me saying so."

"Not at all, Martin. Destructive criticism is the breath of life to me."

He tapped a cigarette on this thumb-nail.

"That third bullet," he remarked, "was of the same type as the other two."

"Wouldn't it 'ave been 'orrible if it 'adn't been," was Martin's reply and Charlton, envisaging all that it meant, nodded agreement.

★ ★ ★

Mr. Farquarson, with a panama-hat tipped over his eyes, was sitting in a deck-chair in his garden and Mrs. Grabbery took the Inspector through the house to him. The old gentleman laid down his paper and told the woman to get the Inspector a chair.

"Well," he said, as Charlton adjusted the chair to his liking and sat down, "what can I do for you this time? Have you managed to establish the identity of the man I saw on the roof yesterday?"

"It was Mr. Pope repairing his wireless aerial," Charlton replied, thinking that, in the circumstances, the truth was best.

"Very odd employment for a man of his advanced age," observed Mr. Farquarson, and then went on, as if recalling something: "Bless my heart and soul! I knew there was another thing I wanted to tell you. Some little time after we left each other yesterday, I was walking down this garden when I happened to look up towards the roofs of the shops in the Square and caught sight of another figure on the top of Mr. Pope's premises. I am quite certain that it was not Mr. Pope himself, because the figure was much broader and more solidly built than his."

"That was myself," replied Charlton, and Mr. Farquarson's "Oh!" sounded like the air leaving a punctured football.

"I have come to ask you," the Inspector went on, "what arrangements you make about cleaning the windows of the Hall."

"Cleaning the windows?" was the amazed reply.

"What a fantastic question! But I suppose the police must carry out their duties without let or hindrance from humble members of the general public. The window cleaning can be divided into two sections: the easily accessible windows that are included in the general cleaning of the building, which takes place once a week and——"

"Which day?"

"Tuesday."

"What time?"

"In the morning. The man calls for the keys at nine o'clock and returns them to me when he has completed the work."

"How long does it take?"

"It all depends. If there has been some sort of show or entertainment on the previous Saturday, it naturally takes longer than if the Hall has not been used. A congregation of persons, however tidy their individual habits——"

"Was the Hall used last Saturday?"

"No. Tomorrow week, when I return from a few days' holiday with my sister in Harrogate, we are to hold the annual——"

"How long did it take the man last Tuesday?"

"About two hours. When he had finished, he deposited the keys with Mrs. Grabbery and she made a note of the time for me, because the man is paid by the hour."

"I suppose there is no doubt that he did return the keys at eleven o'clock?"

From under the brim of his hat, Mr. Farquarson looked at Charlton fixedly for a moment or two.

"I see what you mean," he said significantly at last, then raised his voice to a shout: "Mrs. Grabbery!" The woman came out into the garden, wiping her hands on her apron.

"I wonder whether you will be kind enough to tell me, Mrs. Grabbery," said Mr. Farquarson, with immense punctilio, "at what hour the cleaner gave up the keys of the Hall last Tuesday?"

"Five to eleven," she answered, and withdrew.

"Loquacious old soul, isn't she?" chuckled her employer.

Charlton smilingly agreed and said that he believed the keys, when not in use, were kept in a drawer of Mr. Farquarson's desk.

"Is the drawer locked?" he added and the secretary shook his head.

"Who does the rest of the windows?" was the next question.

"The Downshire Window Cleaning Co. (1922), Ltd.," Mr. Farquarson conscientiously replied. "They do the outsides of the gallery windows once a fortnight—on alternate Mondays.

"When do they do the top-lights?"

"Every fourth Monday."

"Have you any idea how they clean the inside? Rather a difficult job, I should imagine."

"Frankly," admitted Mr. Farquarson, "I'm not sure. I believe—I only *believe*—that they get at them from the roof. Some of the sections can be opened from inside the Hall and I am under the impression that the men crawl through from the roof and rest a board across the wooden surround of the top-light. There are two stout iron bars that run across from left to right. I don't know whether they make use of those."

"Is there any rope kept in the Hall?"

"Yes. We need lengths of it from time to time."

"Are there any duplicates of the keys?"

"Yes. For safety's sake, another set is kept by one of the Committee. I expect you know him: Mr. Cooper, the Southern Counties Bank manager."

"I've just been talking to him. Well, Mr. Farquarson, I mustn't keep you any longer from your paper. Thanks very much for your information."

"Not at all. If you want further particulars about the window cleaning, I suggest you go and see the company. They've a branch in Taunton Street."

"I'll try them. What's the cleaner's name?"

"Frank Baggs."

XX.

The Doctor's Evidence

THE Baggs question must be finally settled: that was Charlton's decision as he climbed into his car outside Mr. Farquarson's house. The Marlings', where Baggs had clipped the hedge, was the obvious starting-point, so he drove round to the eastern side of the Common, along which ran Chesapeake Road. Number fourteen was about ten minutes' walk from the Square. He gave his name to the maid and was shown in to Mrs. Marling, who apologized for her husband not being available.

"He doesn't come in to lunch until half-past one," she explained.

"I think you can be of even greater assistance," smiled Charlton. "Do you employ a man named Frank Baggs?"

"Yes," Mrs. Marling agreed. "We have him to tidy up the garden."

"Was he working here yesterday?"

"He was here in the morning."

"Between what times?"

"He arrived about eleven and left soon after one."

"How soon after? Can you remember the exact time, Mrs. Marling? It's a rather important point."

She looked thoughtful and then said slowly:

"He had been cutting the hedge in the front garden and he brought the tools through the side gate and knocked on the kitchen door. My maid came and told me that he had finished his work and wanted to speak to me. I was rather surprised, because the maid usually gives him his money; but I went out to see him. He was very apologetic and asked whether we could see our way to increase the amount we gave him for his work. I told him that that was for my husband to decide and that, if he liked to wait, my husband would be coming home to lunch.

"Baggs asked how long that would be and I turned round—yes, it's wonderful what you can remember when you set your mind to it—I turned round and looked at the clock on the kitchen mantelpiece, which said twenty-past one. But it's always a quarter of an hour fast, so I told Baggs that my husband wouldn't be in for another five-and-twenty minutes. Baggs said he wouldn't wait, but would I please mention the matter to my husband and let him know what the decision was next time he came."

"So Baggs left here a shade after five-past one?"

"Yes."

"Had he a bicycle?"

"No. Sometimes he comes on one, but yesterday he didn't bring it."

"How do you pay him? So much a visit?"

"No. We give him tenpence an hour. My maid makes a note of the time and pays him accordingly."

"Do you always keep the kitchen clock a quarter of an hour fast?"

"*I* dont," she smiled, "but Agnes does. It seems very foolish of her, but she says it helps with her work."

"Does Baggs know that? But perhaps your maid can answer that question."

Mrs. Marling rang the bell and when the girl appeared, repeated Charlton's enquiry; but Agnes could give no definite reply. She said Baggs never queried the amount she gave him and left it to her to say how many hours he had worked. Charlton asked if it was possible for a person standing at the back door to see the clock, and Agnes said that it was.

Having thanked Mrs. Marling for her assistance, Charlton directed the car towards the Paragon, where, to the north of Effingham Street, Baggs lived with his mother and sister.

Baggs was at home and took him into the clean, but pitifully poverty-stricken, parlour. The man was clearly ill at ease.

"You said this morning, Baggs," said Charlton softly, "that at a quarter past one yesterday you were working in the front garden of number fourteen, Chesapeake Road. Why did you tell me something that wasn't true?"

"It *was* true," protested Baggs. "I was talking to Mrs. Marling, when I'd done the job, at twenty past. I know it was, 'cause the clock in the kitchen said so."

"But that clock is always kept fifteen minutes fast. I thought you knew that."

"*Me?* I never knew nothing about it. If anybody told you I did, it's a blinking lie!"

"Where did you cycle to when you left Mrs. Marling?"

"I didn't cycle. Me bike's in pieces at the moment. I walked along the side of the Common and I 'adn't got very far before the storm broke. I got all the shelter I could from it under a big gorse bush and when it blew over, I came back 'ere for me dinner."

"Did you see anybody you knew at about that time?" Baggs shook his head.

"Did you meet anybody you knew on your way back home?"

The man again shook his head.

"Most folks was indoors 'avin their dinners," he said.

"Tell me what you did with yourself last Tuesday morning, Baggs."

"Chewsday? That would be that day I clean out the 'All. At nine o'clock I got the keys from Mr. Farquarson's 'ouse—Mrs. Grabbery it was that give 'em to me—and from then till close on eleven I was busy in the 'All. Then I give the keys back to Mrs. Grabbery and came 'ome. Soon after twelve o'clock, me sister rushed out to me and said that poor old Tom—"

"You say your sister rushed out to you," interrupted Charlton. "Where were you, then?"

"In the shed at the back. I was taking down my bike."

"Had your sister been in the house since you had returned from the Hall?"

"No. She goes to Mrs. Dodge in Handen Street on Chewsdays and she'd only just got back when she came and told me."

"Was your mother in at the time?"

"She was out washing all day. Didn't get back till gone five."

"So at midday you were alone in the house?"

"That's about the size of it," admitted Baggs.

"And at a quarter to six yesterday morning. Where were you then?"

"In bedner sleep," said Baggs promptly.

"Your mother and sister were also in the house?"

"Yes. . . . Look 'ere, Inspector! I don't like the sound of all these questions. You don't suspect *me* of being mixed up in all these murders, do you? I wasn't to know that Mrs. Marling's clock was fast, was I? I didn't mean to tell you no lies this morning. I . . ."

"It is my business to question every person who is connected in any way with these three occurrences."

"Well, I'm not connected with any of them. Why pick on me?"

"You are the brother-in-law of the first victim and you were employed, until a few weeks ago, by the third victim. You have access to the Horticultural Hall."

"But I gave the keys to Mrs. Grabbery a full hour before Tom was shot. *She'll* tell you that."

"She has already done so, Baggs, but for a man who makes a part of his living by such means, there is very little difficulty in cutting duplicate keys."

Baggs looked completely dumbfounded.

"'Oo told you that?" he demanded.

"I don't suggest for a moment that you were guilty of such a breach of trust," Charlton hastened to console him. "I am merely pointing out to you your connection, as I see it, with these crimes. I have offered you the opportunity to produce an alibi, but you haven't done so."

"'Ow can I?" asked Baggs wretchedly.

"That is a question for you to answer, Baggs. I take it that your mother and sisters are both out now? . . . Well, I must see them another time."

He was late keeping his appointment with Dr. Weston, who apologized for having had to send him away earlier that day.

"That's all right, Doctor," Charlton reassured him, "although I'm very anxious to have your report on Humphries. Will he pull through?"

"No, he won't. We're doing all we can, of course, but the case is hopeless."

Charlton's face did not betray his bitter thoughts.

"I haven't had a chance," he said, "to ask you about the last two affairs. Can you give me any hints about the direction of the bullets?"

"I can tell you something a little more definite than I could about Earnshaw," the doctor replied. "I'll take that poor young devil Ransome first. He was shot, as you know, through the back and I can say quite definitely that the bullet came from a point some distance above him."

"Can you specify the distance?"

"Not with any accuracy. There were complications."

"Was the point to his left or right?"

"If anything, slightly to his left."

"He fell forward," said Charlton reflectively, "in the direction of Heather Street, which suggests that he came out of the passage and was walking straight across towards Heather Street when the Sniper brought him down. And you say that the shot came from his left?"

The doctor grunted assent.

"Can you see what that means?" There was excitement in Charlton's voice. "It means that Ransome couldn't have been shot from the roof of the Horticultural Hall."

"I thought it would interest you," said the doctor calmly.

"It does, most profoundly; and it might interest another gentleman I've just been talking to. That agrees with the opinion I was beginning to form about Humphries. If, as Johnson told me, the bullet tore his ear and then ricocheted off his head, it doesn't seem likely that the shot came from the roof of the Hall, because Humphries would have had to have his head twisted right round over his left shoulder for the bullet to take such a course."

"Perfectly right; and I think we can go still further. The bullet hit Humphries at the base of the skull, just behind the right mastoid bone, fractured the skull, then glanced off and tore his ear badly. If he had been sitting in the car in a normal position—that is, facing ahead—practically the only points from which such a wound could have been inflicted would have been *inside* the car. That, I think, is what saved his life—or, rather, deferred his death. He must have turned his head, at the moment the shot was fired, to see whether everything was clear to the near side of the car before starting off."

"We mustn't lose sight of the possibility," said Charlton, "that he had his elbow over the back seat, with the whole of his body turned to the left. That would have allowed him to be shot, in the way he was, from the roof of the Hall."

"I think not," disagreed Weston. "He wouldn't have fallen as he did. From the position in which I found him, I should think that he was sitting quite naturally in his seat and had just glanced casually round to his left when the Sniper pulled the trigger."

"That's very helpful indeed. We're gradually limiting the possibilities. I've wasted more time than I care to think about on that Hall and now it's beginning to look as if I can wipe it out entirely."

"I wish you would," said the doctor. "Those rococo abortions that our fathers built, with their passion for large chunks of conventional decoration, give me a pain."

He laughed heartily at his own joke; but suddenly his merriment stopped and he laid his hand on Charlton's shoulder.

"I'm sorry about Humphries," he said, "but there's not an earthly. The man has never regained consciousness. It's rough luck on you, old chap. I thought I was going to save him for you. For the Lord's sake don't let another happen, or you'll be for the high jump."

"Don't I know it," said Charlton feelingly.

* * *

Whether or not the Inspector's investigation and the evidence of Dr. Weston finally settled the question of Frank Baggs, there was one other matter that required Charlton's urgent attention. He had only Mrs. Archer's assurance that Humphries was the notorious Geoffrey Ibbotson and it seemed essential to verify the truth of that statement. The man had lived for ten years in Burgeston and appeared to have cut himself off from his old associations—with the exception of Mr. John Smith. That gentleman, who had appeared so fleetingly at Normanhurst, seemed to be the one who could most easily—if not most readily—confirm Mrs. Archer's suspicions. The great difficulty was, of course, to get in touch with him. Neither Miss Steward nor the other members of the staff had any idea who he was, the only available description being that he was tall and middle-aged, with a closely trimmed moustache and horn-rimmed spectacles of an unusual shape. But Charlton somehow had a feeling—call it a hunch, if you like—that Smith's visit to Normanhurst was connected, in some way, with Jack Ransome.

At about the same time as Frank Baggs had overheard Diana and Jack talking of Humphries' promise about the new book, Mr. Smith had visited the house. If Humphries had been using his influence to place the book with a London publisher, it was probable that he had got into touch with someone who had been his friend before the Stevenage divorce. However much he might concern himself with the little doings of Paulsfield and its immediate surroundings, it was hardly likely that he would risk exposure by making new friends in London. Mr. Smith was probably an old acquaintance, whose regard for Humphries had survived the disgrace of eleven years before.

So when Charlton left Dr. Weston, he went round to see Jack Ransome.

"I understood you to say yesterday," he said, "that Mr. Humphries takes a great interest in your work. Has he shown that interest in any practical way?"

"He was always ready to give me advice and I had the free run of his books and garden."

"I see your publishers are Siddons and Hancock."

"Yes, but the next one is going to be done by Gable's."

"Did Mr. Humphries arrange that for you?" Jack hesitated and then agreed.

"You are very fortunate, Mr. Ransome. I understand that Gable's are a far, far better firm than Siddons and Hancock."

"You bet they are!" said Jack. "I mustn't tell you what I think of Siddons and Hancock. I signed the agreement for the new book—it's called *Wild Life*—the other day and the terms are miles better than my old ones."

"Have you met any of Gable's people?"

"No. Mr. Humphries put the thing through for me."

"He didn't mention any of them by name or describe them to you?"

"No, I don't know them from Adam, though I hope to meet some of them soon."

"Thank you, Mr. Ransome. That is all I want to know on that subject. I've just one other question before I go: Where were you at midday last Tuesday?"

"In my room, working on my book—not *Wild Life,* but the next one."

"Were you by yourself?"

"Yes. Mother was out shopping and poor old Arthur was off on some private business."

"Yes," said Charlton with a nod, "your brother was taking photographs in the Square. Where is this room you were working in, Mr. Ransome?"

"It's my bedroom, really, but I use it as a study as well. If you look at the house from the street, it is in the top left-hand corner."

"The one with the window overlooking the corner shop in the High Street?"

"That's it. Arthur had the one on the other side of the same landing."

"Yesterday you said that at a quarter past one, you were once again working upstairs in your room. . . ." Jack moved restlessly in his chair.

"Was your mother out on that occasion also?"

"No," was the rather defiant reply, "she was not. She was lying down in her own room on the floor below. You will probably remember that she had received a terrible shock."

"I am doing my best to save her from another, Mr. Ransome," said Charlton very seriously.

"I don't understand you, Inspector," said Jack, his pale face flushing.

"Why did Miss Steward think you had tried to murder Mr. Humphries?"

"I still don't understand you."

"But she did think so, didn't she, when you spoke to her on the Burgeston road this morning?"

"This is a trick to catch me!" shouted Jack wildly.

"I'll confess that it's a trick to catch somebody, Mr. Ransome, but not necessarily you. Was it because on one occasion about six weeks ago you told her that you would"—he paused—"murder the swine?"

Jack looked in wonder at him.

"What *are* you?" he asked.

"A hard-worked and very harassed Inspector of Police,"

explained Charlton with a twinkle in his eye.

If this boy was responsible for those three crimes, he decided, he would forswear smoking, which was unthinkable.

"I think you're a blasted magician!" said Jack frankly; and smiled. "What you suggest is absolutely true. You know what women are like, don't you?"

Charlton sagely nodded his head.

"That is why I am still celibate," he said.

"When Diana heard that Mr. Humphries had been shot, she immediately leapt to the conclusion that I'd done it. It didn't matter that Earnshaw and my own brother had been shot first. I had threatened to kill Mr. Humphries and that was good enough for her. Of course, when I said I'd kill him (and I don't know how you found out. I'm quite sure Diana didn't tell you) I didn't really mean it literally. It was. . . ."

"'Full of sound and fury, signifying nothing'?"

"That's it. I was frightfully jealous of Mr. Humphries. Anyway, Diana was a bit difficult yesterday afternoon. I couldn't make out quite what was wrong with her. This morning she rang me up, said she had something very important to tell me and would I cycle out to meet her on the Burgeston road. I had a hell of a game to convince her that there was nothing in her suspicions—and that's about all there is to it. She told me that you police have decided to search this house for the gun and I, for one, shall be delighted if you do."

"Where on earth did Miss Steward pick up that yarn?" asked Charlton incredulously.

"She said some newspaper reporter told her."

"That accounts for it! Well, thank you for being so frank. It's so much better to get these things off your chest."

"Are you really going to get a warrant to search here?"

"If the need arises, Mr. Ransome, I shall search every house in Paulsfield. What was your father's Christian name?"

"James Manville Ransome. Why?"

"I just wondered."

XXI.

A Gentleman's Strange Behaviour

THE Sergeant stood in the doorway of the police station and from his expression Charlton judged that his thoughts were far away.

"How now, good Master Martin," he said. "Wherefore the pensive mien? Thinking, as has been said, is but an idle waste of thought, and nought is every thing and every thing is nought."

Martin removed his gaze from the empyrean.

"I was wondering what I'd do," he said, "if my missus or young Ted was next."

"If you'll take my advice," said Charlton as they went inside, "you'll stop being morbid. The only thing you've got to do is keep them well away from the Square."

"'Ow do I know that'll do any good? A pistol's not like a machine-gun. You can carry it about in your pocket."

"Not very easily. A Parabellum's nearly nine inches long and weighs a good two pounds when it's loaded."

"Well," persevered Martin, "you could 'ide it under your mack or put it in an attachy case. What's to stop this murdering devil from prowling about the Common? How do we know that 'e doesn't go out of a night and snoop round looking for someone to kill? Ted plays with the other kids on the Common. Why mightn t 'e be shot, same as young Ransome?"

"We'd soon get him if he tried that game."

"That wouldn't be much satisfaction to me, would it?" demanded Martin.

"People like you and me, Martin," said Charlton musingly, "who earn our bread and butter by preventing it, are likely to come to regard crime impersonally. It is all in the day's work and doesn't affect us very deeply, until we suddenly discover that, as well as being cogs in the machinery of justice, we are also citizen Harry Charlton and citizen Jack Martin."

"Bert," said the Sergeant coyly.

"Spare me your ghastly secrets!" said Charlton with a shudder. "We get case-hardened, cynical, callous, insensible, like a small boy who commits mayhem against a daddy-long-legs because it doesn't really seem to mind. What was it Kipling said about losing the common touch?"

"'East is East and West is West,'" said Martin helpfully.

"But that is by the way," said Charlton more briskly. "I saw the Super this morning and put the whole thing in front of him. I got his authority to do what I think fit."

His voice sank to a confidential murmur.

"I've arranged relays of watchers in the church tower and that roadmenders' shelter during the hours of daylight—it's no good their being there after dark."

"They might see the flash," suggested Martin.

"If their unblinking eyes were fixed every second of the night on the suspected buildings, they undoubtedly would, but I'm gambling against such inhuman concentration. Apart from that, I doubt if the Sniper will try any tricks when the light's not good enough. Even in the hands of an expert, a pistol is a fickle weapon."

"What if 'e goes wandering about the streets and gets close enough to someone for a baby in arms not to miss?"

"That I have also provided for. I've drawn on the available strength at Lulverton and every person who could possibly be concerned in those shootings has now a faithful shadow lurking near, dogging his every step by night and keeping a watchful eye on his comings and goings by day."

"I *thought* the town was getting a bit crowded," chuckled Martin, "and that one or two friendly faces were kicking their 'eels—in a manner of speaking—at street corners, as if they were waiting either for the end of the world or the pubs to open. Young Emerson 'as been fussing round all the morning like a bloke organizing a charity bazaar. Not," he added handsomely, "that anybody but me would 'ave noticed it."

"I've also managed to convey to certain people that their houses are likely to be searched and it's possible that that will make somebody break cover. Who takes over from you to-night?"

"Harwood."

"Right. I'll call in for news on my way back home from London. I'm driving up this afternoon to see some publishers."

"Really?" said Martin, intrigued. "Going to write your reminiscences?"

Charlton shook his head.

"I'm trying my hand at a thriller," he said, "with an amateur detective hero who is *persona grata* at Scotland Yard and who drops a final 'g' every time he picks up a clue. I'm going to have a Detective-inspector who is stolid and unemotional, without a scrap of humour or imagination, and a Police-sergeant who is a figure of fun—'an ordinary fool that has no more brain than a stone.' And, as film rights are more profitable than book royalties, my first consideration shall be not to write a good book, but to write a book that will make a good film—a story that is full of incident and situation, and free from such idle, plot-retarding chatter as you and I are now engaged upon."

"Leave me out," grinned Martin. "You're doing all the talking."

"I always do," said Charlton mournfully. "As Who-was-it said about What's-his-name, I become inebriated with the exuberance of my own verbosity. But jesting apart, I want to make sure that Humphries is really Geoffrey Ibbotson. I don't think it really affects the issue, but I want to settle the point."

Paulsfield was over fifty miles from London and the afternoon was well advanced before Charlton drove down Ludgate Hill into Fleet Street, in a side street off which were the offices of Gable, Ltd. He handed the girl a card that described him perfectly truthfully as Mr. Henry Charlton, of Holmedene, Northern Avenue, Southmouth-by-the-Sea, and said that he was anxious to get in touch with a gentleman whose name he had forgotten and whom he believed to be connected with her firm.

"He's tall and middle-aged," he added, "with a small moustache, and used to wear octagonal horn-rimmed spectacles."

"That'll be Mr. Smith," said the girl without hesitation. "Mr. John Munro Smith, one of the junior partners."

Charlton hid his discomfiture and asked if he could speak to Mr. Smith. The girl took away the card, returned in a few moments and asked him to follow her. Mr. Smith rose from his desk as Charlton was shown into the room.

"Good afternoon, Mr. Charlton," he said with a pleasant smile. "What can I do for you?"

"That is my private card," Charlton explained. "I am a police-inspector."

Mr. Smith raised his eyebrows and played with the card in his hand, waiting for Charlton to continue.

"I think you are going to publish a book entitled *Wild Life,* by a young man called John Ransome?"

"That is so."

"And that the book was brought to your notice by a Mr. Anthony Humphries of Paulsfield in Downshire?"

"Quite."

"Do you know Mr. Humphries well?"

"Yes, our friendship is of some years' standing. I was horrified to read in the paper that he was badly wounded yesterday. How is he, do you know?"

"His condition is very grave, but he is still alive."

"Have you any idea who did it? Personally, I can't really see why anyone should want to shoot the poor chap."

"I am looking into the case now, Mr. Smith, and that is why I have driven up to see *you.*"

"I'm afraid I can help you very little, Inspector. The last time I saw Humphries was about six weeks ago."

"You went to see him, I believe, at his house just outside Paulsfield?"

"Yes," agreed Mr. Smith. "It was actually on the question of *Wild Life* that I went down."

"Probably to be introduced to Mr. John Ransome?"

"No. As a matter of fact, I didn't meet him. I had some tea with Humphries and his secretary, and then Humphries and I went into his study to discuss the question of the book."

"It's funny that Mr. Humphries didn't say anything about it afterwards to Mr. Ransome."

"I think," smiled Smith, "that Humphries is one who likes to do good by stealth. I agreed with him that afternoon that I would get my co-directors to consider the book and when it had been decided to publish it, we wrote direct to Mr. Ransome, stating our terms."

"When was that letter sent?"

"About a fortnight ago. I will have the exact date looked up for you."

"Don't bother," said Charlton, as Smith reached for the bell-push on his desk. "How long have you known Mr. Humphries?"

"More years than I care to think about," said the other with a smile.

"Did you know him before 1925?"

Mr. Smith looked doubtful.

"That was the year," said Charlton, as if to aid the publisher's memory, "when Sir Waldo Stevenage divorced his wife."

"I am more likely to remember it," said Smith with an easy laugh, "as the year when the Oxford boat was swamped! Yes, I knew Humphries some time before that."

"Then you can probably tell me where he lived before he moved to Paulsfield. We are in the difficult position of not being able to communicate with his relations, as we can find no trace of them."

"There you've stumped me! I know nothing of Humphries' family affairs. As to where he used to live, I believe it was somewhere in the Hampstead neighbourhood."

"Did you and he go to the same school?"

"Good heavens, Inspector! That's harking back a bit, isn't it? No, we didn't."

"I understand that he was nicknamed 'Geoff' at the school you both attended."

Smith looked frankly puzzled: then his face cleared. "I see what you're getting at," he said. "When I was down with Humphries, he told his secretary—a pretty, pleasant little girl, whose name I forget—that we used to call him 'Geoff' at school. He only meant it as a joke, of course."

"How did the question arise?"

"I had happened to call him 'Geoff' in the course of conversation."

"Had you any particular reason?"

"It was just a nickname, used, at one time, by his business friends."

"Is that also meant as a joke, Mr. Smith?" asked Charlton quietly.

"I don't follow you."

"I suggest that 'Geoff' was not a nickname Humphries had at school or later among his business associates, but a diminutive of the name decided upon by his parents and given to him at his christening."

He leant forward suddenly in his chair.

"Let us come to the point, Mr. Smith. Is Humphries Geoffrey Ibbotson?"

Smith was silent.

"I already have proof," went on Charlton mendaciously.

"I merely want your confirmation."

"Yes, he is."

"Good."

"I am the only person whose friendship he kept after that ghastly divorce case and although I haven't seen him for years—except on the occasion we've mentioned—we have written to each other from time to time. I'm not trying to defend his behaviour in that Stevenage affair, but I think he was disgracefully treated afterwards. Hounded out is the only way to put it. I gave him my word, just before he went off to bury himself in the country, that I would keep his hiding-place and new name to myself; but now I think I'm justified in breaking my promise."

"I think you are, too."

"But is there any need for the truth to go further than you police people? Poor old Geoffrey has made himself a new life and it doesn't seem fair to—"

"The real facts will have to come out at the inquest," interjected Charlton.

"*Inquest?*" asked Smith sharply. "Is it as bad as that?"

"He's dying."

They were both silent for a while. At length Smith said:

"As it's your job to find out who shot him, I suppose you're anxious to know whether the blow was aimed at Anthony Humphries or Geoffrey Ibbotson?" Charlton maintained a discreet silence.

"Personally," Smith went on, "I should say Humphries. Ibbotson 'died'—if I may use the word—a long time ago and the only connection between him and his old life is myself. Nobody else knew where Ibbotson went—and I don't expect anybody cared very much. The public memory is very short. That's what I told him at the time, but he said he couldn't face it any longer."

He sighed regretfully.

"Now, I suppose, the papers will dish up the Stevenage divorce case again and make a front page story out of the shooting of the mysterious Mr. Humphries."

"I'm afraid so," said Charlton and rose to go.

As he swung the car into Fleet Street, he decided that a hard-working policeman must have a little relaxation sometimes and drove towards Oxford Circus and the Palladium. He arrived in time for the first house and managed, for a couple of hours, to thrust the Sniper out of his mind. By a quarter past nine he had crossed the Thames by Waterloo Bridge and was making his leisurely way homeward.

But before he got to Paulsfield, odd things began to happen there.

★ ★ ★

Young Detective-constable Hartley was getting bored. He had received instructions to keep an eye on things in the Square, which at that hour of the night, in a town where most people went early to bed, was something of a sinecure. Carr and Houseman were watching the back of the block; and if any of the residents took a walk, it was Hartley's duty to follow. He yawned widely and looked at his watch. Eleven-fifteen. A good many hours yet before he would be relieved. It wasn't what you might call an interesting job, standing in a gloomy doorway, not daring to smoke and waiting for something to happen, when you felt quite certain that nothing would. Madge was probably in bed and asleep by then. What would she say about this night duty when they were married? Most likely wouldn't be too keen . . . They'd fixed up to go to the "Majestic" when he got roped in for this business. Rotten to have to put her off. Not the first time, either. But duty came first—not that it was any good telling a girl that. You'd only to drop a hint that, if it was all the same to her, you wouldn't see each other next Tuesday evening, as you'd done every Tuesday and Friday and Saturday and Sunday, work permitting, for the last three years, because you wanted to stay at home and mug up Principles of Local Government or Evidence and Procedure—you only had to do that and she immediately got it into her dear, silly little head that you didn't love her any more and the fat was properly in the fire and in the end you saw her on Tuesday at the usual place, after all . . . The old moon looked good. Just like a face with the mouth going Oh, when you came to look at it carefully . . . Wonder if there was anybody living on it . . . Wonder what sort of house Madge would like to live in. They'd have to get one that was easy to look after. She didn't get much practice at that kind of thing, being in the shop all day . . . What wouldn't he give for a cigarette. Was it worth the risk? No, it was *not* . . . Hullo! Somebody was coming out. That was better!

He waited in his hiding-place until the reliever of his boredom had gone some distance up the High Street and then followed in his rubber-soled shoes. With thirty yards between them, they went along the High Street and turned to the right by the "Queen's Head" into the road that led them to Paulsfield Common. Across the middle of the Common ran a road from east to west and the quarry, who was carrying what looked to Hartley like a brown-paper parcel, turned into it. Half-way across the Common and some fifty yards from the road was a stretch of water that was known locally by the flattering title of the lake. Hartley saw his prey leave the road and take to the roughly formed path between the gorse bushes. The detective hurried silently along the path and, as he reached the last bush before the cleared space around the lake, saw in the moonlight a figure standing by the water's edge. The right arm swung forward and something hit the water and sank about eight yards from the bank.

Hartley had just time to hide behind the bush before the other turned and came back towards the path. He lingered a few moments and then again took up the trail, which led, after they had reached the road, not back the way they had come, but in the other direction towards the western border of the Common, along which ran the main London road. After

Hartley had turned to the left, which would lead him back to the town, a car pulled up by his side and he heard Inspector Charlton's voice say:

"What are you doing here, Hartley?"

The detective pointed to the figure passing under a street lamp some little distance ahead and rapidly explained the position.

"Jump in," said Charlton. He caught up the walker, stopped a few yards in advance, jumped out and strolled back.

"Good evening, Mr. Pope," he said.

"Good evening, Inspector," the old tobacconist courteously responded. "You quite startled me!"

Charlton suggested that he should drive Mr. Pope back to the Square.

"Really no," protested Mr. Pope. "It is very kind of you, but it is but a step and I only came out for the walk."

"As a matter of fact, I rather want to have a chat with you, if it's not too late. Can you spare me five minutes at the police station? We can talk in comfort there."

"If that is the case," Mr. Pope replied, "by all means let me drive back with you."

When they arrived at the police station, Hartley quietly disappeared and Charlton took Mr. Pope into the back office.

"I am delighted to report," said Mr. Pope as he sat down, "a marked improvement in the reception of my wireless set. Everything that the makers of the aerial claimed in their advertisement is true and I can now hear perfectly without straining."

"I'm glad of that."

"I was listening earlier this evening to an hour of Debussy's music and the piano might have been in the same room."

"That's good. What was it you threw in the lake just now, Mr. Pope?"

The agreeable smile disappeared from the tobacconist's face.

"The lake?" he said vaguely.

"The stretch of water on the Common," said Charlton, making it clearer. "You left your shop a few minutes after eleven-fifteen and made your way to the lake, in which you threw a paper package. What was in the package?"

"Oh, yes," said Mr. Pope, as if recalling an event in his boyhood, "I took the package out with me and, as my walk took me near to the lake, I left the road and deposited the package in the lake. I thought that was the safest place for it."

"What was in it?" asked Charlton with great patience. "What was in it?" repeated Mr. Pope. "Oh, I see what you mean. What was in the package? Safety-razor blades. It is always a great problem to know what to do with them, is it not? They gradually accumulate and one hesitates to throw them into the dust-bin for fear of injuring those who take away the refuse, and if you bury them in the garden, they are a constant source of danger to cats when they are digging, as those strange, secretive creatures make a regular habit of doing.

"I remember once reading a highly entertaining article by the late William Caine on this topic and he chose the same method as I have. He threw them in a pond on Hampstead Heath and a friend who was with him said he had thousands at home in a locked box. Then Caine said that, if his friend had thousands in a locked box, he himself had millions under the water of the Vale of Health pond. *Most* amusing."

Charlton did not agree.

"But don't you use an ordinary razor?" he asked.

"Why do you suggest that, Inspector?"

"I remember seeing two of them on your wash-stand yesterday."

"It's very odd that you should have noticed them," smiled Mr. Pope. "It is only recently that I have taken to them again. Many years ago, of course, I used to use what is vulgarly called a 'cut-throat' and then, when the safety type of razor was introduced, I bought one. But a week or two ago I suddenly took it into my head to go back to my old friends, and it was

210

that that prompted me to clear out my large collection of used blades."

"Well," smiled Charlton, "you'll never see them again. After life's fitful fever, they sleep well—in the mud at the bottom of Paulsfield lake."

"Where," said Mr. Pope with a little thankful sigh, "they can lie to rust away, safely and undisturbed."

"You're telling me?" said Charlton, but not aloud.

XXII.

Aunt Sally

BEFORE he went home to bed, Charlton had a word with Hartley.

"Did you make a note," he asked, "of the exact spot where that package hit the water?"

"Yes, sir. It was about seven or eight yards from the bank and I can show you just where the man was standing when he threw it."

"We must get it out. Wait until five o'clock and then go and knock up one of the Common keepers—Harwood will tell you where they live—and go with him to the lake. I shall be back here again at five-thirty and you can pass the package over to me then."

"Right, sir."

"Before I met you to-night, I had decided on a plan. If we discover what we are looking for in that parcel, I needn't make my little experiment, but I'll be here at half-past five, in case we don't."

"And if I can't find the parcel, sir?"

"Don't be ridiculous, Hartley."

At half-past five on the Saturday morning, Charlton drew up outside Paulsfield police station. Hartley was waiting for him inside, with an expression of restrained triumph on his face. Lying on Martin's desk, on several thicknesses of newspaper, was a wet parcel.

"Splendid!" said the Inspector and walked over to it. "Would you say there were razor-blades in that, Hartley?"

"No, sir."

"Neither would I."

He cut the string and pulled away the sodden paper from a brown leather holster. Hartley was a rapt observer. Inside the holster was a pistol, which Charlton extracted—and startled Hartley with a burst of laughter.

"I don't think this will interfere with our experiment!" he said, and passed over to Hartley a very old Colt revolver, coated with the rust of years. It was unloaded and the cylinder revolved reluctantly.

"Razor-blades would have been far more dangerous weapons than that museum piece," he laughed. "Old Pope need not have been so anxious to get rid of it."

"It seems to free *him* of suspicion," ventured Hartley.

"Not if he saw you watching the house and knew that you would follow him to the lake."

"I don't get that, sir," Hartley confessed.

"For ways that are dark, and for tricks that are vain, Hartley, the Heathen Chinee is not nearly so peculiar as a Christian Englishman turned criminal. You have just said that Mr. Pope's behaviour of last night frees him of suspicion. Might it not be, Hartley, that Mr. Pope had that thought in mind when he set out last night to dispose of an ancient relic that no sane person would associate with those shootings? Isn't it a good plan to make the innocent action of a guilty person look like the guilty action of an innocent person?"

He lighted a cigarette, while Hartley thought that out. "Now for my little stratagem," he went on, "in which I shall need your asistance. You know the situation, I think? Someone in that block to the north of the Square, or in one of the adjoining buildings, has already killed two men and seriously wounded another. The only satisfactory way to clear the whole thing up is to catch that someone at it again. I passed on instructions via Harwood to the men now watching from the church tower and the roadmenders' shelter and they're both there with their guns ready—not to kill the killer, but to take his mind off his job just long enough for the stool-pigeon to save his own skin."

"And you want me to be . . . ?" began Hartley diffidently.

"Oh, no," Charlton reassured him. "I have reserved that important rôle for myself. Your job will be to wait just round the corner, ready to pick up the pieces."

"But you might get killed," said Hartley.

"I very much doubt it," Charlton replied and rather wished that he did. "What was it Spenser said in the *Faerie Queene?* 'Be bolde, Be bolde, and everywhere Be bolde.'"

"And didn't Shakespeare say," riposted Hartley, not to be outdone, "that the better part of valour is discretion?"

Charlton laughed gaily.

"He put those words in the mouth of a cowardly old rapscallion, who called himself 'plump Jack.' We, Hartley, are neither plump nor cowardly—well, not plump, anyway!"

Five minutes later, he walked down the High Street and turned the corner into Effingham Street. In the church tower and the shelter, two sharp-eyed men watched the windows and roofs of the suspected buildings; and in the doorway of the Post Office lurked Hartley. The sun was not very high in the sky and the crisp, clean air made sudden death seem preposterous. Murder and criminal homicide were for the dark hours, in foggy November streets or shadowy corners, not for blue skies and the early morning peace of a sleepy little market-town in rural England.

Charlton swung into the passage and broke into a cheerful whistle, not because he was moved to jauntiness, but because he thought that his version of Beethoven's Minuet would prepare the Sniper for his arrival. In the passage he felt safe enough, but when, still whistling, he left the shelter of Beamish's shop and the Hall behind and walked across towards Heather Street, he began to feel uncomfortable and the Minuet did not come so tunefully from his lips.

At the point where the whistle had died with Arthur Ransome as the bullet got the boy through the back, Charlton paused and took his cigarette case from his jacket pocket. No sound broke the silence and when he tapped the cigarette on the case before lighting it, it seemed to him like a cannonade. As he threw away the match and started to walk forward again, with a most unpleasant feeling between his shoulder blades, he glanced first at the shelter and then at the church tower and fervently hoped that his men were alert and ready to shoot before the Sniper could take aim.

Heather Street seemed a long way off. He stopped again, to give the Sniper every chance, but no explosion came. Then, when he had gone a dozen more paces nearer safety, he heard the last thing he expected to hear.

A voice shouted, "Hi!"

He paused, looked round and saw in the entrance to the passage a familiar figure in an overcoat and boxer hat.

It was Mr. Farquarson and he was carrying his neatly rolled umbrella and a paper bag. He emerged from the passage and walked across the Square towards Charlton, who anxiously tried to wave him back into the passage.

"What's the trouble?" the secretary shouted in a stentorian voice. "Somebody else been murdered?"

Blithely swinging his umbrella, he approached the Inspector, who was cautiously scanning the windows and roofs, which showed no sign of human movement.

"The top of the morning to you, Inspector," cried Mr. Farquarson gaily. "It's a treat to be alive!"

"You're right!" was the heartfelt response. "Let's get to somewhere safer."

"Safer?" asked Mr. Farquarson, as he fell into step with Charlton, who had started back towards the Post Office.

"Don't you remember what happened at this time yesterday morning, Mr. Farquarson?"

"Poor young Arthur Ransome was killed," the secretary readily answered. "But surely you don't imagine they'd try to shoot a funny old fellow like me? My dear Inspector, it's unthinkable. What would happen to the Horticultural Society without my guiding hand?"

"If you insist upon walking about the empty Square in that careless way," said Charlton, "you will soon enable me to answer that question."

They passed the doorway of the Post Office, from which the discreet Hartley had vanished, and turned into the High Street.

"You're up early this morning," observed the Inspector.

"I'm always up early," retorted Mr. Farquarson. "It is, without a shadow of doubt, the best time of the day. I should like to rise every morning at dawn, have my breakfast at eight o'clock and then go back to bed again until the next daybreak. Unlike many convivial gentlemen, I go in the opposite direction to the milk. I'm off now to pay a call on Mr. and Mrs. Drake."

"Rather an unconventional hour for visiting," said Charlton, frankly deceived.

"To the contrary," said Mr. Farquarson. "Ducks are notoriously early risers."

The laugh that followed made Charlton look uneasily round, for fear some roused sleeper might throw something.

They parted at the police station and Mr. Farquarson went busily off towards the Common with his umbrella and his bag of bread. Hartley was inside the station, talking to P. C. Harwood. They both looked at Charlton when he came in.

"A melancholy failure, Hartley," he said with a regretful smile.

"I nearly jumped out of my skin," Hartley admitted, "when that old gentleman yelled out like that. I was all keyed up for a shot, but I didn't expect somebody to shout, 'Hi!'"

"Neither did I. Now you'd better go home and get some sleep, Hartley. I shan't want you any more to-day."

"Or to-night?" asked Hartley hopefully.

"No. You'll be able to take her out this evening." Hartley blushed violently and once again faded away. When Sergeant

Martin arrived later, he told Charlton that he had picked up some information the previous evening, and they went together into the private office.

"Somebody told me—no names, no pack-drill—that young Arthur Ransome 'ad a donah," he said. "You remember telling me to find out?"

"What's her name and where does she live?" asked Charlton, immediately interested.

"Noreen Prentice, Dunrovin, Talbot Road. That's a turning out of Heather Street, down at the other end from the Square. Father's a retired business man and Noreen's the only child. Pretty little thing and high-spirited. The old lady's a bit of a battle-cruiser and a big church-worker. Life and soul of the Mothers' Outing."

"Mrs. Ransome knew nothing of it. What about the Prentices?"

"That's what I don't know, but it's likely they didn't. Mrs. Ransome's one of them *sweet* old ladies, with a face like an angel with the stomach ache and a mind so narrow that you couldn't get a fag-paper between the sides of it. *She* wouldn't 'ave the lads going out with the girls, like ordinary lads should. *She* wanted them to stay with their poor widowed mother. You know the kind of thing I mean: 'I've scraped and saved and worked my fingers to the bone for you boys and now all the thanks I get . . .' and so on, until the poor little beggars go and marry a barmaid or, what's twenty times as bad, wrap themselves up inside themselves like a wood-louse and read Paul de Kock in the coal-shed."

Martin was getting quite heated.

"Have *you* never read Paul de Kock in the coal-shed, Martin?" asked Charlton mischievously.

"You bet I have!" admitted Martin openly. "But I didn't let it prey on my mind. As a matter of fact, I always found that sort of thing a bit monot'nous. Where was I? Oh yes: with the old girl that sort, I don't expect young Arthur made 'imself too prominent at Dunrovin. People would've talked if 'e 'ad and it would've got back to 'er ladyship. They more likely did it on the q.t.—clan-what's-it's-name."

"Do you think they'd fix a meeting so early in the day as five-forty-five?"

"I'd think anything if it's two young people in love."

"I'll go round and see the girl."

Martin pursed his lips with his fingers.

"You know best, of course," he said, "but I'm not so sure that it would be quite the thing. It might not do the poor kid any good at home if you told Mrs. P. that you were a Police-inspector and wanted a word with 'er daughter about Arthur Ransome."

"You're a good, thoughtful chap, Martin," said Charlton, "and perfectly right. What do you suggest?"

"Get Miss Molly to ring 'er up. They're on the 'phone. Number 297. If anyone else answers it, they won't 'ave any suspicions, it being a girl's voice at the other end."

Charlton looked at the Sergeant admiringly.

"You display," he said, "an unexpected talent for intrigue. Where did you learn it?"

"Night school," answered Martin with a grin, "but don't breathe a word to the missus. You can ask Miss Molly to say that she wants to 'ave a talk with Noreen on a private matter and will she meet 'er at such-and-such a tea-shop in Lulverton. The girl can get the bus there and you can drop in and join the party. That's, of course, if Miss Molly doesn't mind. Don't tell 'er," he added hurriedly, "that it was my idea."

"We can easily find out what she thinks," said Charlton and pulled the telephone towards him; but he paused before he lifted the receiver. "I was forgetting," he smiled, "that it is still indecently early. I'll give the young woman time to have her breakfast in peace."

He waited until eight o'clock before he rang Molly.

"Hullo, my dear!" he said cheerily. "Sorry to leave you so betimes this morning, but duty's clarion call sounded. Martin has suggested to me ..."

The Sergeant hopped up and down and waved wild signals.

". . . that you should fine me half-a-crown every time I disorganize your household arrangements. Just a moment. Martin wants to speak to me. What is it, Martin?"

"There was a wasp buzzing round you," was Martin's manful lie. "It's gone now."

Molly was delighted to fall in with her uncle's plan, and he arranged for her to try to fix an appointment with Noreen Prentice for eleven o'clock at a particular café in Lulverton.

"All expenses paid?" asked Molly.

"Anything up to fourpence, my dear," he replied and rang off.

When the tobacconist had opened his shop, Charlton went round to see him.

"About those razor-blades, Mr. Pope," he said without preamble. Mr. Pope sighed in resignation.

"I had hoped," he said, "that that particular matter was closed. What more can I tell you than I have already told you?"

"Something rather important."

"And what is that?"

"The truth."

"I fail to understand you, Inspector. I wished to dispose of those razor-blades and chose—"

"Mr. Pope," said Charlton stingingly, "I have treated you from the beginning of this case with the utmost consideration. All I ask in return is that you give me correct answers to my questions. Last night I asked you to tell me what was in the package that you threw into the lake. Your answer was that it contained old razor-blades. I will put the question again: *What was in that package?*"

Mr. Pope looked vastly unhappy and Charlton's heart went out to him. Then he said, after an apprehensive gulp: "A revolver."

"A Colt, with 'C.P.' carved on the stock?"

"Yes . . . But how did you know?"

"It has been removed from the lake. You acted rather unwisely, Mr. Pope."

"I thought it was for the best," the old man replied. "I heard quite by accident that a house on this side of the Square was to be searched for firearms and feared that it might be this one. So I took the first opportunity to rid myself of a weapon that might incriminate me. It is only a curiosity and I have never had any ammunition for it. I have only kept it because my father, under Sir Garnet Wolseley, used it with some distinction at Tel-el-Kebir in the Egyptian campaign of 1882. It was he who carved his initials on the stock."

Charlton's expression suggested greater annoyance than he actually felt. He wished Mr. Pope an abrupt good day and left the shop. If the old gentleman had seen his smile as he walked round into the High Street, he might not have felt so utterly miserable.

★ ★ ★

Charlton strolled into the Lulverton tea-shop and looked round. The place was fairly full, but he caught sight of the two girls over in a far corner. They were chatting gaily, as if they had known each other for years. Molly *had* that faculty. She glanced towards the door and smiled at Charlton, who picked his way, through a tangle of dog-leads, to their table.

"Good morning, Uncle Harry," she said, then turning to Noreen, "This is my uncle, Inspector Charlton—and he's not nearly so ferocious as you'd think."

Noreen Prentice smiled. She was a doll-like little thing, with fair, fluffy hair, large blue eyes that seemed for ever wide with delighted surprise and a mouth that must surely have been made for saying, "Goody-goody!" Charlton decided that she was still in her 'teens and that however deep her grief had been at Arthur Ransome's death, her mind was too volatile to brood for long on the tragedy. Life for her was just one gorgeous picnic and although the wasps and flies were bothersome at times, she soon forgot them. She was not heartless, but she lacked the flair for sustained unhappiness.

"Good morning, Inspector," she said. "I've just been hearing all about you and I've been simply dying to meet you." When he had hung up his hat on a peg and sat down, he glanced at Molly and she nodded slightly. That meant that Noreen knew why she had been invited to Lulverton. He did not, however, immediately broach the subject: Miss Prentice had, first of all, to be studied and appraised. She was more than a pawn in the game that he was trying to win, because on her evidence depended one of the most vital questions of his investigation: was the Sniper sane or mad? If he were sane, Charlton reasoned, there would be a matter-of-fact motive, or even motives, behind the crimes; but if he were mad, there would be no traceable motive and a large proportion of Charlton's work, particularly in connection with Humphries' past life, would be completely wasted. Actually, if one may speak parenthetically, there *was* a traceable motive and it depended on the third victim being not Anthony Humphries, the rival of Jack Ransome for Diana Steward's favours, but Geoffrey Ibbotson, the co-respondent in the Stevenage divorce.

After five minutes' small-talk, Charlton said:

"I think you know, Miss Prentice, why we have asked you to come here to-day?"

A shadow passed over Noreen's vivacious little face.

"Yes," she said, "it's about poor Arthur."

"I want to ask you about only one thing: Did you have an appointment with him early on Thursday morning?"

Noreen nodded and her eyes filled with tears.

"We thought it was going to be such fun," she said with a catch in her voice. "We couldn't often see each other, because Mums is dead against me having boy friends; but at a dance last Saturday night, we fixed up a special private meeting at the bottom of our garden, which you can get at from the road by a little passage-way. We sometimes used to talk over the wall, where we couldn't be seen from the house, and on Thursday morning—we arranged it well in advance, so that we could look forward to it—on Thursday morning I was waiting there ever so long for him to come. Then I got quite cross with him and crept indoors and back to bed, without knowing that . . . he'd . . . just . . . been ..."

Charlton left her to Molly for a while.

"Have you ever fixed a meeting at that time before?" he asked gently when Noreen was more controlled.

"Never," she said with a vehement shake of her head.

"Did you tell anybody about this one?"

"I didn't breathe a word to a soul and I haven't said anything about it since."

"Is it likely that you were overheard when you arranged it at the dance?"

"I don't think we could *possibly* have been. We were dancing together and Arthur whispered in my ear."

"Do you know of anybody he himself might have mentioned it to?"

"There's nobody in the world he would have told. It was our own secret and to let anybody into it would have ruined it."

At a glance from her uncle, Molly guided the conversation to brighter things. Then Charlton saw Noreen on to the Paulsfield bus and came back to Molly.

"Thank you, my dear," he said. "That's proved one thing."

"What's that?"

"The Sniper is mad."

XXIII.

Species Four

ONE thing, as has frequently been said, leads to another.
Acting on instructions received from Superintendent
Kingsley, Charlton swore an information at the Petty Sessional
Court on the following Monday morning and obtained
a warrant to search Beamish's, Pope's and Muttigen's. He
purposely excluded the Ransomes' house, because he no
longer regarded it with any suspicion. With the blue sheet
in his wallet, he called in at Paulsfield police station to see
Martin. It was fortunate, in a way, that he did.

"I'm glad you came in, sir," said the Sergeant. "The Super
was on the 'phone ten minutes ago and he said not to execute
that warrant."

Charlton raised his eyebrows.

"Not till 'e gives you the word, anyway. If you ask me, I
should think there's been a bit of a rumpus and the Super's got
the wind up. He says you're to report to him and 'e'll explain
the position. Probably a bit too fruity for the innocent ears of
yours truly."

Superintendent Kingsley's manner was no less irritable than
when Charlton had seen him last. The poor man was having
a worrying time.

"Have you applied for that Paulsfield warrant?" he asked.

"Yes, sir, but Sergeant Martin tells me that you don't want
it executed."

"Not yet, at any rate. There's been some bother, Charlton.
Inspector Meadows took out a warrant to search a house in
Wantage Road, just round the corner, but the only things he
could find being printed were billheads, visiting cards and

concert programmes. Not even," he smiled bitterly, "anything about Little Audrey."

This, be it added, was at the time when the scurrilous adventures of that laughing maiden were on everybody's lips.

"Meadows said he was dead sure these things"—he picked up by one corner a grimy, much-folded sheet of paper— "which have been flooding the neighbourhood, emanated from that house and now we're having trouble with the mother and father of the young chap Meadows suspected. They're kicking up the devil's own fuss: defamation of character, damaged reputations, injured feelings and all that clutter. So until that dies down, I'm not looking for any more unpleasantness. I know murder's a more serious offence than printing this muck. . . ."

He ran his eye over the sheet with a disgusted curl of his lip.

"That line doesn't scan," he said. "Listen to this."

He read the first few stanzas aloud, beating the rhythm with his hand.

"There, that's wrong, isn't it? If they'd put 'mournfully' instead of 'sadly' it would have made all the difference."

"Or 'disconsolately'," suggested Charlton, falling in with the spirit of the thing.

"That's it!" said the Super enthusiastically. "'Disconsolately dumti–dumti–dum.'"

He coughed.

"As I was saying, murder's a more serious offence than printing this stuff, but see whether you can't put yourself in a stronger position before you execute that warrant. Which premises does it cover—the four you mentioned the other day?"

"Only three of them, sir. I've discarded any idea of the Ransomes' house being concerned with the shootings. I didn't want to have too many on the warrant—it doesn't look too good."

"That's exactly what I mean. Even three are bad enough. Two of them are bound to be wrong and probably the whole lot. Then where should we be, coping with another bunch of outraged innocents? Keep your men watching for any trouble and wait for a few days to see what happens. If you get a real chance, of course, and are sure of your ground, don't hesitate."

So Charlton bided his time, not unwillingly. The week advanced, no further excitement happened in Paulsfield and slowly the townspeople began to drift back into the Square. The panic of the previous Friday did not last and within a week of Arthur Ransome's death, everything had returned to normal.

"It's all over," they said. "The Sniper has most probably fled from the town and there's no need for us to worry our heads any more about him."

They were behaving rather like the celebrated ostrich, but it brought the smiles back to the faces of the stately Mr. Cooper, the cherubic Mr. Harbottle, the manager of Higham's and all the other shopkeepers around the market-place.

But Bradfield, Emerson, Hartley and the others still kept unceasing vigil and waited for the Sniper to try it again.

And Geoffrey Ibbotson lingered in Paulsfield Hospital.

On the Monday afternoon, Charlton cleared up the question of the escaping bull. It will be remembered that the drover had said that he had stumbled and lost his hold on the bullstaff; but Charlton had thought at the time that the man might have been in league with the murderer. He was not still of the same mind, but felt that the point ought to be settled.

He consulted Martin's records and interviewed the other drovers who had been near the Post Office at the time. They said that the incident had had all the appearances of an accident. The man had not stumbled, but slipped, and they all gave vividly descriptive reasons why he had lost his footing.

Farmer Kidd of Burgeston, who employed the drover, said that he had only picked on that particular man at the last minute, and any sort of prearranged plan was therefore out of the question. It might have been fixed on the way to market, but it was highly unlikely.

Then there were two other witnesses to be examined on another matter: the mother and sister of Frank Baggs. Their evidence was completely negative. They had both been sound asleep at the time when Arthur Ransome was shot and therefore could not testify that their unpleasant relation had been with them in the house.

Friday came. In the afternoon, Charlton dropped in to see Martin about something else and the conversation turned to the Sniper.

"D'you think 'e's finished 'is half-larks?" asked Martin. "It's over a week since the last shooting."

"I don't imagine so for a moment," the Inspector replied.

"Probably got wind of the patrols and thinks it's a bit too dangerous to try on again."

"My own opinion is that he's waiting."

"Waiting? What for? There's plenty of victims about the Square now."

"I believe that he's *waiting for Humphries to die.*"

"What makes you think that?"

"The patrols are behaving with the utmost caution and it's unlikely that the Sniper knows about them. He has shown us that he's willing to take the gravest risk of detection, yet for eight days he has been inactive, with five beautiful little cartridges fairly clamouring to kill somebody. My belief is that he is carrying out a fixed scheme, which is now held up until Humphries dies. If that poor chap hadn't turned his head at the last moment—as Dr. Weston says he must have done—his death would have been swiftly followed by an attempt on someone else's life and we might have caught the Sniper by now."

"You think he's really come off the hook?"

"I'm convinced of it. Nobody except Noreen Prentice knew that Arthur Ransome was going out last Thursday morning, so how could his death have been premeditated?"

"P'r'aps the Sniper saw 'is big chance and took it."

"It was a very fortunate accident for him, if he just happened to be in the right place at the right moment. Can you imagine him saying to himself, 'I've never known Arthur Ransome to get up at a quarter to six in the morning and go for a walk across the Square, so tomorrow I'll be lying in wait for him, in case he does'?"

Martin shook his head slowly.

"On the other hand, one can easily conceive the Sniper saying, 'There's a sporting chance that *somebody* will be out and about before six tomorrow morning, so I'll get up nice and early and see if I can pick him off. I was more than lucky to get away with that Earnshaw business like I did, but in future I must make a point of having my little bits of fun when the Square's not quite so crowded. It won't do to take too many risks, even with that ninny-wit, Charlton.'"

"But why should 'e wait for Humphries to die? Homicidal mania's like smoking cigarettes: as soon as you've finished one, you want another."

"Because, as I say, he's carrying out a definite plan, step by step. I can't explain or justify it, but I've got the idea that these murders are all part of some crazy design that will become perfectly clear when we can get hold of the vital clue."

"If 'e's carrying out a definite plan, step by step, and Ransome's death was one of the steps, surely that means the Sniper plotted to kill 'im? I don't mean to be rude, but it looks to me as if you're contradictin' yourself. First you say that it didn't matter to the Sniper whether 'e shot Ransome or the Four 'Orsemen of the Apoca-how-much, and then you say that the killing of Ransome was all a part of some nutty frame-up. It doesn't seem sense to me."

"It doesn't seem sense to me, either, Martin, but that's how I feel about it. I don't think he plotted to kill Ransome, but when Ransome walked across the Square, decided that he would suit his purpose. Ransome had—how can I explain it?—the necessary

227

qualifications. Imagine the Sniper as a lepidopterist who sets out to catch a special kind of butterfly. He doesn't look for one particular insect—Clarissa, the Camberwell Beauty, Roderick the Red Admiral, or Fred Fritillary—but for any member of the class in which he is interested. *That* is what I think was the position with Earnshaw, Ransome and Humphries. Earnshaw was Species One, Ransome was Species Two and Humphries was Species Three. When Humphries dies, as he shortly will, the Sniper will start to look for Species Four—that is, somebody fulfilling the peculiar requirements of that portion of his plan."

"Sounds all right," said Martin apathetically. "What's the position about that search warrant?"

Charlton laughed.

"You're a sensible fellow," he said, "to put more faith in a search warrant than my high-flown theories. That valuable document, which gives a named constable—*id est,* myself—authority to enter at any time, if necessary by force, and search for firearms or ammunition the premises of Messrs. Beamish, Pope and Muttigen, is now in my pocket-book, where it will remain until the Super gives the word, or until I have a sufficiently cast-iron case to justify executing it."

"When you do it," said Martin, "don't leave me out of the fun. The missus and me are going out visiting to-night, so don't make it then."

"I'll try not to," Charlton promised him with a smile.

The telephone bell rang and the Sergeant answered it.

"For you," he said, handing over the instrument.

The conversation was short and Charlton hung up the receiver with a grunt.

"Humphries is dead," he said.

"Poor devil."

"He died half-an-hour ago of hypostatic pneumonia."

"Now, if there's anything in your theory," said Martin practically, "you've got to look out for Species Four. You'd better give the detectives the tip to be extra watchful."

"I don't think there's any need for that," answered Charlton. "They're all on the alert. Their strength has been considerably increased and every night the Horticultural Hall and the adjoining block of shops are surrounded by men with powerful electric torches. As soon as they hear a shot, they'll throw the beams on to the buildings—and if the Sniper can slip away via the roofs, I'll take off my hat to him. We can't use the shelter any longer, because the road-repairing has drifted up the High Street and the shelter has gone with it; but during the daytime I've two men in the church tower and half-a-dozen who take it in turns to hang about the Square, so that none of them ist here long enough to be conspicuous. Have you seen the old boy with the four children and no pension who's been standing with a tray of matches in the High Street just outside 'Voslivres'? That's young Emerson."

"Go *on!*" said Martin incredulously.

"He tells me that he sold a box the other day."

"If 'e keeps that up," chuckled Martin, "'e'll soon be leaving the force and going into the retail business!"

* * *

The electric clock on the mantelpiece of the lounge at Holmedene pointed to a quarter to eleven. An atmosphere of tranquillity rested on the room, the only sounds being the clicking of Molly's knitting-needles and the rustling of the pages of her uncle's book. Outside, the air was heavy and pregnant with the storm to come, and the leaves stirred uneasily in the tiny breeze that was its forerunner.

Molly broke a long silence.

"Was that thunder, or only a train?"

"Thunder," replied Charlton, raising his eyes from his book. "It's been working up for some time."

"I hope it won't keep us awake."

"It'll have its work cut out to disturb me. I'm dead tired and have made an early appointment to-night with Nature's soft nurse. Felony and his little sister, Misdemeanour, are quiet for the moment and I may as well take full advantage of it."

As his hand masked a wide yawn, the telephone in the hall burst into sudden life.

"I spoke too soon," he said with a grimace.

"It may be Mrs. Eldersley," suggested Molly. "I think she wants us to go to a whist-drive tomorrow week."

"Give me Felony every time," smiled her uncle, as he got out of his chair and went to answer the insistent summons of the bell.

"Inspector Charlton here," he announced when he had lifted the hand-microphone. "Oh, yes, Mrs. Archer. Good evening. . . . Now? . . . It's rather late. Can't it wait until the morning? . . . All right, Mrs. Archer. I'll come over. . . . Yes, within half-an-hour. . . . Good-bye." He slammed back the receiver with an impatient and uncharacteristically lurid oath.

"Naughty, naughty!" remonstrated Molly through the open doorway.

"Some of these women have about as much consideration for a fellow as a . . . as a . . ."

His usual fluency deserted him.

"Couldn't you put her off?" asked Molly. "Say you had spots and were afraid it was something?"

"I tried to, but she was insistent. She's got something important to tell me and she wants me to go over at once. If I don't, there may be trouble, even though she *has* only discovered that Humphries was good at Algebra or that Earnshaw's cousin is in the North-West Mounted."

"You must take your raincoat," instructed Molly.

"I shall *not* take my raincoat," he retorted.

He took his raincoat.

The storm did not break before he reached Paulsfield. He parked the car by the statue and, as he walked across towards the shops, saw a figure that he immediately recognized as Mr.

Farquarson's walking from the direction of the High Street. They met and exchanged greetings outside Beamish's.

"The very man I want to see!" said the secretary heartily. "I have tidings for you. Early this evening, I went to the hospital to enquire about Mr. Humphries and was told that the hapless man"—his voice sank theatrically—"had expired."

Charlton said nothing.

"He is dead," said Mr. Farquarson, putting it another way.

"Quite," was the brief reply.

"I imagined that that would be news to you," said the old gentleman in a mortified tone.

"I'm afraid it isn't."

"His death leaves you faced, does it not, with another baffling murder? I hope that your investigation into the three crimes is progressing favourably, Inspector?"

"I am glad to say that it is," Charlton lied brightly. "in spite of many hindrances and a considerable wasting of my time."

"Splendid!" said Mr. Farquarson, and disappeared into the obscurity of the passage like a stately spook.

Mrs. Archer herself answered Charlton's ring. She smiled a welcome, thanked him for coming so promptly and led the way up to her room.

"I'm sorry," she said, as they sat down, "to bring you out so late at night, but there is something that I simply *must* tell you. My conscience has been troubling me so much during the last week that I can't stand it any longer."

She went to a drawer in the bookcase and came back to her seat carrying a Webley revolver.

"Be careful," she warned him, as she handed it over. "Some of the chambers are loaded."

Charlton immediately "broke" it and removed the three cartridges that it contained.

"It was my husband's," explained Mrs. Archer. "It went through the War with him and he brought it back home with him when he was invalided out in 1918. I've always treasured it because of its associations, though I've hardly dared to touch it, as I knew it was loaded and am terrified of such things. It was only when Ruth told me that you police were applying for a warrant to search houses in the Square that I began to get anxious about having it in my possession. I've had the awful feeling that you would search my room, find that revolver and immediately suspect me of shooting those three poor men, particularly as some of the cartridges are missing."

"I'll keep it, if you don't mind, Mrs. Archer," said the Inspector, mastering his vexation. "Have you a certificate for it?"

"Oh, no. It has been locked away ever since Richard— my late husband—brought it back from France. He won the D.S.O. at Cambrai, you know, and was badly wounded at Bapaume in August, 1918—so badly that it lead to his death five years afterwards."

"Very tragic," said Charlton sympathetically. "I need hardly tell you, I think, Mrs. Archer, that it is against the law to be in possession of a loaded firearm without a certificate."

"I know," she answered, "but I do hope you're not going to be nasty about it. After all, it's only a souvenir."

"It is more than that. It is a dangerous weapon and a menace to the public safety. If you wanted to keep it as a War trophy you should have surrendered the ammunition to the police and applied to the Chief Constable for permission to dispense with a firearm certificate."

"Oh, *dear!*" almost wailed Mrs. Archer. "It isn't going to get me into trouble, is it?"

Charlton called to mind his conversation with Mrs. Symes on the same subject, but he was too sleepy and splenetic to be compassionate with Mrs. Archer.

"I must hand it over to the Chief Constable," he said severely, "and let him decide."

"Now you're being horribly official!" she complained, her brilliant blue eyes looking reproachfully at him from behind her gold-rimmed spectacles. "I've had that revolver on my mind ever since last week and now that I've confessed everything, it hasn't made me any happier!"

This was not the masterful, almost masculine woman that he had come to know.

"I am sorry, Mrs. Archer," he said, "but it is a very serious offence to have a loaded firearm without a proper permit. The penalty is a fifty pounds fine and the possibility of three months' imprisonment."

"I'm beginning to feel sorry that I asked you to come," she said. "Not that I mind about your silly punishments. Don't think that! I can easily afford to pay the fine and I've always wanted to go to gaol. But I was *so* looking forward to a comfortable little talk with you. I am a lonely old woman, Inspector, with too few really intelligent friends. My husband's death left a gap in my life that has never been filled since. I don't think the terrible position and feelings of a widow are really understood by most people. She may be a widow, but she is still a woman."

A tremor of absolute terror ran through Charlton. Mrs. Archer was *ogling* him.

"We must be keeping Miss Beamish awake with our talking," he said hastily, fidgeting uncomfortably in his chair.

"That's all right," said Mrs. Archer reassuringly. "She isn't in. She's staying for a few days with friends in Littleworth; and Joseph, my brother, is out visiting this evening and is not back yet."

Charlton leapt from his chair, as if a pin had been jabbed through the seat. He already heard the excited wagging of the Paulsfield tongues. Old Farquarson had left him at the door of Beamish's and he was the biggest gibble-gabbler at large.

"I must get back home," he said. "My niece is waiting up for me."

"Let me make you some coffee," offered Mrs. Archer. "They say mine is very good."

She held out the cigarette-box towards him.

"No, really!" he protested. "It is getting very late and I have to drive back to Southmouth."

"Good night, then, Inspector," she said and inclined her head like a *grande dame*.

With a sigh of relief, he closed the door of her room behind him and turned to go down the stairs. As he did so, he heard clumsy feet ascending the upper flight. Mr. Joseph Beamish had returned home, he thought. He slipped the Webley into his raincoat pocket and went down into the dark shop. The door was bolted on the inside. He pulled back the fastening, closed the door gently on the Yale lock and strode across the Square to where his car stood pointing towards the High Street.

As he walked into the area of light cast by the side-lamps, he was shot through the back.

XXIV.

Martin's Hour

THE Sergeant had won two shillings and fourpence at solo and was in a sunny mood as he walked up the High Street with Mrs. Martin. They were in a hurry to get home, because the thunder was getting steadily louder and Martin's new grey flannel suit would have lost its splendour in a rainstorm. As they got near to the Square, a staccato report cracked out above the sullen rumble of the thunder.

"Jumping Pete!" ejaculated Martin. "The Sniper's at it again!"

He pushed his wife into a doorway.

"Knock up Mrs. Bennett," he said urgently, "and wait till I call for you."

Without more words he sprinted along the High Street into the Square, which was gloomy under the heavy sky, except where the street lamps inadequately shone. Just to the other side of the statue, in front of a car, a man lay on his face and another came running from the Paragon. Martin met the blinding glare of an electric torch.

"Hartley here, Sergeant," said a voice and the light was snapped off, leaving Martin blinking in the darkness.

"Get that block floodlit," snapped Martin, "and stop anybody who tries to leave. Tell 'em to watch the roofs, then ring for Dr. Weston and the ambulance. Send one of the men here with a flash-lamp." Hartley ran off and Martin stood out of range of the car's lights until a plain-clothes man arrived.

"Got a gun?" asked Martin. "Good. Play your torch over the front of them buildings and if you see anything fishy, *shoot*. I want to 'ave a look at *him*."

He knelt down in front of the car by the raincoated body. As he did so, lightning ran jaggedly down the sky, heavy drops began to fall and a vicious ripple of thunder sounded overhead.

"God Almighty!" he said aghast. "It's Inspector Charlton!"

He feverishly felt the outstretched wrist.

"Pulse is all right," he said in relieved tones to the detective, who was busily flashing his torch over the shops and Hall.

Martin lighted a match and searched the back of Charlton's coat for the rent left by the bullet. He found it in the left shoulder.

"Hope it hasn't pierced 'is chest," he muttered.

He pulled off his own jacket and, after gently turning the unconscious man on to his side, rolled up the jacket and slipped it under Charlton's head. Then standing in his shirtsleeves, completely unmindful of the now torrential rain and crashing thunder, he waited fretfully for Dr. Weston and the ambulance.

All round the block on the north side of the Square the narrow beams of light kept playing.

"We'll get the tricky illegitimate this time," said Martin vengefully, and the man with the gun grunted agreement.

By the time Dr. Weston arrived, Charlton was beginning to stir uneasily. The car screamed in protest as the doctor tugged savagely at the hand-brake, flung open the door and jumped out. The vitriolic little man had been just off to bed, after eighteen hours' work, and was inclined to be peevish.

"I hope," he said acidly, "that I have not been invited to a searchlight demonstration? Is enemy aircraft expected?"

"Inspector Charlton's been shot, sir," said Martin quietly.

"*What?*"

The Sergeant pointed to the injured man and the doctor plunged forward on to his knee by the side of his greatest friend.

"'E's coming to," said Martin. "'E must 've fallen forward and stunned himself on the ground."

Weston turned his head towards the detective, who, with the torch in one hand and the gun in the other, was conscientiously "hosing" the building with a stream of light.

"Stop playing Zeppelins," he said, "and point that torch over here."

"Mustn't do that, sir," warned Martin. "He's holding us covered from another attack. I think the Inspector keeps a torch in his car."

A mighty crash of thunder broke almost above them and the rain came down so fiercely that the drops bounced back like tennis balls.

Martin got the torch and held it so that the doctor could carry out his examination.

"There doesn't *seem* to be much real harm done," said Weston at length, and Martin sighed deeply with relief. "I think the bullet's lodged in the shoulder muscles."

Charlton groaned.

"You're all right, old fellow," the doctor said to him.

"Just a bit of an accident. We'll have you in bed in a minute or two."

They heard a clanging bell and the ambulance swung into the Square. Charlton was lifted gently into it and Dr. Weston, leaving his own car to take care of itself, followed.

"Just a tick," said Martin, as the door was about to be closed. "Will you get the wallet out of 'is breast-pocket, Doctor? I'll take the responsibility."

Without protest, Weston did as he was asked.

"There's a blue paper in it," explained Martin, "which I'd like to have."

The doctor looked through the wallet and handed the search warrant out to Martin, who stuffed it quickly in the pocket of his trousers before the rain could reduce it to pulp.

The door was pulled shut and the ambulance slid away. Martin picked up a limp thing from the ground.

"That cost me four and a half guineas," he said mournfully, as he gingerly insinuated his arms into the sodden sleeves. "Thank the Lord I left the weskit at 'ome. That's *something* saved from the wreck."

The detective chuckled and the ray of light shot skywards.

"Oi!" cried Martin. "'E's not up there. More likely to've gone the other way. Keep at it, Trafford, until the battery wears out. Now, Mr. perishing Sniper! You've got your work cut out to get away with it this time, you sneakin', murderin' little drip of hog-wash!"

And with his completely shapeless cloth cap flung on his head at a rakehelly angle, Police-sergeant Albert Martin swaggered truculently across the Square.

He spoke to the three detectives at the back of the block: the first between Mrs. Ransome's house and the multiple store, the second in the passage and the third in the Paragon. They each told him that nobody had come within range of their lights.

"Stick to it," he said. "We mustn't let 'imslip by." From the top floor of the empty block of shops on the other side of the High Street, another beam played over the multiple store, the newspaper offices, Mr. Muttigen's and the ironmonger's.

Martin took Hartley with him and rang Mr. Muttigen's bell.

"We'll go up on the roofs afterwards," he said, as they waited on the step, "and work from one end to the other. 'E may be hiding behind the parapet till us slops go 'ome to sleepy-bye."

Most of the residents round the Square must have been roused by the noise and the flashing lights, and it was not long before the apologetic little chemist, in a purple dressing-gown, opened the door. Martin spent no time on a polite interchange of greetings, but waved the paper in front of Mr. Muttigen.

"I've a warrant to search this house for firearms," he said.

"Certainly, Sergeant," replied the little man humbly, and stood back for them to enter.

"Who's in?" demanded Martin.

"My wife and son."

"Any firearms kept?"

Mr. Muttigen shook his head in horror.

"Please warn Mrs. Muttigen that we shall want to come upstairs."

When the chemist had gone, Martin looked round the shop, with its bottles, tins and photographic materials, and scratched his head forlornly.

"It's one thing to say, 'I'll frisk every inch of this place,' Hartley," he said, "but it's another thing to do it!"

They searched the ground floor and, when Mr. Muttigen returned, required of him the keys of certain drawers and cupboards. Then the three of them went up to the first floor, where Mrs. Muttigen had come down to wait for them on the landing.

"This is laughable," she said.

"I'm glad you think so, madam," answered Martin.

"It's too utterly preposterous for words!"

She was the complete antithesis of her husband and did not mince matters.

"I want to search your bedroom, if you please," said the Sergeant firmly, but quailing inwardly.

"How *dare* you!" she flared up. "I know who you are. You're Sergeant Martin and you've no right to come in here like this! I shall see that my husband makes a complaint to the——"

"Hush, my dear," said Mr. Muttigen. "The Sergeant's only doing his duty. It is all a matter of police routine and is as distasteful to him as it is to us."

"Quite so, sir," said Martin, warming towards him.

"The living-rooms are on this floor," the chemist said, "if you would care to glance round them?"

Martin and Hartley did far more than glance round them, but found no lethal weapon. Mr. Muttigen led them up to the top floor, while his wife stayed behind, "to tidy up."

There were two bedrooms upstairs and a bathroom. The front bedroom was shared by the pair, and the two policemen ran through the wardrobe, the dressing-table and all other possible hiding-places, including, to the vast displeasure of Mrs. Muttigen, who came up at the wrong moment, the bed itself.

"Now the back room, please," said Martin, whose finer feelings were bruised by the necessity for such antics.

"That is my son's room," said Mr. Muttigen timidly.

"I thought as much."

"I ... We ... He ... He is rather shy."

"I'm sorry about that, sir, but it's my duty to search the room. P'r'aps you'd like to let 'im know we're 'ere, in case he's asleep."

They went out on to the landing and Mrs. Muttigen slammed and locked the door behind them. The anxious father sighed heavily and knocked on the boy's door.

"Harold!" he called.

There was no answer and Mr. Muttigen raised his voice.

"Harold!"

He turned the handle and pushed the door, but it did not move.

"That is very strange," he whispered to Martin. "We have purposely taken the key away. He must have wedged a chair underneath the handle on the other side."

"Call him again," Martin whispered back.

"Harold," appealed Mr. Muttigen, "this is Dad here. Open the door, Harold."

The only reply was a distant rumble of thunder. The chemist moved from the door and went to lead the way downstairs.

"*Just* a minute," Martin detained him. "I want a look inside that room and if Master Muttigen won't open to us, we'll 'ave to take steps."

"Won't you be satisfied with the parts of the house you have already seen?"

"'Fraid not, sir, but I'll give you another chance to persuade the lad to let us in."

He walked away from the door to where Hartley stood, while the chemist called supplications through the panels.

"The poor old chap," he muttered to the detective. "'E's got enough to put up with, without us bargin' in, what with that and that." He jerked his thumb in the direction of the two closed doors. "I feel a dirty cad."

"Duty's duty," answered Hartley, who was younger and harder-hearted.

Mr. Muttigen ceased pleading, turned towards them and raised his hands in a gesture of pathetic surrender.

"I have done all I can," he said. "You gentlemen must now do as you think fit."

Martin nudged Hartley and nodded towards the door. The young detective stepped forward and applied a lusty shoulder to it. On the second thrust, the chair inside slipped on the linoleum and the door swung open. The room was in darkness, except for a moment, when one of the busy torches outside flashed across the window.

"Where's the switch?" asked Martin.

"Just to the right," replied Mr. Muttigen.

When Hartley had turned it on, Martin followed him into the room and looked round.

"'E's not here!" he said.

"I am afraid he will be under the bed," said the chemist contritely.

He was. The room was filled with books, piled copies of the *Boys' Own Paper* and Meccano models. Hartley and the Sergeant searched through the jumble, while Mr. Muttigen stood in the doorway and his son lay crouched beneath the bed, as near to the wall as he could get. Then, when they had satisfied themselves that no firearm was concealed in the room, Martin went to the window, threw up the sash and was instantly dazzled by the full glare of the torch held by the watchful man below. Martin waved his hand and the shaft of light moved away. He beckoned Hartley to the window.

"Could you get up on the roof from 'ere?" he asked in a low tone.

"You bet!" replied Hartley confidently, and started to climb out, but Martin restrained him.

"Save that for the Police Sports," he advised.

He turned from the window to Mr. Muttigen, nodded towards Harold's retreat and jerked his arm.

"Yank him out," the movement suggested.

The little man was about to shake his head, but checked himself and moved across to the bed.

"Harold," he said, bending down, "won't you come out and meet the gentlemen?"

"That's a jolly good model of a crane, Hartley," said Martin guilefully. "How does it work?"

"I suppose you turn this bit," Hartley took his cue. "No, that doesn't do it."

"'Ow d'you make it lift things, Mr. Muttigen?" asked Martin with a meaning glance and a movement of his head that brought the chemist over to the table with them.

"I really don't know. Harold is the only one who knows anything about cranes in this house," he admitted; then added in a soft voice, "*It won't do any good.*"

"Turn it the other way, Hartley," suggested the Sergeant. "Look out, or you'll break it! Gosh, but it's a fine piece of work. Pity it doesn't operate properly."

The boy under the bed stirred. The three of them clustered round the model and feigned a close attention to it. They heard Harold crawl out. Then there was the thud of bare feet and, before they thought to turn their heads, a crash sounded outside on the landing.

"Good God!" said Martin with a start. "What was that?"

"He has shut himself in the lavatory," replied Mr. Muttigen, with something that might have been relief in his tones.

Martin started out across the room, but the chemist caught his arm.

"Sergeant," he said earnestly, "if you have any consideration for us at all, for God's sake don't pursue this any further. Let the poor boy stay where he is. I'm afraid that his reason is already in the greatest danger and I shudder to think of what may follow continued persecution."

"I never saw 'im slip out of here. How do I know 'e didn't take—" began Martin, and stopped suddenly.

"I know what you mean," said Mr. Muttigen quietly. "but if I give you my word of honour that I know of no opportunity Harold has ever had of getting hold of a dangerous weapon and that, to my knowledge, no firearm of any description has ever been brought into this house, will you go?"

Martin studied the man's face intently.

"Come on, Hartley," he said at last, and went down the stairs.

The chemist came with them to the shop door.

"Mr. Muttigen, sir," said Martin, "I've never felt a bigger swine in my life than I 'ave to-night."

The bald little man held out his hand and smiled slightly.

"*I* have to sell people castor-oil," he answered.

The rain had stopped. As the two of them were passing the ironmonger's, Martin paused.

"What was that?" he asked sharply.

"I heard nothing," said Hartley.

"I thought it was someone laughing. Probably only my fancy. That boy's given me the heeby-jeebies."

"He couldn't have got back from the roof to his room," Hartley answered the question that was in both their minds. "As soon as the shot went, all our men switched on their lights."

"A little conjuring trick like that," scoffed Martin, "wouldn't trouble a bloke who's already got away with three of the sauciest murders I've ever heard of."

Detective-constable Trafford was still at his post in the Square. They went over to him, but he had nothing to report. A sustained push on Mr. Pope's bell eventually brought the tobacconist down in his dressing-gown. He seemed barely awake, but when Martin produced his search warrant, readily placed his home at their disposal.

"I have half expected such a visitation," he said, "but not at such an unusual hour."

"Sorry, sir," said Martin, "but it wasn't of our choosing." The tobacconist violently drew in a breath.

"Don't tell me," he said, "that there has been more shooting?"

"Didn't you hear anything?" asked the Sergeant in astonishment.

"Not a thing," confessed Mr. Pope. "I must have been very soundly asleep. You awakened me when you rang the bell. I earnestly hope that no one has been killed?"

The Sergeant brushed aside the question and suggested that he and Hartley had better get on with their job. They ransacked the house from top to bottom, but without result; and allowed Mr. Pope to return to his bed.

The light in Mrs. Archer's room was still on when Hartley pressed the bell. She came down at once and they heard her fumbling with the bolt.

"Good evening, Sergeant," she said gravely. "I have waited up for you. It seems almost incredible to me. I practically saw it happen. He had only just left me."

"He'd been here, had 'e?" said Martin. "I wondered what 'e was doing in the Square so late."

"He let himself out. I heard him unbolt the shop door and guessed that my brother had come in while we were talking and gone up to bed, after closing up for the night. So I went downstairs to refasten the bolt and when I came up here again, went to the window to shut out the storm and saw him lying in front of his car, with you standing near him. I *do* hope he's not dangerously wounded?"

"We don't know," was Martin's guarded answer.

"They've taken 'im to hospital. Now, Mrs. Archer, I'm sorry to bother you at this time of the night, but I've got to search this house."

Mrs. Archer smiled faintly.

"Inspector Charlton has just taken away the only firearm we had," she said, "but please do just what you like."

Hartley and the Sergeant started with the shop, which was quite a hopeless proposition. The needle and the haystack were nothing to it. Then they went up into Mrs. Archer's room, the orderliness of which came as a relief to them. They conscientiously pried into every corner: the bed and the cabinet beside it, the drawers of the bookcase and the radio-gramophone. Martin tried the drawers of the card-index.

"Can I ask you for the key of this, madam?" he enquired politely.

"You can ask, Sergeant," she responded sweetly, "but you're not going to get it."

"Sorry, Mrs. Archer, but I've got to insist."

"I refuse to let you see into those drawers," she said definitely. "All they contain is private papers."

"It's not a good thing," said Martin with great severity, "to obstruct the police. You've seen the warrant I hold to search this house and if you try to prevent me doing it, you're guilty of misdemeanour."

Mrs. Archer capitulated.

"Very well, then," she said, and handed over the key. Martin pulled out the drawers, one by one. When he opened the third, his hand hovered over the section devoted to "M"; but Mrs. Archer coughed significantly and he hastily continued his search for the Parabellum.

"Is Miss Beamish in her room?" he enquired, as he turned the key in the lock of the bottom drawer.

"No," said Mrs. Archer shortly.

"And Mr. Beamish?"

"Yes."

"Before we go up, we'd like to take a look round the back room on this floor, if you don't mind."

"Does it really matter, Sergeant, whether I mind or not?" she asked. The affair of the cabinet seemed to be rankling.

The policemen scrutinized the back sitting-room and then Mrs. Archer led them up to Miss Beamish's apartment on the top floor.

"Would that be your brother's room?" asked Martin, as they came out again on to the landing.

"Yes," answered the widow, "but he is so deaf that it will be impossible to rouse him by knocking on the door. If you *must* interrupt his well-earned sleep, you had better go in."

With the dignity of an insulted queen, she went downstairs to her room.

Martin looked at Hartley and Hartley did the same to Martin. Then the Sergeant squared his shoulders, took hold of the knob and opened the door. They caught the sound of heavy breathing.

"Mr. Beamish!" called Martin, but the old curio dealer did not stir.

Martin switched on the light and they saw Mr. Beamish, in his shirt and trousers, lying on his back on top of the bedclothes. A pair of boots stood on the dressing-table and a suit of pyjamas was neatly arranged on a coat-hanger hooked to the key of the wardrobe.

"Looks like Lodge Night," grunted Martin.

Taking no further notice of the snoring man, they scouted round the room. Then Martin said:

"Shall we wake 'im up?"

"Better," suggested Hartley. "He may have slipped the gun under the bedclothes and be lying on top of it." They took it in turns to shake Mr. Beamish's shoulder and at last aroused him. He blinked owlishly in the bright light, closed his eyes and went to sleep again.

"'E's too full for words," said the Sergeant. "Roll 'im over, but don't let 'im fall on the floor, or we'll 'ave the duchess up."

There was nothing hidden in the bed.

"Might as well tuck 'im in nice and comfy," said the considerate Martin and they threw the bedclothes over the gentleman so profoundly *in poculis,* and left him to sleep it off.

"Where do we go from here?" enquired Hartley, as Mrs. Archer savagely shot the bolt behind them.

"Rout out old Farquarson and get into the Hall."

"Does the warrant cover that?"

"No. It doesn't even cover *us,* if the truth must be told. It's in Inspector Charlton's name and ought to've been executed by him, but I'm risking that."

"Any Court would uphold you," encouraged Hartley. Immediately after they rang the bell of number seven, Effingham Street, the light was switched on in the first floor bedroom, but it was five minutes before Mr. Farquarson opened the door in all the conventional splendour of his everyday attire.

"Why, Sergeant!" he said with a welcoming smile. "This *is* a pleasant surprise. Sorry to keep you waiting, but I couldn't allow even such an old friend as yourself to see me in my nightie!"

Effingham Street reeled under the shock of his sudden mighty laugh.

"And is this your son?" he asked with interest.

"No," Martin flashed back. "'E's my sister's eldest boy. Mr. Farquarson, sir, we're rather keen on getting into the 'All, if you can arrange it. I've no real authority, but I'd feel it a great—"

"My dear Sergeant," threw in the secretary warmly, "I don't expect you to produce a search warrant every time you wish to enter the Hall. My only regret is that you cannot defer your visit until 7.30 tomorrow evening, when we are to hold a concert; but that perhaps is not convenient?"

"I'd come with pleasure," lied Martin, "only I shall be on duty. Will you give me the keys, sir, or would you like to come with us?"

"I have had a long day," the old gentleman responded, "and am very sleepy. I think I can trust you with the keys overnight, Sergeant, if you will be kind enough to return them to me without fail in the morning?"

"Certainly, sir."

Mr. Farquarson procured the keys from his desk, handed them to Martin and genially wished them both good night.

"Don't keep your nephew up too late," were his last words. "Lads need plenty of sleep."

"Saucy old scoundrel," grumbled Hartley, as they went down the garden path.

The detectives in the Paragon and the passage had kept close guard over the back of the Hall and assured Martin that nobody had come through the gates, shinned over the fence, or descended by the ladder from the roof. Hartley and Martin walked along the Paragon and unlocked the gate that led into the yard. They entered the Hall through the back door and carried out a thorough search for intruders. The only living things they met were two mice and a spider.

"We must do the roof, while we're here," decided Martin.

Hartley led the way up the iron ladder and they walked round the domed top-light.

"What about the other roofs?" asked the detective.

The Sergeant scratched his head.

"We can't get on them now, can we?" he said. "I hadn't thought of that. Could we get across from 'ere?"

"Too risky to jump it. What about those boards? Will one reach across?"

"Good idea! As long as you don't expect *me* to join your Suicide Club!"

"There's nothing in it," said Hartley, as they got the plank into position, and immediately proved it by leaping on to the parapet and striding casually down the swaying bridge to the roof of Beamish's shop.

He was gone five minutes.

"Nothing doing," he said, as he came back across the plank. "I've been right round and even looked down all the chimney-pots."

Martin pushed his damp cap to the back of his head.

"Beats me," was his unreserved admission.

XXV.

Jeff

THE day after Martin's sleeveless errand, things came to a head.

In the morning, after an X-ray examination of the wound, Dr. Weston extracted the bullet from the bunch of muscles above Charlton's left shoulder blade.

"A couple of days' rest will put you right," he said afterwards in the patient's private room.

"I can go home, then?"

"*Rest,* I said. You're going to stay here in bed until I give you permission to get up."

"How do you suggest that I should pass the time? Except for a sore shoulder and an even sorer head, I have never felt better."

"Ask yourself riddles."

"I shall be able to do that," was the significant reply.

The doctor rose and picked up his hat.

"Sit down again, please," instructed Charlton, and Weston obeyed.

"What's the trouble?" he demanded. "I'm in a deuce of a hurry."

"I am going to die."

"Nonsense!" laughed the doctor. "I've already told you that you'll be ambulatory in a couple of days."

"On second thoughts," amended Charlton, "I had better die last night. I've been toying with the idea of lingering for several days, but I think it will be more convincing if I died on the way to hospital."

Weston looked anxiously at his patient and Charlton laughed at his expression.

"It's all right, Weston!" he said. "I may be clothed in the wrong pyjamas, but I am nevertheless in my right mind. I merely propose to emulate the gentleman in one of Hood's poems, who was not quite—but only rather dead."

"If that bullet had been a few inches lower, there wouldn't have been any *rather* about it. Do you mind letting me into your confidence and telling me what the devil you're talking about?"

"I have come to the conclusion that this Sniper fellow never attempts another murder until his previous victim has reached the undiscovered country, from whose bourn no Hollingsworth returns."

"I laugh only at my own jokes before lunch," said Weston severely. "I see your idea, though: to arrange for your obituary notice to be published, so that you can lure the Sniper into trying again. But apart from the fact that the whole thing seems to me to be too wildly silly, I think you are taking a grave risk with other people's lives. Wouldn't it be safer to tie the Sniper's hands by protracting your illness indefinitely—or, at any rate, until you can formulate a case against him?"

"I don't believe it would, because it's only a theory of mine and I should look very foolish if I skulked here, dawdling away my last hours, as it were, and allowed the Sniper to get away with another murder. I'm not asking you to spread the news that I am dead, Weston, but please don't tell everybody that it's only a scratch and that I shall be out and about again early next week."

Soon after the doctor went, Martin arrived, and Charlton outlined the scheme to him. The Sergeant promised to start the rumour and the hospital staff were instructed to refuse to answer any questions about the Inspector's condition.

"What happened last night, Martin," Charlton asked, "after I was called away?"

"I 'appened to be on the spot and took the liberty of getting the search warrant out of your wallet. Was that all right, sir?"

"What did you do with it?"

"Executed it."

"I think we can plead extenuating circumstances, if there's a riot. I take it you found nothing? No, I didn't think you would. Give me the details."

"As soon as the shot went off, all the men round the block switched on their torches and kept the buildings under constant observation until I'd finished my search. They've been on the watch all night and nobody 'as left the shops or the Hall. I took Hartley with me and went to Muttigen's first. He 'imself opened the door and we searched the whole place. Mrs. M. cut up a bit rough."

"What about Harold, the son?"

"We 'ad a terrible time with 'im. 'Ad to break open the bedroom door and then found 'im 'iding under the bed. Then, when we weren't looking, 'e slipped out and locked 'imself in the 'Ouse of Commons."

"Did you get him out?"

"No, I left 'im there. Old Mutt got tearful and staked 'is oath——"

"Old who?"

"Mutt, short for Muttigen."

"What does Mutt immediately suggest to you, Martin?"

"Jeff!" laughed Martin.

"Exactly so."

The Sergeant's mouth fell open.

"Jigger me gently!" he said.

They both fell silent. At length, Martin said:

"Nobody could 'ave got back into that house from the roof."

"Just a quaint coincidence, I expect. What had the egregious Pope to say for himself?"

"Nothing very much. 'E'd slept through it all, 'e said, and didn't wake till we rang the bell. We frisked 'is place pretty thoroughly and the same with next door. Mrs. Archer got shirty when I asked for the key of 'er precious cabinet, and Beamish, who I'd never 'ave thought it of, 'ad been out on the oil. If it was somebody's birthday, they must 'ave been quads."

"Did you search the Hall?"

"Got the keys from Farquarson—which reminds me I must take them back—and went over every square inch of it. Then we climbed on to the roof, pushed a board across to Beamish's place and Hartley made dead sure that nobody was 'anging about on the other roofs."

"Did you catch any whiffs of burnt powder in Beamish's or Pope's?"

"No, and I was on the look-out for it."

"It's not likely that you would. Nitrocellulose powder doesn't hang about like the old black stuff."

Martin looked awkward, and then said in a rush:

"Look 'ere, sir. You can choke me off for me sauce, if you like, but I've been cudgelling my brains to think what you were doing at Beamish's last night. You 'adn't been taking old Vat 69 'ome, I suppose ? Mrs. Archer said something to me about a gun."

"I've been wondering about that myself, Martin. Mrs. Archer rang me up and said she had something important to tell me. I came straight over and she immediately produced a loaded Webley revolver that had belonged to her husband. She said that it had been troubling her conscience and that she wanted to make full confession to me. Then—and you needn't let this go any further—she began to make what I can only call overtures. She said what a sad and lonely life a widow's was and how nobody understood their position; and I had the sudden horrible suspicion that she was offering herself for the post of Mrs. Henry Charlton."

Martin whistled softly.

"What interests me is her exact reason for summoning me. That her only motive was to deliver up the Webley is absurd and if she *was* setting her cap at me, she chose a funny time to do it. The only thing is, of course, that her brother and sister were both out, which perhaps doesn't often happen."

He paused and looked at Martin meaningly.

"There is only one other alternative."

The Sergeant nodded his head in comprehension.

"The trouble is," Charlton changed the subject, "that a search warrant is like a bee's stinging apparatus: it can only be used once. If we want to search those places again, we shall have to swear another information and get a brand new warrant."

"'Ope I didn't overlook the Parabellum," said Martin fervently.

"You did the best you could under rather difficult conditions. By the way, before you arrange for me to be mourned by all, you'd better tell the patrols what the position is and warn them to be on the *qui vive,* because as soon as the Sniper hears of my regrettable departure from this life, he'll probably give a glad cry and murder the mayor, aldermen and burgesses."

When Martin had gone, Charlton settled his head on the pillow and gazed at the ceiling in profound thought. The white distemper must have had a soporific effect upon him, for his eyes closed and he slept until noon.

When he awoke, his mind reverted to the Sniper. He tried to put his ideas into some sort of order, feeling that somewhere there lurked the key to the whole problem. He rang the bell and asked the young and winsome nurse for a pencil and paper and, when she had propped up the pillows behind him, rested the writing-pad on his knees and jotted down some notes, his main purpose being to establish a connection between the four shootings. He thought, first of all, that there were only three to consider, but then remembered that there had been another. He took them in order and scribbled down the following memoranda:—

"Earnshaw. A workman for the U.D.C. Happily married.

Apparently no enemies or financial worries. Gambled, but not heavily. Brother-in-law of Frank Baggs, discharged by Humphries (Ibbotson). He and brother Albert served in War (Parabellum?).

"Ransome. Carrying on secret love affair with girl. Rival? Took photos endangering Sniper's safety, but photos publshd before murdered. Killed to prevent giving evidence in court of exact moment first photo taken? Brother, Jack Ransome, lover of Diana Steward, secretary to Ibbotson. No connection with Earnshaw, except through Frank Baggs. Arthur Ransome— Jack Ransome —Ibbotson—Baggs—Thomas Earnshaw.

"Ibbotson. Living under name Anthony Humphries. Real Christian name Geoffrey. C/f Jeff. Nothing in that. Probably made enemies in old life in London. Only known connection, John M. Smith, who not the only one to know secret. Mrs. Archer also. Did she tell anyone else? Sacked Baggs. No real motive for murder by Baggs. No real motive for murder by Jack Ransome. Just windy talk to impress Diana Stwrd. Ibbotson cut off for ten years from old life. Surely killed before this if for smthng done then? What happened to Sir W. Stvnge and ex-wife?

"Charlton. In charge of case. Shot for that or personal reasons? Shot because gettng too near solution? No private connectn with other three victims. If gettng too near solution, how? Last witnesses questioned, mother and sister of Baggs. They not able to say Baggs at home when Rnsme shot."

The Inspector read through what he had written and grunted. That didn't seem to be much help. He wrote down other points as they occurred to him.

"Cartridge case of Ransome bullet found in passage. Therefore not fired from Pope's window. Side window Archer's room? Pope not on roof when Ransome shot. Seen at front room window. Good point.

"Muttigen. Mutt and Jeff. No use. Coincidence. Harold. Gun under bed, then took into lavatory? Impossible get down from roof without being seen.

"Keys of Hall kept in desk of James E. Farquarson, secretary. Desk drawer not locked. Mrs. Grabbery? Baggs cleans Hall. Cuts keys for living. Weston's evidence sggsts shot not fired from roof of Hall. Hartley—plank. Broad daylight? Not feasible.

"Beamish really drunk? Jumble in shop. Pebble on beach.

"Duplicate keys of Hall kept Cooper, mgr. S. Counties Bank. Humphries kept A/c there. Nothing in it."

He paused, glanced down the page and, with an impatient ejaculation, ripped it off the pad. Then, when he was about to crumple it in his hand, something riveted his attention and he gave a shout that brought the nurse running into the room.

"I've got it!" he told her excitedly.

★ ★ ★

Martin called at number seven, Effingham Street, to return the keys of the Hall.

"Show the Sergeant in, Mrs. Grabbery," Mr. Farquarson called from his study.

"I hope the Inspector's wound was not serious, Sergeant?" he said, as he replaced the keys in the drawer of the desk at which he sat.

"'E died last night," Martin replied, with a histrionic catch in his voice.

The smile went suddenly from the secretary's face and his cheeks lost something of their healthy colour. He pulled at his collar and Martin, alarmed, half rose to his feet.

"Sorry I didn't break it easier," he said apologetically.

"You have given me a nasty shock, Sergeant, and my heart is not all it should be. Perhaps you will ask Mrs. Grabbery to bring me in some water?"

Martin jumped up and called to the woman, who hurried in with a glass. The old man had slumped down into his chair and, with one arm supporting him, she held the glass to his lips.

"You'll be all right directly, sir," she said with a gentleness at which Charlton would have marvelled. "Just take it quietly for a bit. Didn't you ought to 'ave one of yer tablets?"

Mr. Farquarson gulped down the water and waved her away.

"I took one ten minutes ago," he said.

"'Adn't I better send for the doctor?"

"*Doctor?*" he snorted with some of his old heartiness. " Don't talk such balderdash, woman!" Then he added courteously, "Thank you, Mrs. Grabbery. I feel quite revived now."

With a last doubtful glance at him, she left them.

"I'm sorry for all this performance, Sergeant," said the secretary, "but your news came as a very severe blow to me. I have known Inspector Charlton only for a few days, but I have found him to be one of the finest and most charming men I have ever met. I already begin to regret that my perverted sense of humour didn't make his task any easier for him."

"Anyway," said Martin unctuously, "'e died in harness and that's what he always wanted to do."

"I shall cancel the concert this evening," decided Mr. Farquarson, "and keep the Hall closed up. If there is any other way in which I can help, Sergeant, don't hesitate to call upon my services. Inspector Charlton's death has brought home to me the real tragedy of these shootings. I am afraid that, up to now, I have treated them too lightly."

His fleshy chin stuck out and his eyes gleamed.

"The murderer shall be brought to justice," he said fiercely, "if I have to do it myself!"

★ ★ ★

A few minutes after Charlton's triumphant declaration to the nurse, P.C. Chandler arrived at the hospital with a letter addressed to the Inspector by Sergeant Martin. Inside was a memorandum from Martin that read:—

"This was found in the Square at 11.45 a.m. to-day by a

man whose name I have taken. It was wrapped round a piece of india-rubber and fixed by an elastic band, both of which are retained for your inspection later. News spread as instructed, after warning patrols. Mr. F. took it badly."

The wording on the enclosure was shorter.

"To Inspector Charlton's successor.

"Rev. xxii, 13."

He studied it with a puzzled frown. Then his face cleared and he asked the nurse for a copy of the New Testament. On the last page of it, he found the thirteenth verse of the twenty-second chapter of the Book of Revelation. It read:—

"I am Alpha and Omega, the beginning and the end, the first and the last."

He returned the Testament to her with a polite smile that hid his immense inner excitement.

"Thank you, Nurse," he said. "That clinches it, I think. Now I should like my clothes, if you please, as quickly as you can get them."

"Doctor says you are to stay in bed," she replied firmly.

"If you don't bring me my clothes," he said with a ferocious frown that was calculated to intimidate her, "I shall arrest you for complicity."

"Where's your warrant?" she asked serenely.

"I can get one."

"Not without your clothes!"

"That's where you're wrong, young woman!" he retorted.

He swung himself out of bed, pulled open the door and ran down the passage to a wall telephone. He was put through to Martin, exchanged a few terse remarks, and hung up. The girl was by his elbow, trying to look stern.

"Nurse," he said earnestly, "if I can't be there in time to stop it, there's going to be another death in the Square. Be a sweet creature and get me some clothes. If you don't, I'll fight my way out of here in these revolting pyjamas!"

"Go back to your room," she said, "and I'll bring them to you."

★ ★ ★

Martin slammed back the receiver, snatched up his cap, shouted some instructions through the inner door and hurried down the steps of the police station. As he turned into the High Street, he heard something that made him break into a run. He swung round into the Square, past the Bank and Pope's, and flung himself panting into Beamish's shop.

It was empty.

His heavy feet shook the staircase and a war-shield fell in front of him, wedged itself in the banisters and brought him sprawling. With a furious oath, he tore it out of the way, leapt up the remaining stairs and burst into Mrs. Archer's room.

Miss Beamish was bending over the body of her sister. The fawn carpet was stained with blood from the jagged hole where the bullet had emerged from the head of the dead woman, who lay on the floor in front of the chair by the window.

Martin took three swift strides.

"Let's 'ave a look at 'er," he said and knelt down.

He scrambled to his feet with a grunt and went to the telephone. Dr. Weston was out, but Hayling promised to be round in two minutes.

"You'd better sit over there, madam," said Martin.

Miss Beamish, whose face was ashen, moved across the room, dabbing at her eyes. As she sat down, her handkerchief dropped from her hand and lay unheeded by her chair until she pulled herself together and picked it up.

While he waited for Dr. Hayling and the Inspector, Martin examined the room. The windows overlooking the Square were closed, but the one at the side was open at the top. On the table were the cardboard squares for "Word Making and Word Taking." Most of them were scattered haphazard, but five had been placed together to form the name, "Erica." Lying also on the table was a Chubb key that Martin recognised as belonging to the card-index cabinets.

An electric horn sounded imperatively and Martin went to the window. A curious crowd had already gathered outside the shop and eddied away from Hayling's car.

Martin opened the window as the young doctor jumped out of the car and called to him to come straight up.

★ ★ ★

When Charlton came out of the hospital, there was a large private car in the drive. He walked up to the chauffeur, produced his credentials and asked to be driven to the Square with all possible speed. The man's employer was not due to come out for some time, so he started up the engine without demur.

In less than three minutes, Charlton was pushing his way through the mob round Beamish's shop door. His face was set in hard lines, because it was obvious that the thing he had feared had happened before he or Martin could prevent it. He hurried up the stairs and went into the front room. Dr. Hayling was talking to Martin and Miss Beamish was still huddled in her chair.

"Is she dead?" was his first eager question.

"Yes," answered Hayling.

Charlton glanced swiftly round the room and took in everything that Martin had seen. He went over and stood by the stricken woman.

"Where have you put the pistol, Miss Beamish?" he asked softly.

She turned her red-rimmed eyes up to his and shook her head.

"I know that Mrs. Archer was the Sniper," he said with great gentleness, "and you cannot save her name." She buried her head in her hands and her body shook with sobs.

"I think I know where it is," he said.

As he moved across the room, Martin muttered in his ear:

"She's got the cartridge-case in 'er 'andkerchief. I saw 'er pick it up."

Charlton went to the bookcase and took down the big black Bible. He walked with it to the table and turned back the cover. Inside, in a cavity cut through the pages, was a Parabellum self-loader.

He took up the key from the table and then glanced again at the letters on the cloth.

"Proper names are not allowed," he murmured wryly to himself, and went to the filing-cabinet.

He opened the second drawer and took out Thomas Earnshaw's card. The red-ink note at the foot now read:

"Shot in Paulsfield Square by Erica Archer (q.v.)."

He ran through the cards in the top drawer and extracted one, which he read and then showed to Martin. It related to Captain Richard ("Jeff") Archer, D.S.O.

★ ★ ★

The body was taken to the mortuary and Charlton walked back with Martin to the police station.

"I couldn't make 'ead or tail of that message," admitted Martin, as they went into the charge-room. "What did it mean?"

"It was a reference to a verse in the New Testament: 'I am Alpha and Omega, the beginning and the end, the first and the last.'"

"I don't savvy."

"Alpha is the first letter in the Greek alphabet. It corresponds to our 'A', which is the first letter of Archer—and Mrs. Archer was the last of the five to die—or, rather, she thought she was."

"Explain it to me in simple words," said Martin.

"Earnshaw, Ransome, Ibbotson, Charlton, Archer. E—R—I—C—A. Species One to Five. Surely the most damnable acrostic that was ever conceived!"

"I never thought it was *her.* I thought it was more likely to be old Farquarson."

"So did a lot of other people, I'll wager!" answered Charlton. He sat down suddenly on a chair and swayed.

"I don't feel so good, Martin," he said with a weak smile, and the Sergeant caught him as he fainted.

★ ★ ★

And that was all there was to it. Those who like happy endings will be pleased to learn that Jack Ransome's *Wild Life* ran into four editions and he married Diana Steward on the strength of it; and that Harold Muttigen is now the willing slave of an out-of-doors girl, who hardly gives the poor fellow a moment for a decent mope.

We know that the Detection Club, under the presidency of Mr. E. C. Bentley, do not like mad murderers, but there it is.

THE END